Scarlet

KAYLEIGH HILTON

Cover: Lena Yang
Formatter: Lorna Reid
Editor: Morgana Stewart

Socials:
Facebook: Kayleigh Hilton- Author
Instagram/Tiktok: Kaylzbookadventures

To all the people who have never felt good enough…

You are worthy.

<3

The antidote to my depression was this book. It picked me up from my weakest moments and made me whole. The deeper we fall, the weaker we feel, the stronger we come out of it.

<3

Trigger Warnings

This book will contain triggers, so please read this book at your own discretion.

Triggers that may be involved:

* Age difference romance
* Correction Facility
* Mental Health: PTSD, Anxiety, Depression, Suicidal Thoughts, Suicidal Pact and Panic Attacks.
* May contain themes/comments related to Sexual Assault, Emotional Manipulation and Rape.
* Contains themes of trauma from Water Boarding, Electrocution, Assault, Torture and Murder.
* Contains brief themes of graphic detail related to Death and Blood.

Prologue

T o Hunt. To Kill. To Serve. That is the mission.

There are thousands of us.

Everyone was numbered, tattooed, and categorized like animals for slaughter.

The tattoos were etched on the right side of our ribs, a number that assigned us a place within the programme. Branded, burned, and scorned. Forever marked.

From such a young age we were given away to them. It was a programme for the unwanted children in the world. The deserted, the broken, the fallen, the lost souls.

Instead of having an abortion, people were offered money, lots of it, going into the hundreds of thousands, to sell their infant to them.

What they did to us further down the line would be forever unknown to the world. The truth was as infants, as children, we were trained, manipulated, and controlled into becoming highly trained assassins. To steal. To hunt. To kill. To fight.

This programme was known as SCARLET.

We had no life. No freedom. No peace.

Chess pieces that moved one by one, like toys in a game. Until some of us got out.

Check mate.

There were only seven of us that were lucky enough to escape. The rest who tried were either killed and slaughtered like the animals we were to him. Bodies piled high, blood of the fallen with trails of bloody footprints around them. Anyone who survived was taken back and brainwashed, making them forget everything.

More torture, more pain, and more control, that was the only thing waiting for them.

The escaped however, were in hiding, staying hidden in the shadows for the last six years, just because of me.

I was his missing piece.

He saw me as his most prized possession, someone who he took under his wing and moulded to be the perfect assassin there was. Just for him

He loved me like a daughter because I was his everything.

His control. His weakness. His life.

His love.

Chapter One

A beautiful start for the damned; a morning breeze, birds tweeting their own tune, the smell of freshly brewed coffee and the clatter of cupboards to signal people in the kitchen.

I always thought that a new day would bring new adventures, new possibilities, and many other things to life, like normal civilised human beings do in their own personal day to day mundane life, things I could no longer do, even when in Scarlet.

***

I opened my eyes to see daylight pouring in through the miniature gap between the blue curtains that moved with the breeze flickering through; signalling the day had begun and that I really needed to get out of bed. But I just couldn't find the motivation.

Since escaping from Scarlet, I've had nothing to do anymore, no motives, no functional life to live. The only thing I could ever really do was just live the day, survive it and stay hidden in the darkest of shadows. Living a life of fractured glass, never being whole again. The anticipation of memories, the continuous torment of control Hugo had over us, the daily struggle to even open my eyes, let alone leave the comfort of my own bed, was a cycle I was forever stuck in. A new reality never being reached. Just simply navigating myself slowly through time on a routine not wanted and never changeable.

Picking up the book that laid next to me on the bed, the book I had been reading before falling asleep, I quickly flicked through the pages and chucked it back down again. Throughout the years, books had become my own personal comfort because of the endless possibilities and number of mysteries a world could have. It was a land of lost souls, a future romance kindling, a place I could lose my mind in, by deconstructing the words written on a page, letting my imagination grow without any fear, pain, or concern, creating dreams and worlds just out of reach.

Around the room I had a wall of memories, photos of my family, the people that I loved, trying to create some normality to our lives. They were the people who held my broken heart. It was the first thing I could do in a place I could finally call home. I could plant seeds, form roots and blossom. After all, it was the first place we could finally feel safe in.

Further around the room, I had fairy lights that lined the walls that at night would create a complexion of fixed stars, a galaxy. To me, they made me think of the stars in the night sky, the eternity of light, time and beauty. The darkness and serenity of eternity, the beam of hope, life, fates, and endless possibilities. It was finally a place where I could breathe and where the stars could align and show me my dreams.

Over the last few years, my own room had become my

safe zone, a place where I didn't need to hide anything, where I could be free by not trying to control myself and could finally let everything out, without the world knowing the truth.

Slowly sitting up in bed as the green silk sheets scrunched up around me, I slid my legs out, putting my feet on the ground, just to get hit with the smell of coffee that made my brain scream for a morning cup. I needed it, my mind and body desperate for the substance itself to course through my veins. It was something to cause a sensation that would make my body tingle, my energy sore and fulfil me in ways nothing else could.

**

Standing up and looking straight into the long-lined mirror that was on the back of my door, I could instantly see the shell of someone I didn't recognise anymore. A past, a haunting memory scorned into my brain. A ghost of my former self. Every morning I would do this and every morning I would despise what was staring back at me. All I could see was the complexion of a ghost, something hollow and bare, a girl once tortured and made to be strong, but now weak and frail and full of self-pity, instead of the girl who always saw happiness, treasured family, friends, and endless stories in her head.

After what seemed like forever watching my reflection, staring into soulless eyes of broken glass, I walked over to my bedroom door and opened it, only to walk down the stairs and into the opened planned kitchen to see Jack.

The beauty of his golden hair glowed in the sunlight, and the fluffiness of it was evident as he ran his hand through it. His somewhat of a beard still had a few toast crumbs still sat in it, while his arms bulked out from his fitted top, with tattoos etched on his skin flexing as he moved about. He was lounging on the ugliest of sofas, cup of coffee in hand, with Amelie and her ever blossoming pink hair, pink hair that she had to represent her twin, the brother who we suspected had died during the escape. She was sitting there in her comfiest of baggy clothing, while her laughter bubbled around the room as she tried her best to cover her mouth with her hand as it echoed, getting lost in conversation with him. Her legs draped over his, while she wore her perfectly imperfect odd socks, showing off the tattoos displayed on her legs as she got lost in the one person she loved the most in this world. Just by the way they looked at each other you could tell they adored one another. A connection like no other. Star crossed lovers.

They had been tied at the hip for the last six years, finding comfort in one another. The love they had for one another was more than just chemicals, magical formulas, and internet quizzes to find the one, it was a simple life of elegance and grace with a few minor bumps in the road. The stars themselves had joined and made sure their fates crossed, like time itself was making sure they would find one another in this life and the next, a constant beautiful sentence for the damned. They had faced many battles side by side and that wasn't going to change anytime soon. Fate had another story for them. A fate none of us could ever see.

Turning my head to look across the room at the middle counter, I saw Sebastian sat on a stool with his back to me, while he read the newspaper in one hand and held his coffee in the other. He was a sculpture of a man with defined cheekbones and masculine beauty, enough to make me bite my lip at the sight of him. To me, he was made by

Gods who had master craftsmanship, with a slice of Heaven and Hell.

Like all the times he had done with me, it was the most perfect time to scare him. Well try to. Every other time that I had tried, I wasn't successful. He would always catch me and say the same stupid words to me on a continuous and expected loop.

Slowly creeping up to him, tip toe, by tip toe, I caught the attention of Jack and Amelie, only for their voices to still, making the room turn quiet.

Putting my hands on Sebastian's shoulders, I shouted "Boo!"

He looked at me with a straight face, unimpressed by my actions. I had failed miserably and could instantly hear Amelie and Jack laugh as the man in front of me looked unfazed.

"You're as quiet as a dinosaur," he muttered the words I hated the most, with the most enchanting smile spread across his face. "Morning, Beautiful."

"Morning," I mumbled.

Hearing my response, he started to laugh, knowing full well I was annoyed and disappointed. I was an assassin, highly trained to kill people by being able to stay hidden in the shadows and yet...I couldn't scare him.

Just by looking at him, I could see that his hair was ruffled, bed set, and untouched, oak brown and sun kissed. His eyes...well they were something else. His eyes represented him, deep pool blue eyes that would pull you under and my god did I want to drown. I could spend eternity looking at his eyes, just losing myself in them, forgetting everything around me. Not far from his eyes was a scar, nothing big but noticeable, a scar that I had caused many years ago. The scar was a symbol of heroism, caused by him saving me, a permanent reminder of who he was. My hero. And my god...that scar... did something. Sebastian was the type of man who had a heart of a lover, the strength of a man, purity, and the courage of a hero. But just like the rest of us, he was damaged by his inner demons and yet he would never let them stop him.

With him still sat there laughing, with his eyes set on me, I walked around the counter towards the coffee pot to get the substance I needed. I grabbed the closet mug I could and put it down only to reach forward for the coffee and see it was empty. Fucking brilliant. The one thing I wanted more than anything.

The sound of a deeper chuckle filled my ears, causing me to turn and look at Sebastian. The cheeky fucker had a grin that went ear to ear, finding amusement at my own disappoint, especially after my failed attempt at 'trying' to scare him. Luckily, there were a few things I was good at, and he knew it, but somehow, he'd forgotten. Tricks and skills once used before. A mastermind behind the beauty. Brains and boldness lurking in the shadows deep within.

Taking a few steps forward, I leant on the counter in front of Sebastian, just standing there with my own cheeky smile on my face as his eyebrows furrowed together.

"What?" he asked.

Meeting his question with silence, I left him to think about what I was doing. When he least expected it, I quickly reached forward and grabbed his coffee mug, only to then take a few steps back and lean my back against the counter.

"That was mine!" He frowned, trying his best puppy dog eyes.

The fucker was trying to get me to feel guilty and playing me at my own game. He knew full well it was hard to resist his charm and was trying to use it to his own leverage.

There were many things I felt guilty about daily. One of them being that everyone was trapped here. Trapped because of me. Trapped in these four walls of a house hiding, just waiting, and praying we wouldn't be found. A guilt that was the Devil sat on my shoulder.

I carried on watching him, not moving, not falling, not giving in to his trap. He quickly gave up and rolled his eyes, causing me to quietly chuckle at his response. "Always stealing my things, Adi," he winked.

Feeling my own cheeks warm up, I knew they had more than likely turned red, bringing colour to my face, while the daily occurrence of fluttering in my chest, a feeling I never wanted to lose appeared. He always called me Adi; it was his nickname for me. He wasn't the kind of person who would give people nicknames, but for some reason I was special, special enough to be graced with one, even though it was simple.

Slowly bringing the coffee mug to my lips to take a sip, I kept my eyes locked on his while he kept his slightly squinted at me, watching my every move. Feeling the hot liquid running down my throat, warming me up from the inside, I hummed to myself.

With a smug smile, I lowered the mug and gave out a satisfied sigh. "Nothing is better than a freshly brewed coffee in the morning," I taunted, knowing full well anything I said would irritate him.

"Freshly brewed stolen coffee more like," he fired back, rolling his eyes, with another fluttering in my chest appearing.

I loved the way I felt with him, especially in moments like this. He made me feel special, making all my fears, pain and torment disappear. I felt like I was someone with him, instead of nothing. He was the sun in the sky that would light up my darkness.

"Good morning to you too, Sebastian," I smirked.

Just by staring at each other, I always felt an unimaginable bond and connection with him. It was something strong but confusing due to it never being talked about.

An untold story. An untold connection.

Moments like this made the rest of the world disappear, making me feel like it was just me and him alone in this room, in a world that consumed us daily, like one of the fictional worlds I had created in my head, a world above the clouds.

A happy ending.

One that would never come.

***

The sound of a coffee mug hitting the counter snapped me out of the trance I was in. Well, a trance we were in.

Turning my head to the sound of the noise, I saw Amelie standing there looking between us both. She stood there with a grin on her face, with her peachy lips slightly parted, watching us, while her hair flowed, moving in the breeze that came from the parted window behind.

With her eyes flickering between us, she knew something was happening. "You love birds...okay?" she asked, hinting at the connection she could visibly see.

Everyone must have been able to see it, but nobody talked about it, not even us. Not even to each other.

Taking a small glance at Sebastian, I could see he was now sitting there awkwardly, stiff as a board, scratching the back of his head while he stared off into the distance. But surely, he felt something to...right?

Turning back to Amelie, I smiled. "Just drinking my coffee," I muttered, to catch Sebastian in the corner of my eye watching me.

"You mean stolen coffee," he chimed in, with a small, yet devilish smirk on his face. My god was that man beautiful.

All I did was roll my eyes at his comment, just to be caught by his stare and a laugh to erupt from Amelie. Busted. "This time it was Adeline, next time it will be you, Sebastian," Amelie said, pointing out the obvious.

"She started it," Sebastian responded quickly.

"Did not!" I exclaimed.

"Did too!"

"Did not!"

"Did too!"

"You are both as bad as each other," Amelie butted in, causing us to stop our miniature debate and to look at her.

As we all stood there, Jack came up behind Amelie and wrapped his arm around her waist, causing her to melt into him. We all watched as he placed a kiss against her cheek and how she instantly blushed from his romantic gesture. Rosey cheeks, eyes full of love and beauty. Flawless emotions flying from them both.

Love.

It was a moment that got me to sneakily glance towards Sebastian and bite my lip, only to then turn my attention quickly back to them before I got caught.

Tilting his head to the side, Jack studied us both as wrinkled his nose. "Are they arguing again?" he asked.

Snorting a laugh, Amelie responded, "About coffee this time."

"Who stole it this time?"

Soon as those words left his lips, Sebastian looked at

me, dead set, finger pointing. "That little minx," he expressed, as I flipped him off.

"Well, one of us needs to run to the store and get supplies," Amelie mentioned, with her eyes shooting between us both, asking without truly asking.

Amelie hated going to the store and doing the supply run. Plus, she would splash the cash, spend way too much, and get things we didn't really need.

"I'll go and I'll take the Jeep," I responded with an eye roll, getting the hint that Amelie was giving, with her face lighting up as soon as the words left my lips.

"I'll go with you," Sebastian quickly chimed in, looking at me with a smirk on his face. "I'm driving." He hated my driving and loved control. The man wanted some sort of power. What's better than speeding in a car?

"Fine! Just don't crash the car," I teased, getting a deep chuckle from him.

As he grabbed his leather jacket and slipped it on, I looked him up and down, hungry eyed. He wore the bad boy look to a 'T'.

He paused in his movements and his eyebrows furrowed like he had a desire to investigate any thoughts in my head. I really hoped my eyes didn't deceive me, because if they did...I was well and truly fucked.

Watching his eyes lock on to me, he asked, "Shouldn't you be going to get dressed?"

Only to snap me out of my own intrusive thoughts.

Please stop staring at me like that.

Looking down at myself, he did have a point, I was still in my pyjamas.

"I'll go and get dressed now," I sighed.

***

In a matter of moments, I was up the stairs and changed, into my mundane clothes. It was the easiest way to blend into the shadows, something that was a daily occurrence for us over the last six years. We needed normality, we had to act as if we knew what normal meant.

I would happily take a normal day of living over the daily nightmare I lived within my head. I wanted to explore, travel and get lost in the world. I wanted to spread my wings and create a life meeting new people, falling in love; a life of being free without the feeling of being trapped in a world of terror, from the outside looking in.

Part of me didn't want to join the society I could see. I didn't feel like I deserved to, due to the amount of blood I had spilled under the devil's control. I was my own monster.

I had been the cause of many things that went wrong and seemed to drag everyone around me into it, into this nightmare. I'd forever be the Devil that would cause people's lives to go up in flames. Like Hell itself.

***

Quickly appearing back downstairs, I saw Sebastian standing there, swinging the keys around his finger, waiting impatiently. The sound of my feet coming down the stairs got him to turn towards me and smile, as he looked me up and down.

"Took you long enough," he let out, just for me to instantly flip him off, yet again.

The fucker had nerve. He usually took longer than me.

The instant reaction of me flipping him off caused him to laugh and for that small twinkle in his beautiful crystal eyes to appear, causing my legs to wobble down the final steps as I reached his side.

Breaking me out of my fourth trance of the day, Jessie came skipping through the door, blonde locks curled like a poodle, bouncing up and down with every energetic step she took. Her skin was fair with a slight pigment of colour, just the right tone of peach. She was a girl who was always full of energy and someone who had a smile that would instantly light up any room she walked in, bringing the darkest of places to life. A rare beauty with a lot of patience.

With a quick glance at her hand, I noticed she was carrying a stack of cash. It was an untraceable means of living for us.

She reached her hand forward and slapped it in Sebastian's hand. "Don't forget this," she said.

Jessie would do this often. Being one of the youngest, but yet the most technical at the age of twenty, she would take bitcoin money she had hidden deep in the dark web and turn it into cash for us, so we had no trail being left behind. Forever in the shadows, forever going unnoticed, forever in the dark.

"Should be enough for the trip."

"Thank you," I smiled.

"Anytime! Make sure you get coffee…Oh! I also want Cheetos, Ben and Jerry's and marshmallows!" The girl could eat anything and everything, never gaining a pound.

"You want us to just buy the whole store?" Sebastian wittingly commented, just for me to playfully smack his arm, basically telling him to cut it out and behave.

"Come on then!" Sebastian piped up, turning around, and opening the door, leading us into the outside world.

***

As the door opened, I could see it was throwing it down, with puddles forming on the floor, with raindrops echoing as they bounced off every surface available, like the rain was washing away the sins of everyone in the world. Clearing the slate. The sky was crying its own tears at what we do to the world and what we do to ourselves. Failing and falling.

Splish! Splash! Splosh!

There was some beauty to the rain, a beauty that enchanted me. Maybe it was the countless movies and books I had read that made me think this way. The idea of kissing someone I loved in the rain, a dance, losing oneself in the moment. A fictional reality setting in my own brain. A dream.

***

Feeling the burn of eyes lingering, a warm presence summoning me, I turned to see Sebastian watching me. His beautiful eyes were etched on me. Eyes I could happily stare at for the rest of my life. If only he knew.

"What?" I asked.

"Worried you're going to get wet, Princess?" he teased, causing me to let out a giggle.

"Nope."

I watched how he held his hand out to me, waiting for me to hold it. He was a gentleman; a man of many things and I knew I was falling in love with him, but I still didn't understand his connection to me.

Happily taking his hand, he whisked us out the house in seconds, running headfirst into the rain, with raindrops hitting us in the face as we ran for protection.

***

Once we got in the car I looked towards him to see his eyes on me and for both of us to burst out laughing. We'd been

15

in the rain for a mere few seconds, but we still looked like drowned rats. It was a laughter that couldn't be controlled. Contagious. As one of us finished, the other would start. A never-ending cycle. A laughter where we couldn't catch our own breath. Moments like this scorned my heart and left it forever imprinted. A tattoo on my brain that would forever have a permanent place.

Once calmed down from the amusement of our own laughter and our near drowning experience in the rain, Sebastian started the car. With an engine roaring, a slap of the gear stick into gear, the volume of the music being turned up and a symphony of tunes filling the void, to then be filled with the most unsettling voices singing completely out of tune, we set off on our journey.

Chapter Two

L iving in the countryside had many blessings for us. A serenity of breathable air, toxicity being left behind, beauty in the horizon. A wilderness of freedom. All that surrounded us were crops thigh high, sights unseen, beautiful animals singing their own tune and nature being free to explore and grow.

I loved being in the countryside. I would spend endless summer nights on a flat piece of grass in the middle of the corn field, blanket out, picnic set, book in hand, sun in the sky, feeling the heat caress my skin. Beautiful summer nights of peace.

It was a place where we could stay hidden due to the low-level amount of security cameras around us. A place where we were secluded with no one ever bothering us.

We were close to the city, but not close enough to be noticed. It was the best place we could find, somewhere close enough to access what we needed like food and resources, depending on our needs at the time, but far enough to have the peace we all craved for, a peace we could use to our advantage to get away from the hauntings that followed. The bogey man hiding in the dark, the monster in the closet.

The journey to the store wasn't too long, but it did consist of a long, winding country road, surrounded by yellow-green fields, countless sheep and mountains that created a beautiful silhouette when the sun hit it just right. It was like the trees enclosed it, a tunnel of green enclosing us in the nature of beauty. The journey itself was drowned out by the sound of uncontrollable amounts of out of tune singing. A moment in itself that I treasured. I loved spending time with him come rain or shine. Being human, joining society, being a stranger and mystery to others. Living a normal life.

The car park when we finally arrived was fairly empty, ten cars at the most. Usually, it was crowded, with seas of cars and people around. Coming during the quiet period was always the best option, easier to stay under the radar. I did love to come during the busier periods to watch life around me and see how everyone went about their day to day, a life I couldn't have. It made me dream better and bigger, hoping one day I would have that. Another dream added to the stars.

Even though we had arrived, we sat there in the car because the rain was still flying down. You could hear it bouncing off the car to the beat of a drum, making its own music, a beat you could listen to for eternity, a melody you could play over and over again. I loved rainy days. My rainy days consisted of sitting on my pillowed windowsill, book in hand, blanket over me, cup of coffee or a hot chocolate next to me, while watching the rain outside as it slowly crept down my window. All I wanted as an added bonus was someone to share it with. Well, to share it with him. Sebastian.

Through all the years we had spent by each-other's side, I've never once had the courage to admit how I felt; I didn't want to destroy what we already had between us, and God forbid he didn't feel the same way. It would break me and then there would be a completely awkward distance between us. What would I do then?

"You ready?" he asked, making me look towards him.

He had been sat there watching me get lost in thought, head in the clouds.

I smiled back. "Yeah."

"You were out of it."

"You know me, away with the fairies!" I emphasized with jazz hands, gaining a deep chuckle from him.

"Wouldn't have it any other way," he smiled, causing me to blush slightly. Just the simplest of things and I was lost in him. It was like his voice, his presence, summoned my body to respond, yet he didn't see it.

***

Before I knew it, I was running again, making the great escape for the store. Raindrops hitting my face again. It was like the rain itself was trying to rid me of my sorrows of the world around me, washing away all my fears for just a moment. A moment of freedom from my demons. If only the rain did truly carry magical powers.

As soon as we got through the doors, I turned towards him and pointed to the trolley next to me. "You're pushing!"

He rolled his eyes. "So, demanding," he mumbled, causing me to laugh.

"Says you!"

He waved me off. "Yeah, yeah! Yeah, yeah!"

Watching as he walked towards the trolleys and

grabbed one, he turned towards me and gave me one of his best sarcastic smiles ever, a smile I wanted to get lost in, only for us to head straight through the next set of doors.

Walking through, the place was full of rainbow shelves, colour coming to life, a vibrant atmosphere, and a small thing of beauty. I had never truly stepped into a store until I was sixteen, but as soon as I did, I loved it. Not for the fact it was a store, but more for the fact I felt like everyone else, part of the world outside that was constantly hidden from me. What I loved most, was to people watch and imagine people's stories, giving them a life that wasn't theirs, but a life I wanted for myself. It was the one way I could live outside my head rent free, a life of being able to explore endless possibilities.

Slowly making our way through the store, we grabbed what we needed; fruit, vegetables, dairy produce, necessary things. It was a cycle that seemed to follow us every time we came together.

All we did was push the trolley around in silence, until I felt a hand accidentally touch mine, causing me to instantly turn and look at him, to watch him watch me. It was like our eyes were dead set on one another, soul searching, thinking about what could possibly be going through one another's minds and wanting to know the truth.

Another puzzle that needed solving.

There was always hope of figuring out what the other was thinking. Truth on the verge of being revealed, but fate had another ruling, never letting us know, even when I craved for it.

It was painstakingly cruel, being left in the unknown of an untold story.

I was supposed to be someone who could read people

well, but when it came to Sebastian I couldn't. A power being burned by a single flame, a single look. By him.

This hard shell that stood in front of me prevented anyone from being able to get anything out of him. Only ever being revealed when wanted. Just by looking at him, I couldn't help feeling like his eyes were dragging me deeper into them, like a sinking ship in the sea and by holding his hand, he was taking me down with him. Forever drowning in the unknown. A drowning I would happily let sweep me off the coastline, willingly letting it submerge and consume me in one.

I pulled away knowing I had to, as I felt my cheeks heating up once again and knew instantly they had gone all rosy, enchanted by his presence. I let out a small cough which seemed to snap him out of the moment, breaking the connection holding us together. There was never going to be the perfect moment to talk about it. I needed to bring up the conversation, but I stood there biting my tongue, refusing to speak, thinking about the paths and doors that might open if I did, the good, the bad and the ugly.

Standing there paralysed, I let my own thoughts consume me again as I watched his confused expression grow.

"What? Have I got something on my face?" he asked.

Not knowing what to say to him, I just stood there, starring. I had accidently created a void in my head and let the emptiness expand, letting it take control. "Hello? Earth to Adi!" He waved in front of me.

I quickly shook my head, blinking a few times, snapping myself into the real world again. "Sorry," I mumbled, as I turned away, still feeling his eyes lingering on me, like he was trying to read my mind and see into my very own soul.

"What's wrong?" he asked, reaching out towards me, and grabbing my hand, causing me to look at him again.

My eyes locked on his perfectly sculptured face, a face that was written full of concern.

"It's nothing," I said.

Hearing my words, he pulled more of a puzzled look, refusing to move even an inch until he knew more. "Spill!"

I knew in that moment he wouldn't leave me alone until I said something. He was someone who would try to dig till he got any answer from me. Even if I had to come up with a fictional lie, a compelling story to distract him from the truth. A complete bullshit story.

I let out a sigh and pulled my hand out of his, scratching my own head due to nerves consuming me. I knew if I didn't speak, he would make me speak, so I had to say something to him, anything to him. I needed to break the silence. I knew if I didn't force myself to say anything now, it could be another month, maybe another year until I finally did, and six years was long enough.

"I...I....," I stuttered, letting out another big sigh again. Knowing full well I was fully swept under the sea by now, drowning in my own thoughts. "Am I the only one who feels it?"

Watching him standing there, confusion completely written all over his face, he opened his mouth to speak. "Feel what?"

Hearing his response, I didn't know if he was just stupid or oblivious to what I was talking about. Maybe I did need to explain it to him? Maybe it was fiction after all? Maybe it was only me who could see it?

"Don't play stupid, you know what I mean!" I fired back at him, letting my emotions overtake my own voice. It was like the flames I was trying to keep back had burnt through the wall I was building, that they had set me ablaze, making me strike, scorning me to the core.

Shit.

He sighed, looking away, scratching his head, contemplating.

Was he deciding how best to reject me?

I just stood there frozen, anger boiling from the silence, watching him. Waiting. Hoping. Needing an answer. An awkward silence fell while he tried to avoid looking at me. The silence itself started to become a ticking time bomb, not from his reaction, but because of my pure stupidity for thinking now was the right time. I knew I should have planned it better, waited for the right moment, I should have thought it through. I should have known that anything I wanted in life wasn't going to happen to me, I didn't deserve that kind of life, the one I really wanted. I deserved what was already given.

"Why are you asking?" he questioned, turning to lock eyes with me once again.

I instantly frowned. Why was I asking? Was he that stupid? Did he not feel it? Did he? Was he just not interested? Thousands of questions/ went through my head all at once. My brain was scrambling for the right thing to say, overloading with data, like it had run out of room but was still trying to cram more information in and process it. Many possibilities flooded my mind.

I looked away and then back at him, filled with emotion and rage.

"It's a conversation well overdue, don't you think?" I asked. His expression was blank. He looked like he wanted to speak but wouldn't. "I've known you since I was seventeen! I've grown up around you and we have been extremely close for years! Are you really telling me that when you look at me and we just end up staring at each other, that you don't feel something going on? That it's one sided? That I'm just imagining things? I'm twenty-five! I'm not a child!" I had finally cracked. "Jack and Amelie have the same age gap! She's twenty-six and he's thirty-seven and that's not an issue."

He still stood there, watching, acknowledging everything I was saying and more than likely going through it all in his own head. Part of me didn't get why he was acting the way he was; it was obvious something was going on, even Amelie had noticed that there was something and joked about it earlier. Yet still nothing.

Watching him stare and feeling my emotions tipping way over the edge, even further than I thought was possible, I knew the love I had for this man made me do questionable things, made my emotions more explosive than I ever thought possible. "Well…why don't you have a think then! When you decide what you want to say to me, I'll be around the corner down the next aisle…away from you."

I turned away from him quickly in a huff, pacing myself away and around the corner to the next aisle. I knew I had just caused a scene and that all eyes were probably on us, but I didn't care. I was telling him the truth and he couldn't even tell me anything. I didn't get what the issue was, but I also knew I had technically ambushed him about it, but what else was I supposed to do?

Stay quiet? Never acknowledge this? Forget about it? Wait for another rainy day?

***

As soon as I was around the corner, I made eye contact with a guy, a sheepish looking guy. Once our eyes locked, he quickly turned away from me, like he was ashamed I caught

24

him…like he didn't want to be caught. I felt the hairs on the back of my neck rise, while my skin started to tingle, causing me to shiver. Goosebumps crept all over me, something wasn't quite right.

I turned to look at the shelves, thinking there could be a possibility that I was imagining everything, maybe like the scenario with Sebastian. Fuck my imagination.

I took another glance towards him and saw that he was looking at me again.

He was definitely watching me. Why was he watching me?

Suddenly, I heard a noise. The noise of a trolley being pushed with a lot of emotion behind it, coming around the corner at full force.

"Why do you always walk off in such a……."

"Shh!" I snapped at Sebastian, facing him in seconds, making him stop in his tracks, taken back by my sudden outburst.

"Why are you shushing me? You're the one who's just had a fucking hissy fit!" he shouted.

Facing away from the man further down the aisle, I made full on eye contact with Sebastian, with my hands resting on the back of the trolley, while Sebastian watched me, trying his best to read me. I could tell by looking at him he was annoyed, but I knew we had to table the conversation right now.

"Gently look over my shoulder. The man in the dark clothing and cap," I said, to see his eyes flicker over me. "He was watching me; he keeps watching me. I don't know if I'm being paranoid or what, but there is something fishy going on."

He quickly looked towards the man again for a few

seconds and then back at me. He knew I was right; he could see him watching me, watching us. But why?

I turned towards the shelving again and took another look towards the man, acting like I was looking further down the shelves for something. I was trying my best to gauge the situation and using my ability to read people. My eyes searched him, inch by inch, piece by piece, until I could make out a small bulge coming from the back of his pants. He had a gun.

He was loaded. Weaponised. Ready for action.

To make things look normal, I grabbed a box of cereal and turned to face Sebastian again, chucking it into the trolley. "Gun back pocket," I mentioned, while I watched Sebastian look again and then back at me.

"Best thing to do is carry on, act normal and get to the car."

"What if he is here for us? For me?"

"We don't know anything yet. Don't overthink it. Don't worry."

But I did. Frozen. I was standing here terrified. Heart racing. Palpitations of fear increasing. What if after all this time they had found us?

Everything around me came to a standstill. Time itself came to a stop, while my heart felt like it was racing a hundred miles an hour. I could feel the fog gathering, my mind shutting down, my body frozen in what to do next. This couldn't be real, this had to be a dream...right?

***

Without even thinking, I felt Sebastian grab me and drag me along, making us carry on down the aisle, pretending to scan the shelves as Sebastian carried on pushing the trolley. My body was walking closer and closer to the mystery man, the man of suspicion, without my say so. It had taken over and I had lost control, it was autopiloting, and I couldn't stop it. As soon as I got close, I tripped and fell into the man. The man quickly caught me as I looked up at him, noticing his facial expression alone reflected how nervous he was. Just from looking in his eyes, you could see the pain behind them, like tears were on the brink but he was shoving it all down. They also gave him away, as they showed recognition.

That in itself terrified me.

I could clearly make out the gun at the back of him and the Apple watch on his arm with a picture of me on it, before it disappeared, hiding his tracks. A picture from when I was at Scarlet. Fuck.

"I'm so sorry," I said, embarrassed about my fall, as he helped me back to my feet and let me go. "I'm so clumsy, I really am sorry."

Looking at me, he let out a small smile. "No harm done, hope your ankle is ok."

"Thank you for catching me."

"Anytime."

I carried on past the man and walked around the corner as quickly as I could, Sebastian following me as I did.

As soon as I got around the corner, I turned towards him. "He has my face on his watch," I stated, as I tried my best to stay composed, but my voice to broke as I started to hyperventilate.

I needed to breathe, but I couldn't. Fear itself had taken over me. The air in my lungs became a painful dagger, stabbing me. It was like my lungs were screaming for more, wanting to be filled, as the tightness in my chest started to grow. My heart thudded against my chest and my hands shook, causing a ripple effect to take over the rest of my body. I felt sick, stomach churning, the feeling of bile being stuck at the bottom of my throat.

The feeling of two hands touching my arms caused me to look up, coming face to face with Sebastian. He was concerned, he could sense my fear, sense what was happening to me.

"Breathe," he calmly spoke, slowly rubbing my arms, keeping his eyes locked on mine. "Breathe in... one... two...three. Breathe out...one...two...three." Listening to his voice, I tried to follow his instructions, while he did it with me. He kept doing it with me until my breathing started to return to normal, then pulled me towards him in seconds, wrapping his arms around me, holding me close, giving me that reassuring hug. "Look, we will just go and pay and then head to the car. It's going to be okay."

It was like time didn't exist for me. Before I knew it, we had walked towards the till and the women behind had scanned all our items, Sebastian had already packed the bags, paid, and was leading the way out of the store. The next thing I knew, Sebastian had let go of my hand and there was a loud bang. I turned around to look and saw clothing scrunched in Sebastian's hand and a man being pinned to the wall behind him. The man from in the store.

"Who are you!" Sebastian shouted, his face red in anger. The man stayed quiet, so Sebastian pulled him forward and chucked him against the wall again. The way his eyes opened wide and how his body started to shake said it all. He was terrified. He then looked towards me for help. "Don't look at her! Look at me! She isn't going to help you! You tell me right now why you are following us!"

"Ok! Ok! Ok!" the man said. "Just let me go and I'll talk." Sebastian let go off the man, but you could still see the rage in his face; he wasn't going to let the man get away with anything and was certainly going to do his best to get answers. The man straightened up his clothing and took a look between me and Sebastian again, as I stood frozen in place.

"Tell me!" Sebastian shouted once again, taking a step towards the man again.

He raised his hands up in protest. "I'm not here to hurt you, any of you!" he said. "He knows where you are. He's biding his time, something is happening within the programme, he's got more powerful people looking for you." He took a deep breath. "The programme has moved locations; I don't know where it is anymore. I got out before the move, it's taken me several months to find you, but I know he isn't going to be far behind. I came to warn you." The man took a large gulp, proving to me that he was just as frightened of them as I was. "I promise I just came to tell you! You need to either run or fight, he's not going to stop."

"He's coming?" I whispered. My terror coming to life.

"He's throwing one of his annual masquerade balls tomorrow night at the theatre, in the middle of the city," the man said. "The best place to find out more details about the programme will be in the office there, on his computer. Only if you want to put a stop to this because it's him or you guys. He won't stop till one of you is on top and I hope it's you."

Standing like the ice sculpture I was, the world around me crumbled and swallowed me whole. This couldn't be real, we had been careful, and it had been six years. I honestly didn't think this would happen anytime soon. I stood there watching the man, as his eyes locked on me.

"Just go," I said. "Go! Run!"

The man just let out a small smile and started to walk

off. He then stopped and looked towards me once more. "Be careful, there's more than there ever was," he spoke before he turned back around and ran away.

Numb to the touch of Sebastian trying to hold my hand. It felt like it was just me stood there in that moment. Fear, pain, and torment scrambled through my head and body. There were moments in the past I'd wished would stay there, but deep down I always knew this life would be too good to be true. This was only a matter of time.

"Come on, let's get you home," Sebastian said, his voice calm and soothing.

Nodding at his words, I turned towards the car, putting the shopping on the back seat, just to then get in the passenger side. I was soaking head to toe from standing in the rain too long, but I didn't care because I was stuck and drowning in my own head. I never wanted to go back to Scarlet, the idea, the thought of going back and being under his control again made me sick to my stomach, no matter where the programme was. It made my head spin, it made traumatic moments come flooding back; seeing friends being shot, being captured as they all tried to escape. Dead bodies lying on the concrete floor in their own pools of blood, blood stains on my clothes, screams so deafening and agonising they would scar you for life. These were the memories he had left me with, left all of us with. These were moments I would forever be haunted by, for the rest of my life.

The bogey man was coming.

Chapter Three

We'd both sat there silently in the car not saying a word. I could feel Sebastian's eyes lingering on me.

"Just say what you want to say," I stated, not looking at him, but knowing he wanted to say something.

"Everything will be ok," he reassured me, as he reached over and grabbed my hand, only for me to pull it away. I hated myself, I was the reason he came in the first place and now I was taking it out on him, which was something I never meant to do, but comfort was too much right now. My own demons were taking control.

"Let's just get back home and tell the others," I sighed, not making eye contact with him in the slightest.

"Ok."

***

After a few minutes of driving, I noticed Sebastian was frequently checking the middle mirror, causing me to be a little confused; he seemed to be way over checking it for a normal drive. I could tell by the grip on the wheel, by his breathing becoming heavier, that something was wrong, and it wasn't about the man from only a few minutes ago.

"What's up?" I asked. No response. "Sebastian!" I shouted, as I watched him glance at me, then the mirror and then the road.

"We have a tail," he stated, making me turn around and look out the back window. That's when I saw it, a black Jeep was following us. I only knew this due to Sebastian changing lanes and the car following every move he was making.

"Fuck! I knew it was too good to be true. He led them to us!"

I turned back around and clicked a button on the dashboard, just for a small screen to appear where the glove compartment was. In literally five seconds, Jessie appeared on screen, taking a bite out of a donut, stuffing her face. The screen was installed for situations like this, for us to get an instant connection to the others if it was ever needed, after Jessie and her bitcoin money ways got us the car in the first place. As soon as it was activated it would automatically connect to Jessie's computer at home with a live feed. Jessie had also installed other technology devices on the car, from heat sensors on the front and back, to hidden compartments where we could hide weapons and ammunition, just in case of scenarios like this one.

"What's up?" she mumbled, mouth full of food, enjoying and savouring every bite of the donut.

"Being followed," I said.

Jessie then started to choke on her donut, coughing and spitting it out.

"You need to lose them," Jack spoke, as he appeared on the screen next to Jessie.

"No shit," Sebastian replied.

I looked towards him, a wicked grin suddenly on my face.

"What's that face for?" he asked.

"You heard the old man! Lose them," I winked at him, causing him to laugh.

"I heard that!" Jack stated.

Sebastian smirked as he knew what he had to do and that was to floor it. "Don't have to tell me twice!"

As soon as the words left his lips, his foot hit the accelerator, chucking me back further into my seat as the car picked up speed. I slowly reached forward, putting my hand under the seat, pulling out a gun and some ammunition,

"Since when did you carry a gun in the car?" he asked.

"Always and there is more."

I loaded the gun and undid my seatbelt, as I watched Sebastian dart between the sea of cars in front of us, making our way down the carriage way. Cars started to honk their horns at us repeatedly as we cut them off. We were clearly going to piss a lot of people off today. I turned around once more to see the Jeep behind us picking up speed, making it known we definitely had a tail on us.

Before I could do anything else, I heard gun fire and one of the side mirrors get taken out, smashing into pieces.

"They're shooting at us!" I stated, letting Jack and Jessie know what was happening.

"I'm looking at the heat sensors on the back of the car. I can make out four people, all loaded," Jessie stated. "Amelie, Jack and Arthur are on their way to help."

"Don't compromise yourselves, we can deal with this," Sebastian said.

It was true we didn't want anyone else getting caught up in this mess and we would do anything to protect them as much as we could, even if it meant sacrificing ourselves. I knew Sebastian thought the same as me, it was something that drew us together.

I could hear more bullets hitting the car, trying their best to take out our tyres. I could feel Sebastian trying to get the car to go faster, as he tried to put his foot down even more. I knew I needed to do something. I quickly pushed myself through the gap, to get into the back of the Jeep, to then pull the sunroof open and stand up, with the wind blowing through my hair, the noise of cars honking their horns and the sound of gunfire filling my ears, making the situation feel more real. Sebastian was trying his best to weave through the sea of cars, keeping himself focused, keeping the car going and keeping it as smooth as possible, for me anyways. I could see and hear the sound of cars crashing, another moment of leaving destruction following us and for the guilt of destroying and combusting innocent lives to swallow me whole.

I aimed and fired my gun, trying my best to aim for the tyres, but not being able to hit them due to the speed. I could still hear muffled talking in the car but knew I wouldn't be able to make a word out because of the cars and gun fire. I ducked back under and leant over the middle, to grab a small grey spec next to the screen, to then place it into my ear. It was a comms earpiece just in case I needed to know what was happening and being said. I quickly got back up through the gap and started firing once again, only to feel a bullet graze my ear, causing my hand to instantly reach up and touch it and then look at it, to see my fingers covered in blood.

Out of nowhere, I could hear the raw of two motorbikes, just to look up and see two come speeding off a ramp, flying high in the air over cars and landing near us, with some cars swerving out of the way and honking their horns once again. The motorbikes got closer to us, only for me to notice it was Amelie, Jack, and Arthur and that they had come to the rescue, even when I told them not to.

"Need a hand?" Amelie asked down the comms.

I laughed but it was cut short as pain exploded across my arm.

"Fuck!" I hissed. I looked down to see another bullet had grazed me, thankfully nothing actually impacting, but enough for it to bleed. Nothing I couldn't handle, but still the pain was there.

"What's happening?" Sebastian asked, concerned about my reaction.

"I got grazed by a bullet. I'm fine," I reassured him

I focused back on the road as Jack got the motorbike closer to the Jeep that was following us, to see Amelie shoot through the window, taking two of them out. They soon got closer to the Jeep, Amelie slowly standing up on the back of the motorbike, hands on Jack's shoulders, while Jack kept it under control. She then jumped onto the car, quickly pulling herself through the smashed back window. I couldn't see much from that point on, only the Jeep swerving side to side, crashing into the side of cars as it followed. Debris and car parts scattered everywhere, causing a car pile-up behind.

Before I knew it, the car took a sharp turn and ran into the dual carriageway wall, causing it to instantly go up in flames.

"Amelie!" I shouted.

"What?" she replied.

Relief filled me as I saw her on the back of Arthur's motorbike, waving at me.

"How?"

"I'm a girl of many talents," she laughed down the comms.

I rolled my eyes and pulled myself down back through the sunroof, sitting on the backseat.

"Guys just get yourself here safely and keep an eye out," Jessie mentioned, knowing our problem had been solved. For now.

As we left the scene, we all kept checking behind us, making sure nobody else was following. All I could see was the disaster we had left behind. All I could do was hope nobody else was hurt due to our actions.

While we got home, Jessie was busy erasing all the camera footage from the events of the day, helping us stay hidden and making sure we couldn't be followed home any more than we had been.

The journey went by quickly. I wasn't really paying attention to anything or anyone, just staying zoned out for the whole car journey home. I could hear Sebastian talking to me, but it was just mumbles, I couldn't make a word out. I knew he was talking to me, probably reassuring me about everything, but I didn't want to hear it. This was my fault.

***

The next thing I knew, I was sitting there on the ugly sofa, staring blankly into space, voices behind me, talking, arguing, sounds that I wasn't paying much attention to, until I felt someone grab hold of my hand. I snapped out of my trance to see Amelie looking at me, concern in her expression.

"Are you okay?" she asked.

"Best that I can be," I said.

I couldn't even register my own emotions right now, let alone tell them how I was doing. It was like my mind couldn't focus on one thing anymore and everything just blurred together, like the boundaries and walls I had built up had slipped away.

Malcom walked over to me and started checking my ear and arm, where I had been grazed by the bullets. He cleaned them up and made sure no other damage had been done and then quickly went to chuck the rubbish in the bin.

"What do you want to do?" Amelie asked, just for my eyes to scan the rest of the room and see everyone watching me.

"What do you mean?" I had no idea what had been discussed as I was completely out of it.

"About the man? About them finding us?" Amelie asked.

"What about it?"

"Do you want to leave it and just hope it's a one off, or do you want to go digging?"

"I'm not sure," I responded, looking down at my hands.

I felt the sofa next to me dip, just for Sebastian to rest his hand on my leg, giving it a reassuring squeeze, just for me to brush his hand away and take another look around and see Jessie sat at a computer desk in the corner, legs folded and a cup of coffee in hand. I then saw Arthur sat on the middle counter just watching, Jack sat next to Amelie, looking directly at me and Malcom just stood in the middle of the room, making me realise all eyes were on me. They were all waiting for me. Waiting for an answer.

I honestly didn't know what to say. What did I want to do? Did I just want to run and flee? Did I want to fight? Did I want it to all end?

There were so many questions I was asking myself, without knowing the answer to any of them. And they were all waiting on me, for me to decide everyone's fate.

"What do you guys think?" I asked. It was the only way I could actually decide on what to do; I didn't want to be the one choosing and rather it be a mutual agreement, so then I wasn't sealing a destiny for them, a destiny none of them wanted.

"I say we move; we run and find somewhere else. We have been hiding for the last six years! We can carry on running," Arthur said from across the room.

Arthur being the youngest at the age of eighteen, was always trying to develop his skills in everything by learning all the skills we each possessed, taking on too much at once and seemed to be the only one who Hugo hadn't corrupted. He only knew the basics; he never really knew the truth. All he knew was how to run.

"We can't keep running," Malcom spoke up. "What happens if they find us again? Just run? We can't run forever!"

Malcom being the oldest, prime age of thirty-eight, knew the most. His skills were to make endless poisons and explosives, but he also had the hands of a healer, learning to stitch, mend and fix broken objects, let alone people. He was and always had been our surgical hero.

Jack sat on the sofa nodding in agreement with the words Malcom spoke, because like Malcom, Jack too was one of the eldest. Unlike Malcom, Jack had been one of the front runners, leading a team of men and women into combat and missions that led to thousands of deaths, that included children and that was a burden he would forever carry.

"Agreed!" Jessie exclaimed.

"I say we do what Adeline thinks is best to do," Sebastian said, taking hold of my hand this time, making sure I couldn't brush him off.

"If we fight, we have to take the whole programme down," I stated. "We can't just take part of it down. It will have to be the whole thing. It's the only way it can be done."

I looked around looking at everyone, with everyone doing the same thing, looking at each other, trying to gauge what might be said next in the room.

"So, we fight?" Sebastian asked.

"I agree, we fight," Jack said. "Who's in agreement?" he asked.

"Agreed," everyone spoke.

I felt the seat next to me shift again, to see Sebastian pushing himself closer to me, just to then wrap his arms around me and pull me in for a hug, a hug which I instantly melted into feeling safe and warm.

"He isn't going to get any of us," he whispered, trying to reassure me that everything would be ok.

"It's my fault he's after you all, if it wasn't for me being his favourite and leaving, you would all be free out here," I muttered, my words breaking as I did.

"It's not your fault. He will be after everyone who left and without you, we would all be stuck there," Malcom spoke up.

"You're the reason we are free in the first place," Jack agreed.

"Forever on the run! How is that freedom?" I cried, tears falling down my face, finally cracking under the pressure. Sebastian's arms around me got tighter, trying his best to comfort me and make me feel safer than I felt. I shifted in his arms, nuzzling myself more into them, as he rested his chin on top of my head.

"I'd rather be forever on the run than stuck in there, doing their dirty work. They manipulated us constantly and don't forget the stuff they did to us," Amelie stated.

Out of us all, Amelie was the one who had the worse experience. Not only was she the best person for anything mechanical and trained to drive or fly anything that moved, she was also the one that had to constantly relive a nightmare. After all, she had spent most of her time there being tortured and manipulated by Hugo and his men and had the scars to prove it.

"We owe you our lives," Jessie added to the mix of statements everyone was saying.

I sat there feeling loved by them all, but still feeling guilty for everything that was happening in the first place. I should have known Hugo wasn't going to stop till he found me. I wished I could give them a better life than what they had, a life of freedom where they could plant roots, instead of a time stamp of a place, where they would only stay for a short amount of time.

But that was it. We were going to fight. Fight for our lives, fight for our freedom, fight for our future. Fight for us.

Chapter Four

The day itself flew by in a blur; time itself didn't stay still for one moment. People ran around doing things, shadows of figures moving around, preparations being made to infiltrate the annual ball. The task at hand was to get in, go to the office and strip the computer of all its data and secrets and then come back home. In and out, what could possibly go wrong?

Sebastian and Jack spent the day getting supplies from the twins. The twins where called Hannah and Luke. Jessie had found them on the dark web two years ago and they were the ones who would supply us with weapons, equipment, electronics and more. It was hard to trust people at the beginning, especially when we first met them, but after a while they became part of the extended family.

We kept them out of the loop a lot of the time because of the danger that followed. Dragging them into this war we were in wouldn't have been fair, but we knew that our secret was safe with them.

Two Years Ago...

Arrangements had been made to meet them and get the supplies we needed, from the people Jessie had found on the dark web. We were all stood there outside the van, leaning against it, or sat inside it with the side door open, in the middle of nowhere, waiting for the suppliers to arrive. Amelie was impatiently pacing with a cigarette in hand because we had been waiting far too long and because she was forever impatient.

"Didn't they say they were going to be here ten minutes ago? How hard is it to turn up on time?" she asked, looking towards Jessie.

Rolling her eyes Jessie spoke, "Already told you they are running late."

"What if they don't come? We are shark bait!" she expressed, taking another drag from her cigarette.

With a sharp huff, and a clench of her fists, Jessie shouted, "They will be here!"

"Just calm down! Both of you!" Jack snapped, causing my eyes to land on Amelie to see her reaction.

"Your meant to be on my side," Amelie said, turning to him with heartbreak in her eyes. "I am your girlfriend, or did you forget that?"

"Sorry, just be patient, ok?" he spoke, walking towards her, just to give her a kiss on the forehead. He looked down at her and she gave him a smile, only to then give him a small peck on the lips.

"You're lucky you're cute," she stated, causing him to let out a small chuckle, as she pulled him forward and kissed him. They pulled away a few seconds later, just for him to rest his forehead against hers.

"Oh...am I now?" he laughed.

"I'll show you how cute later," she teased him.

"Oh really?"

"Just got to wait and see. I am a girl of many talents after all…"

He smirked, clearly picturing things I really didn't want to know about.

"I'm seriously going to be sick," Arthur chimed in, miming himself vomiting, causing Amelie to flip him off. He chuckled.

"Amelie is right to be impatient, we are in the middle of nowhere," Sebastian spoke, as he climbed out the van to stretch his legs, changing the subject. "Plus, we have been here an hour."

"I told you; they are coming. Are you forgetting how much we are getting?' Jessie exclaimed, frowning at us all.

"We do need them supplies! If one of us gets hurt, how am I going to save any of you?" Malcom asked from the passenger seat, with the window down.

"Yeah… I'd rather wait," Arthur spoke up, while he sat at the edge of the van door, feet on the ground. I just silently watched them all sitting there, letting them all say what they wanted. I was happy to wait, unlike most.

"Finally!" Amelie said, chucking the cigarette to the floor, twisting her boot on it.

We all looked up and saw another black van coming towards us. They had finally showed up. Every one of us got to our feet and stood there waiting for them to get closer and pull up.

When they did, a tall guy with blue hair and a tall girl with short purple hair got out of the van and walked towards us.

"Jessie?" the female asked, looking at all of us, clearly wondering which one she was.

"Hannah!" Jessie spoke, walking up and shaking the girl's hand. "Nice to meet you."

Pointing to the guy with the blue hair next to her, she smiled, "This is Luke, my twin brother."

"Nice to meet you," Jessie said again, shaking Luke's hand.

Looking at the rest of us near the van, Hannah raised a brow. "See you brought the gang?"

"Yeah, I did."

"Just so you know, you don't have to worry about us. We are always on the run ourselves, especially with what we do," Luke spoke up.

"We don't trust easily," Amelie chimed in, walking towards them, standing only inches away, looking like she was ready to fight and clearly not trusting a word coming from either of them. "Especially just on your word alone."

With a smug look on her face, Hannah replied, "I get it. It might take time, but it's true."

Knowing the potential threat, Jack walked towards Amelie. "Come on," he said, getting her to take a few steps back, basically gesturing for her to calm down and leave it alone.

Amelie sighed, but willingly walked away with him, backing away from the situation, defusing the bomb waiting to go off. Jack was the only one who was able to actually get her to calm down quickly, especially in moments like this. She had such a short fuse nowadays due to everything she had gone through, and nobody could blame her for that. A small flame could easily light the match.

"She's got bite," Luke spoke with a smirk on his face, watching Amelie.

The look Amelie gave him looked like she would happily oblige in ripping his head off, but the small squeeze of Jack's hand holding hers made her look at him, bringing her home. After all, home wasn't a place, it was a person. Her person.

"I wouldn't do that," Sebastian chimed in, making them aware not to push her buttons.

"I'm only kidding," Luke smiled.

"Yeah right," Amelie mumbled under her breath, simply rolling her eyes.

Hannah shook her head. "Luke, just go and do the wire transfer with Jessie."

Listening to Hannah, Luke walked off with Jessie, so they could do their thing, while Amelie kept her eyes locked on Luke, following them.

"Who is the medic?" Hannah asked, her eyes scanning the rest of us.

Walking towards her, Malcom held his hand out, "Names Malcom," he spoke, as Hannah happily shook his hand.

Seconds later, Hannah turned around and slid their van door open, pointing at two extremely large grey cases. "Medical supplies you asked for."

Malcom turned to look at Arthur, who quickly came to join him so they could lift one between them, carrying it to our van and sliding it in. They then came back and did the same with the other box.

"What about the ammunition?" I asked, just for Jack to let go of Amelie's hand and walk towards the van.

"Here," Hannah spoke again, climbing into the van to point at another two large black cases.

Looking at each other and then the boxes, Jack and Sebastian walked forward and lifted both of them one by one, loading them into our van.

Luke and Jessie soon came back over and joined us.

Luke nodded towards his sister. "Done," he said, getting his sister to smile.

"Just need the security stuff," Jessie mentioned, for Hannah to point at another large black box.

Sebastian and Jack once again walked towards it and lifted it, taking the last box to the van, only to re-join us seconds later.

"I guess that's it, nice meeting you both," Jessie smiled, making it clear that the transaction was over with, the job was done.

"If you need anything else, don't hesitate to ask," Hannah smiled back. "I know you're not going to believe us, but in this kind of world you need allies. We are willing to help you, but you must trust us. We know what it's like to struggle and if you ever find yourself needing a place to stay, just ask."

"We are fine on our own and have been for years," Amelie didn't hesitate to mention.

"We want to help, just remember that," Hannah said, looking directly at Amelie.

"We didn't ask for it!"

"Well technically you did."

"I don't like you."

"Well, we don't do this job to be liked."

"Cat fight!" Arthur shouted, only for Hannah and Amelie to look at him.

"I'll kick your ass in a minute," Amelie hissed towards Arthur.

"Come on then!" Arthur egged her on. She stepped towards him but was then blocked by Jack standing in front of her.

"Leave it," he tried to reassure her, trying to get her to look at him.

"Pretty boy got a mouth on him," she snapped, looking directly at Arthur, who was stood there smiling and waving at her. "He needs to be put in his place."

"I'd like to see you try," Arthur teased. That boy had a death wish and soon enough it was going to be granted.

"Arthur! Stop it!" Jack shouted, taking a glance at him.

Arthur raised both hands in the air like he was surrendering, admitting defeat. "She started it," he shot back.

"I'll finish it!" Amelie took another step towards him.

"Stop!" Jack shouted at Amelie. He clearly instantly regretted the words as soon as he saw the way she looked at him.

I watched as she pulled her arm out of his grip, not happy with him in the slightest. Then again, I wouldn't be either if he was my partner and spoke to me like that. Just from the frown that etched across his face and the guilt ridden look in his eyes, he clearly knew in that moment that he had fucked up for shouting at her. Everyone including myself knew it was something she had experienced constantly in the programme and that his actions would make her have flashbacks of events that traumatised her.

Watching as Jack tried to reach out to her again, she shouted. "Leave it!" She then pushed him away, not wanting to be touched.

In that moment, we could all see the pain in her eyes from him shouting, meaning she was playing every moment in her mind on a loop. The torment, the control, the unsteadiness that she constantly faced, like everything within her was fighting against itself to stop her from breaking the control she had over herself.

My instinct was to run up to her and hug her, but I knew, like most, she had to approach you. If you were to go up to her now, she would shut you down and not engage with you. It had to be her call.

In a huff, she turned around and walked towards me. As she got closer to me, she reached out for me, causing me to hold my arms out towards her. She instantly wrapped her arms around me and buried her face into my neck as I wrapped my arms around her, embracing her in a hug.

"It's ok," I soothed her, as my hand gently rubbed her back. "He didn't mean it. You know he loves you," I stated. I was simply trying my best to comfort her from her own thoughts, thoughts I knew so much about being her best friend and all.

After a few minutes, she pulled away and gave me a weak smile, just to then turn and jump into the van, slamming the door shut behind her, clearly wanting a moment to herself.

Jack, standing there looking defeated and annoyed at himself for what he had done, sighed. "Well…that's me in the doghouse."

Knowing Jack, I knew he always wanted to do right by her, protect her from the world and always did. I could tell that sometimes he felt like he was the monster, but he wasn't, I knew this because it was the same way I looked when I thought about the same thing.

"Sorry," Arthur said sheepishly.

"Just forget it and stop taunting her," Jack said to Arthur, just for him to nod in agreement. "You know how she gets, especially after everything."

After a few minutes of awkward silence, Hannah got back into the van, while Luke walked around to the other side.

"Thank you for your help. I know we don't seem like the friendliest of people right now, but I'm sure you understand," I said, with Hannah nodding at me, paying her respects.

"We get it. When you come from such a shitty background it's bound to cause some changes and the world around you becomes harder. We understand that more than most," Hannah explained, as the vans engine started. "See you around and stay safe."

"You too," I smiled.

Soon enough the van started to move, leaving us all watching the van disappear into the distance. The deal had been done and a new chapter had started.

Present...

Jessie had spent the day busy at her big four screen computer desk, trying to put our fake identities on the list for the annual ball so we had a way of infiltrating them. The rest were just prepping for anything and everything they could as we had to be ready.

Me on the other hand, I stayed to myself for the day. I just wanted space and had spent that time sat in my room, cup of coffee in hand, staring at the countryside out my window. I watched how the crops swayed in the breeze and how all the warm colours blended together. The sun had hit its highest peak of the day and had slowly faded away and let the sunset appear. All the pinks, oranges and yellows blended together, creating a beautiful moment that made the perfect photograph in my mind.

I needed to be away from the others, to get my head in the right frame of mind. It was the moment I had always dreaded; I'd known it was coming, but part of me had always hoped that it wouldn't be anytime soon. I'd even hoped it would never come at all and that maybe we would have a clean future, a future I should have known would never exist, a future that would forever be a dream. Fiction.

The ball itself was a way for Hugo to show off, show his power, his wealth; for him to make connections and show off his prized possessions. Once I loved the balls too, when I was in the programme, but that first time was just a distant memory.

Eight years ago…

I was sat on my bed in a luxury room, filled with bookshelves, expensive jewellery, clothes, and furniture, being treated like royalty by Hugo. I was his pride and joy. He would do anything he could for me, trying his best to please me and show me how much I meant to him.

The book in my hand was my favourite, something fictional but full of love, something that made me cry. The emotions I felt throughout this book made my heart bleed and my tears fall. It then went on to heal the broken pieces it created. It was a world I wanted to be in. A world I could read on my rainy days.

**

KNOCK! KNOCK!

Someone banging on the door caused me to slide my bookmark in and put the book on my bed.

"Come in!" I shouted.

With a creak from my bedroom door, it opened just for Hugo to walk in with a smile plastered across his face. Hugo had his longish black hair slicked back, while he wore his dark shades, something he would wear more than anything, same with his suited and booted look. He didn't look bad for a man in early fifties, but then again, I never really knew his exact age, even with being by his side for many years. We never celebrated any birthdays. Nothing ever got celebrated unless Hugo made an exception, like my birthday only. It was something I hated because he would make a big deal about it. I would celebrate my friend's birthdays secretly, but not enough to cause Hugo to pay attention. Truth was, he just hated the attention not being on him. He had the power, the control and he thrived on it. Thrived on it so much it consumed him.

Watching him enter the room, I saw him carrying a large purple box with a green ribbon wrapped around it, a present of some sort. I slowly got to my feet as Hugo got closer to me and put the box at the end of my bed. He then looked at me with a smile.

"What's in the elegant box?" I asked, pointing to it; my curiosity getting the better of me. I never did like surprises and Hugo knew that, but yet still did them as it pleased him.

"That, my darling, is for you," he beamed.

"For me?" I questioned.

"Yes, my dear," he grinned; his smile as wide as the Cheshire Cat's.

I sat down next to the box admiring it, wondering what secrets it had hidden inside.

"How would you like to finally come to the annual ball?"

A smile plastered across my face, I shouted. "Really!" With the happiness taking over my body.

From the upturned look on his face, the raised prominent cheekbones and the overall visage that glowed, my reaction made him beyond happy. It was clearly a reaction he was hoping for, a reaction to boost his ego.

"Really," he smiled, only for me to shoot up and hug him, as fast as I could.

I pulled away smiling and looked at the box, still

curious about what was inside it. "So, what's in there?"

"Open it," he encouraged me, with a nod of his head in the direction of the box.

I ribbed opened the box in seconds, to reveal the most stunning red celestial dress I had ever seen. I was mesmerised by its beauty.

The dress was elegant and delicate from what I could see, causing me to pull the dress out of the box and look at it properly. It was out of this world, a dress from the fairy-tales. It was radiantly long and flowing, covered in small glittered embedded stars, that where etched into the lace material that covered the red silk underneath. The sleeves were slightly off the shoulder and short, but this was a dress for royalty, a dress fit for a princess, which was definitely not me, but a dress I would wear in a heartbeat.

"You will be the Belle of the ball," Hugo beamed.

I took another look at the box to see there was a mask that was red and laced to go with the dress and next to it was a silver flower crown. It had a small red dangling bead in the middle that would rest on your forehead with two silver strands coming from it, connecting beautiful red roses that wrapped around the rest of the crown itself. I was beyond happy and couldn't believe what he had given me.

Quickly placing the dress back onto the bed, I ran and hugged him again, causing him to laugh. "Thank you! Thank you! Thank you!" I squealed, over excited that I was finally attending a ball, especially in a dress like that. A child on a sugar rush high.

Hugo pulled away soon enough and clicked his fingers, causing a man to walk in with another box, the same as mine.

"Can't let you go on your own. Pick a friend to attend,"

he smiled, as the man placed the box on the bed next to mine. It was a no brainer who I wanted to invite.

"Amelie," I didn't hesitate to pick. Hugo to sighed and pulled his face at Amelie's name.

From the clench of his jaw, the visible vein in the middle of his forehead throbbing and the small flare of his nostrils, the hate and dislike of hearing Amelie's name became prominent. He always believed that girl did wrong, stepped out of line, didn't obey the simple rules he set in place and because of his 'belief', he made her pay the price with the reward of a thousand nightmares.

If it was up to him, I would have different people around me, ones he would personally love to pick, but I knew that he knew he couldn't control me too much. The risk in controlling me too much, the risk of losing me, wasn't a risk he wanted to take.

"I know you don't like her, but please?" I asked, hoping, praying he would accept.

"For you, anything," he smiled, giving me a kiss on the forehead, causing me to smile even more. Hugo then turned on his heels and started to walk back to the door, but before he got to it, he turned around and looked at me again. "I've chosen Sebastian and Jack to look after you all, so they will come get you beforehand." He then walked out, leaving me full of happiness and full of love.

Present...

A simple knock at the door snapped me out of my memories, strangely feeling connected to my own thoughts. Déjà vu, a feeling I always felt, especially now. Time was playing on a constant loop, a never-ending cycle.

"Come in!" I shouted, not even looking in the

direction of the creaking door and the footsteps entering.

A small figure in the corner of my eye sat down at the end of my bed and watched me. I knew that they had come to talk to me, that they had come to make sure I was alright and that I hadn't snapped or broke, not just yet anyways.

I sighed to myself and turned towards Amelie who was sat there in her training gear, with a concerned look on her face. "I'm sorry that it's come to this," I muttered, feeling my tears building up, praying they wouldn't make an appearance.

"Not your fault," she quickly replied. "We all knew this day was coming… it just came sooner than we hoped for." I knew that deep down she was right; we had all prepared for this day. It was just that the day of reckoning had hit us faster than we could blink, but then again, when would be the perfect time?

"I wish our lives were different," I slipped out. "I wanted a life of having fun, finding someone to love, having a family…. being free. I wish there was some kind of cosmic loophole that could let us restart, have different lives away from Scarlet. A life where we still had each other without running or fearing for our lives every second of the day."

Amelie just sat there looking at me, reading me and reading the pain on my face and in my eyes. It was a pain I knew she felt too because she also wished for the same restart. However, we both knew this was the card we had been dealt and we had to accept that. We just wished the fear didn't exist and that it wasn't lurking in the shadows waiting to jump out of the dark. Horror resurfacing and coming back to life.

"I promise once this is over, we can have the life we want," Amelie smiled at me. It was a promise I knew

Amelie would try her best to keep because it was a promise, she was trying to keep to herself too. "Try and get some sleep, okay?" she said, just for me to nod. "If you fancy coming to train, feel free to join, but in the meantime, just relax and sleep." As soon as the words had left her lips she was gone, leaving me sat there again on my own, with my memories haunting me and my own personal Devil that sat on my shoulder, holding his pitchfork, waiting for the perfect moment to strike.

Chapter Five

I spent the next hour lounging in bed, thinking rest would be the answer, but my brain was too wide awake for me to relax, let alone sleep. Everything was haunting me. Eternal happiness, destruction, pain, death, the fate of us all, my mind thought about everything. Eternal happiness was something I wished for, but my brain wouldn't let me forget it wasn't possible, especially with the lives we lived. Destruction, how it followed and how no matter where we went, we left the place in despair, a foundation waiting to crack.

***

I dabbled with the idea of doing some training like Amelie had said, that it might help me get rid of the tension my body seemed to be holding onto.

Maybe I could beat a punching bag picturing Hugo's face, take all my anger out on the man I hated the most in this world, a man I grew up loving like a father, only for it to all be a fabricated lie.

I shot myself up and out of bed, jumping at the idea of

taking my stress out on something so then I could focus, even if it meant I could only sleep for a few hours.

Quickly changing into some workout attire, I walked out of my room and down the stairs to see Sebastian coming out of the kitchen with a bottle of water in hand.

"Training too?" he asked, while I watched him look me up and down.

I hesitated in responding due to the last conversation we had being me confessing my love to him and him standing there silently. For now, I had to bury it, pretend, and act like I was fine, like I was doing with everything else.

"Best way to get some stress out," I smiled slightly, knowing he fully knew what I was hinting at, as he seemed to be in the same mindset.

"Train with me?" he asked. I hesitated.

Could I still be myself with him? Even when he knew the truth?

"Sure," I agreed, causing Sebastian to smile more and lead the way down the long hallway.

I always knew we were blessed to find such a big house that had multiple rooms, especially so we could set up our own training room, medical room, and anything we really needed. This was a place of possibilities, a place we could one day maybe call our eternal home.

**

The training room was filled high and low with equipment. It had a climbing wall, archery boards, mats, treadmills, weights, and some punching bags in the corner.

It was a good thing we had eventually trusted Hannah and Luke, as they supplied us with everything. We were extremely lucky they did, without them I don't know where we would be.

As soon as we both entered, we could see Amelie and Jack training together. Amelie had two small wooden objects in her hands, symbolising knives and so did Jack. She was swinging them at Jack, but he was able to block every blow she tried to give. She was trying with everything she had to land a blow, but nothing was working. Jack then slipped his leg under hers, bringing her down to the floor on her back, but she grabbed him, causing him to fall with her, just to then land on top of her and them both to start instantly laughing.

Watching them together was like watching a romantic film in reality, something so pure and innocent that it made you believe in true love. It was something for the hopeless romantics, like me.

Jack leant down and kissed her. Amelie instantly started returning the gesture, both smiling into the kiss. They both seemed to get swept up in the moment and the next thing me and Sebastian saw was roaming hands and Jack kissing down Amelie's neck, not realising we were stood there.

The moment before us started to heat up instantly, until Sebastian walked further in and spoke. "Just to let you know there is such a thing as a bed for those kinds of things."

They both suddenly stopped and turned their heads to face us, only to look at each other and burst out laughing again. Jack then quickly stood up and put his hand out towards Amelie, just for her to accept and for him to pull her to her feet. They both looked flustered and red at the cheeks as they turned to look at us, with Amelie biting her lip, trying to contain another laugh.

Rubbing the back of his neck, Jack looked between us. "How long were you stood there for?" he asked.

"Long enough," Sebastian said.

Jack let out a small chuckle and looked towards Amelie. "Oops," he spoke, causing her to laugh. He turned back to face us and smiled. I just stood there watching Amelie, who was admiring Jack with so much love and desire in her eyes and a smile on her face. I watched how Jack took a glance at her and how he instantly smiled at seeing her looking at him the way she was. Both just standing there with so much love between them.

Amelie walked closer to Jack, wrapping her arms loosely around his waist, only for him to wrap one of his arms around her shoulders. It was a love and devotion I wanted for myself, causing me to take a small glance towards Sebastian. It was what I wanted with him. Clearly, I had a hopeless crush on a man that didn't want me and more than likely never would. Fairy tales always said a man wanted a damsel in distress, but as much as I could be seen as one, I wasn't wanted.

What was worse than a damsel?

A broken heart.

***

"We will leave you two to train," Jack said, causing me to look back at them both and to catch Amelie watching me. I could clearly see on her face that she knew what I was thinking.

Him. *Always* him.

Jack removed his arm from around Amelie's shoulders, just to quickly pick her up and chuck her over his shoulder, causing her to squeal, "Jack!"

He let out a chuckle and started walking towards the door with her. "I've got plans for you," he said, smacking her ass, causing her to giggle louder. Jack walked past us with Amelie waving as they exited the room, just for her giggling to echo down the corridor, filling the house with life.

***

I turned to see Sebastian looking at me, just for us both to start laughing.

"Lovers eh!" Sebastian nervously laughed. I just nodded, my laughter falling away. Part of me felt jealous, jealous of the fact they both had someone to love and to love them back. I always thought that maybe I would find it one day, but I knew I had to realise it may not be written in my story anymore.

My star in the sky wouldn't be the star to fall.

I felt a hand touch my shoulder and I looked up towards Sebastian, meaning I had got lost in my own thoughts again.

"You ok?" he asked.

"Yeah, I'm fine," I slightly smiled, not revealing the truth about my own thoughts to him.

Sebastian stood looking at me and from his reaction alone, I knew he didn't believe me, but I also knew that he knew, if I wanted to talk about it, I would.

"What do you want to do first?" he asked me, changing the subject. I just shrugged.

I really wanted to tell him the truth first. I wanted to tell him about my feelings and find out how he felt, but that wasn't going to happen. We had already tried that.

He looked down and picked up the wooden objects Amelie and Jack had left on the floor and held them up. "Want to train with these?" he asked.

"Sure," I hesitantly smiled, wishing I had the guts to bring up this conversation playing over in my head, but knowing I did it this morning and it had to blown up in my face, I wouldn't do it again, I couldn't.

Sebastian chucked them at me one at a time, causing me to catch both of them as I walked over to him and stood in front of him.

As soon as I was close enough, he grabbed my arms and put them in a better position. "Put one arm like this and the other like that," he said, his touch making my body shiver. It was a touch that was forever imprinted on my skin like a tattoo. Something I wanted to feel forever.

He looked down at my feet and laughed. "Put your feet, here and here." He kicked my feet so I would move them, making sure I looked ready and was in the right position to train. "Stand like that because when you swing this arm, you can aim for here." His hands slowly touched my left arm, while his other hand pointed to his right shoulder. "Try it." At that comment I did, I aimed with my left arm like he said. He blocked my blow. "Now aim for other areas and move your feet. Make sure you try to kick and slide your feet under your opponent, try take them by surprise." He smiled, as I rolled my eyes at him. "Yeah, yeah. I know you already know this, but I'm improving your skills Adi." He laughed and I swung at him, trying to take him by surprise, but failing due to him blocking it again.

He just stood there laughing at me, knowing full well what I was trying to do. I took this as my sign to start swinging at him repeatedly, trying to land that hit.

However, everything I tried was failing, so I started to use my legs, trying to kick him, but he seemed to either dodge them or block them too.

At this rate, I felt like I wouldn't be able to knock him off his feet, as much as I would love to prove him wrong. Put him in his place, just this once.

Without realising, we were both in full combat mode, trying to get the other to the ground. I went to spin around and get him from another angle, only for him to wrap his arm around me with the wooden object against my neck and the other at my side, with my back pressed against his chest. I could feel his hot breath against the side of my face.

"Got you," he softly spoke, causing the hairs on the back of my neck to stand up tall.

I turned my head slightly to the side to see his face only inches from mine, his eyes locking onto mine. We were both breathing heavily, staring at each other, not being able to break the gaze. I could feel the heat of his chest against my back, my heart beating as fast as his, the air in the room growing thinner, the tension between us building.

Before I knew it, I had turned around in his arms and was facing him, still only inches away. His arms were still wrapped around me, but lowering down to my waist, while my hands rested against his chest, feeling the beat of his heart and his chest rise and fall. I could feel the heat in the room intensifying and the feeling between us getting stronger, as everything around us seemed to disappear, leaving just us. We were both looking into each other's eyes and then to each other's lips, the tension growing by the second. I could feel us both getting closer and closer with our lips almost touching. I felt his hand slowly making its way to cup the side of my face, just for me to relax into his touch. I wanted this, I wanted to kiss him, and I wasn't going to stop it.

Suddenly, there was the noise of wooden objects hitting the floor, the noise breaking us out of the moment. We instantly and quickly took a few steps away from each other and looked away. Sebastian had accidentally dropped them from his right hand in the moment.

I took a glance towards him and saw his cheeks were flustered red just like mine.

His eyes met mine as he scratched his head, something he would do when he was nervous. "I...I...I should go and shower," he got out. I sighed, the moment clearly over.

"Yeah, same here," I disappointingly agreed, knowing we didn't seem to know how to act with each other in moments like this.

Secretly I wished I had the nerve to just walk up to him right now and pull him forward, kissing him in seconds and taking him by surprise, but I knew I didn't have the guts to do it. I wished it would happen, then maybe I would finally know the truth about what was going on between us, but I knew it wouldn't be right to chuck it on him again. I saw how that went in the store and how it didn't seem to do anything good for me or for us.

I just stood there not knowing what to do, as Sebastian picked up the wooden objects and put them away, only then to stop and look at me; both still not knowing what to say to the other. I hated the silence more than anything and knew I had to say something, but I also knew I would be better not mentioning it.

"I guess I'll see you in the morning," I slightly smiled, slowly walking past him.

He instantly grabbed hold of my arm, causing me to stop and look at him.

Our eyes locked once again, as we both stood there not saying a word. There was something about this gesture that made me think he had stopped me for the reason I was hoping for. His touch was all I craved and the feeling of his hands on me instantly warmed my insides, as they screamed for more of him. I watched as he tried to speak, but nothing seemed to be coming out.

He seemed to give up and let me go. "See you in the morning," he spoke.

I could feel my insides crumbling at the loss of his touch as I turned away and walked towards the door. I then suddenly stopped and turned towards him again, catching him watching me.

"Night Sebastian," I weakly smiled once more and turned to disappear out of the room, up the stairs to my own room. I then took a quick shower and chucked myself into bed, falling into a deep sleep quickly.

My last thought being him.

Chapter Six

The night was quiet, not even a creak in the house. Silent as a mouse, enough to hear a pin drop. Everyone was sleeping, getting in their rest for the adventures of the night coming. The rest would be needed, the battle was coming, a fight we had to win and control. We had to stop Hugo. The only way to stop him was to kill him, destroy the building and put an end to it all. Challenge accepted.

Suddenly, there was a noise, causing me to shoot up from my bed and wonder what was going on. I sat there listening, no longer being able to hear anything, thinking it was all in my head, till there was a bang against my wall. I stayed still listening and heard another bang against the wall, realising it was coming from Sebastian's room, as his room was next door.

BANG! BANG! BANG!

From the sounds I could hear, I knew there was something wrong and I needed to know what was happening. I got up as fast as I could and ran out of my room to his, knocking on his door, only to get no answer.

"NO! NO! NO!" I heard coming from inside, causing me to push the door open, to see him thrashing in the sheets.

I instantly ran towards him, trying to shake him awake. "Seb! Seb! Wake up! You're safe," I shouted.

He shot up panting, breathing heavily. His eyes were vacant, like nobody was there. Like he hadn't realised what was really happening. When he suddenly noticed me sitting there, he instantly grabbed me, hugging me, holding me tight. Though I was taken by surprise, I soon hugged him back instinctively, holding him close, giving him the reassurance he needed in that moment.

After a few minutes, I still felt him breathing heavily and holding onto me tightly, like he was scared. "You're safe," I whispered to him. "I'm here for you." I tried my best to reassure him, rubbing his back lightly, feeling him slowly calm down and his breathing return to normal.

After a few more minutes, he pulled away and pushed himself back, resting himself against the headboard as I sat there quietly watching. "I'm sorry," he let out, closing his eyes in embarrassment.

"Why are you sorry?" I asked.

He opened his eyes and looked towards me. "Sorry you had to see me like that."

"No need to be sorry. Were you having a nightmare?"

He sat there frozen and gulped. I knew deep down he didn't want to talk about it, but I was giving him the option. The ball was in his court, and he didn't need to play it if he didn't want to.

"Yeah, I always have them," he hesitantly said. "Some nights they are worse than normal... like tonight."

"What about?" I asked wanting to help him, only if he wanted to talk about it.

"I...I...," he tried to get out. He couldn't speak. "Losing someone."

I sat there, a little puzzled by his answer. "You're not going to lose us."

"I'm not talking about them," he spoke. "I'm talking about you; I don't want to lose you."

I sat there silently, just watching him. I could see how broken and weak he felt in that moment. He hated feeling vulnerable, hated showing his weaknesses. I stood up and moved closer to him, taking a seat next to him and pulling him in for a hug, holding him tightly, to feel him melt into me. He then pulled away and led down, resting his head on my lap, causing me to instantly play with his hair, giving him a soothing gesture. All I wanted to do in that moment was hold him, protect him and be there for him, like he always was for me. Two broken souls trying to fix each other.

"I'm always going to be here for you, Sebastian," I softly spoke, still running my fingers through his hair. "I'm not going anywhere."

He turned around onto his back to look up at me, my palm instantly going to his face, rubbing his cheek with my thumb.

"You're the one person that I can't lose," he whispered, pain and heartache laced in his voice.

We sat there just looking at each other, with me still holding him, caressing his face, only for his hand to come and rest on mine, the one that was on the side of his face. We sat there just taking in one another, finding comfort, peace and serenity. A simple gesture greatly appreciated.

I could feel the pull towards him again just like every other time, giving me the butterflies. It was times like this where he showed me his true self, where I felt honoured for even knowing him. But I knew that despite what this was to me, this was just a moment of friendship to him.

"Will you stay the night?" he asked me, just wanting me to be there with him.

"Always," I smiled, for the light in his beautiful blue eyes to come back to life.

He sat himself up and put himself back on the right side of the bed, as climbed into the other side, lying myself down to face him.

I watched how he seemed to be studying me, like he was searching for something. "Can I ask you a question?" he asked.

"Sure."

"Will you...erm...hold me?" he asked hesitantly.

I slowly let out a weak smile towards him, feeling privileged he would ask me something like that, like he felt comforted by me the most out of anyone. I turned myself over onto my back and held my arm out. He then shuffled himself closer to me, resting his head against my chest. He wrapped his arm over my waist, and I wrapped my arm around his back. In this moment, he just wanted the support I was offering. It was moments like this that I would never take for granted, a moment where he would break down his walls and just let me be there to guide him.

"I'll always hold you," I reassured him, slowly playing with his hair once again.

"Thank you," he said, melting into me.

"I promise I'm not going anywhere. If you want me here, I'll be here."

After a few minutes of silence, I could hear small sniffles and slowly ran my finger across his cheek, noticing it was wet to touch. I pulled him in tighter. "No need to cry," I comforted, hoping that all he could feel was love, the love I had for him, the kind of love that makes you feel whole again and the world a brighter place.

"They are happy tears. I feel safe with you," he admitted, making it known he was feeling the love I was giving him. Especially with the fact I had a tight hold on him. A blanket of cover.

"You never need to ask for anything like this. Just tell me and I'll do it."

"How did I end up so lucky to have you?"

"I ask myself the same question about you."

"We are quite the pair. Aren't we?" he laughed.

"We certainly are."

"The sound of your heart beating soothes me, makes me relax, makes me feel better," he stated, not knowing his words made me smile.

I sat there silently, listening to his breathing and how it got heavier, meaning he had fallen asleep. Knowing this made me smile more than I already was. He had felt that reassured by me and comforted because I was there, he could sleep peacefully, away from the terrors and nightmares that followed him. Away from the horrors that were once inflicted on him to cause him hell, to haunt him for the rest of his days to come, until the end of the line. I wanted to tell him I felt the same way about him, about the nightmares I faced of losing him and how it killed me, but I didn't want to burden him with my own problems as I was there for him, not for myself. I slowly closed my own eyes, feeling warm and toasty with him around me and I let sleep sweep over me, taking me into the clouds of my dreams and away from reality.

A dream world where we could be happy.

Chapter Seven

T he smell of coffee filled the air once again, light draping through the curtains, and I could feel my head on something solid. When I opened my eyes, I saw that I had my head on Sebastian's chest, my arm draped over him and his arms wrapped around me, holding me close. During the night we had switched without realising. I was comfy and content and didn't want to move, but I knew I had to.

I pulled myself away and sat up with my head against the bed frame, to see Sebastian was already awake, his eyes glued on me. He had clearly been watching me sleep.

"Sorry," I apologised, for being asleep on him, feeling like he only stayed there because he didn't want to wake me.

"No need to be sorry. I liked it. Plus, it's the first night I've not had any nightmares," he reassured me.

Hearing this made me smile, knowing I had helped him meant everything to me and more. I wanted to support him more than anything. If I couldn't love him the way I so badly wished I could, at least I could love him this way and still have something.

"All I did was fall asleep," I shot back at him, causing him to have a small chuckle.

"By you being here, it made everything better," he beamed, his cheeks blushing.

His words made the butterflies in my stomach come back to life and my cheeks to turn that extra shade of red, just like they always did.

He looked at me again, holding his hand out in my direction. I looked at him and then his hand, only to lift mine and place it in his and for him to tightly hold onto it.

"Can I say something?" he asked, looking down at our hands as he slowly traced the lines on my palm with his fingertips. A sensitive touch that sent shivers through me.

"Sure," I smiled, curious to know what he wanted to talk about.

"That talk...the one we were having in the store," he mentioned, his eyes landing on mine.

"You mean the talk I was having with you, where you stood silent?" I asked, raising a brow, as he scratched his and looked away from me.

He turned to face me again, with his eyes watching me once more. "Yes, that talk," he blushed.

"What about it?" I asked.

"I didn't know what to say to you, it's why I didn't say anything at the time."

"We don't have to talk about it."

"No, we do need to talk about it," he responded quickly. "I just don't know how to put it in words."

"You can tell me anything, you should know that by now," I reassured him, not wanting him to feel pressured into the conversation, even though I wanted to know everything right now.

Deep down my stomach was doing flips, my heart was

beating out of my chest, this was the moment. Then out of nowhere fear took over and I started to doubt myself. What if he was going to say he didn't feel the same way? What if he said he actually did love me? Was this going to affect our friendship?

"I know I can tell you anything, but I just wanted to say the right thing," he admitted, making me realise it was all he had been thinking about...but was it good or bad?

"Just tell me...the good, bad or the ugly, just tell me," I stated, putting my other hand on his, causing him to look up at me.

I knew I had to hear what he had to say because I would spend every second of every minute, of every hour, of every day, weeks, or months with it eating away at me. A question I wanted the answer to, a riddle needing to be solved.

"I feel it too," he awkwardly smiled, taking me by surprise. I couldn't believe I had heard him say he felt it too, I knew there was something and I couldn't believe I was right. "Just promise me you will be careful tonight and then we can have a proper talk tomorrow."

I sat there frozen and disappointed that this was the end of the talk, that something he brought up and something I desperately wanted to talk about, lasted only seconds. I hoped there would be more than just him saying he felt it too, but I knew I couldn't rush him to talk about it, it wouldn't be fair. I wanted to know his thoughts about it, about what he truly felt besides the tension, like was it good? Was it bad? What was it?

There were too many questions on a loop in my head. I looked at him and nodded, nonetheless. Sebastian then let go of my hand as he got out of the bed and then walked straight to his drawers. I watched as he pulled out some clothes and headed straight into the bathroom, leaving me sitting there speechless. I just sat there waiting, waiting for him to come out and when he did, he appeared fully dressed, chucking his dirty boxers straight into the washing basket.

Sebastian then stopped and stood there, cocking his head to the side while he looked at me. "I thought you might have gone," he smiled, making me smile back.

"Was that my sign to leave?" I asked, causing him to laugh.

"No! Never! I just assumed you would have gone to get changed. We have a busy day ahead," he replied quickly. I knew he was right; it was a day of strategy and planning ahead for tonight's events.

"Well as I know we aren't going out till later; I think I'll stay in what I'm already in," I grinned. He just rolled his eyes at my comment and walked towards his bedroom door, opening it, signalling the way for me. I shook my head at him, causing him to let out a slight laugh.

"The cheek," he pointed at me, making my insides turn to jelly, just from the simplest of flirty things.

"Takes one to know one," I teased, as I got up out of the bed and walked towards the door and through it, with Sebastian following not far behind me.

***

Walking straight into the open planned kitchen, we saw Amelie and Jack having a make out session once again. They both clearly couldn't take their hands off each other. It was lovely to see people so in love, especially in the world we lived in, but not like that on the couch, in a room where everyone sits. Sebastian stopped in his tracks and coughed, signalling people had entered the room. They both pulled apart and looked towards us, realising they had been caught once again.

"Morning," Amelie smiled, red at the cheeks, looking extremely flustered.

"Morning," I smiled back.

"Didn't expect to walk into something this morning, after the sounds I could hear last night," Sebastian shot at them, as they both laughed.

"Sorry," Jack spoke, as Amelie sat there biting her lip.

"Save it for the bedroom, not the sofa," Sebastian teased them both.

"Not stopped us before," Amelie muttered under her breath, only for us both to quickly turn and look at her, hearing every word.

"I'm never sitting there ever again," Sebastian expressed, looking disgusted by the comment, making Amelie realise how loud she had said it.

"Oops?" she sarcastically replied, with an amused look on her face.

Sebastian shook his head and walked over to the counter with me not far behind. As I reached the first counter, I sat down on a stool and leant forward, watching him make two coffees and some toast. He then turned towards me and placed one in front of me, while he stood there munching on a slice of toast with the other one on a plate in front of him. I quickly reached forward and grabbed the extra, only to take a bite out of it and for his mouth to open, shocked at my action.

"That was mine," he frowned.

I smiled and took another bite. "Sharing's caring," I mumbled, stuffing my face.

"If it was anybody else, I would be mad. When it's you, I find it cute," he smiled, causing me to blush, making me remember the first time we met all those years ago.

Wait...did he just call me cute?

Nine Years Ago...

Like every morning, I walked through the grand doors into the dining room to meet Hugo. When I walked in there was a long table in the middle that could happily sit up to ten people, while the walls were decorated with famous paintings from Van Gogh to Andy Warhol, pieces of history that I loved to see every morning, making me realise the beauty of untold stories. There was also an elegant chandelier above, a signature piece of furniture that Hugo seemed to put everywhere. Hugo loved the expensive taste and was a man who would flash his cash, not caring who saw or what anyone thought. After all, he was a very wealthy man, due to the business he ran and the company he kept around him.

I walked in the room and saw Hugo sat at the top of the table, coffee in hand and newspaper in the other, just like every other morning.

As soon as Hugo saw me, he put the newspaper down and smiled. "Morning, Dear."

"Morning," I responded, taking the seat next to him.

In front of me was a selection of toast, fruit, cereal, a glass of apple juice and a full English. I was always spoilt for choice; I could have anything I fancied. I reached over and grabbed a slice of toast, while I added a fried egg, just to then dig in, enjoying the food in front of me.

"So, I have someone I'd like you to meet," Hugo said, causing me to look at him. "He's someone I trust and someone I'd like you to get to know."

As soon as Hugo finished his sentence, the doors

opened and in walked a man I couldn't take my eyes off. He was breathtakingly handsome and was definitely a fine-looking man. Some eye candy.

"Sebastian!" Hugo exclaimed, with a smile on his face.

Sebastian walked around the table and sat opposite me, both of us staring at each other as he did, like we were both drawn to each other, causing me to feel a funny feeling I had never experienced before. "Sebastian, this is Adeline. Adeline, this is Sebastian," Hugo pointed at us both.

"Nice to meet you, Adeline," he smiled, causing me to blush and push a loose piece of hair behind my ear.

"Nice to meet you, Sebastian," I smiled. We both carried on looking at each other not saying a word, memorised and intrigued by each other. I could feel myself getting lost in his eyes, as ours remained locked to each other. There was something about him that was so hypnotising that I couldn't resist. It was like he was putting me under a spell, like he was the Pied Piper, and I was the prey.

"Adeline here is my best female fighter," Hugo spoke, breaking the moment we were both having.

"Is she now?" Sebastian asked, raising his eyebrow, a smirk on his face, like he didn't believe a word Hugo was saying or just wanted to get under my skin. Well, as much as he was a dreamboat, he seemed to be an asshole.

"She is. And Sebastian is my best male fighter," he told me, causing me to lean back in my chair with a smug look on my face.

"Oh really?" I added, looking at Sebastian.

Two could play at this game, pretty boy.

"I could take her down," Sebastian teased. I scoffed.

I could tell that Sebastian had balls, suspected balls of

steel. I would happily chop them and 'it' right off just to bring him down a peg or two.

"I'd like to see you try."

"Don't tempt me."

"Bite me," I smirked, causing him to laugh again. I hated to admit it, but I kind of liked this Sebastian guy, there was something about him, even if he was 'slightly' an asshole.

"You two are going to get along nicely," Hugo smiled, as he stood up from the table. "I've got things to do, so I will leave you two to get to know each other."

We both watched how he made his way across the room and left, leaving the two of us, with both of us instantly looking at each other again once the door closed.

Sebastian lent forward on the table. His eyes seemed to search mine, like he was trying to take a photographic picture in his head.

"Take a picture it'll last longer," I teased him. He just rolled his eyes at me, making the funny feeling inside me grow stronger.

What was it about him?

"I like you, you got attitude," he smirked, causing me to pull a face and feel giggly on the inside. There was something so intriguing about him, but I couldn't seem to put my finger on it

"So, what has he told you to do for me?" I asked him, curious why Hugo got us to meet and my strange infatuation with him already.

"To train you, look after you and basically be your babysitter," he stated, with a smug look on his face, trying his best to tease me and lie through his teeth.

Oh Sebastian, don't bullshit a bullshitter.

"I highly doubt that," I shot back at him, knowing full well he was just saying it all for a laugh.

"It's true."

"Lies."

"Want to bet on it?"

"Try me," I shot back at him again, both of us realising we were both just firing answers back at each other.

"I'll win," he smirked.

"Doubtful," I scoffed.

"You're psychotic."

"You're insatiable."

"You can't be serious?"

"Deadly serious," I smirked again, causing him to laugh.

"This is going to be the start of a beautiful friendship," he smiled.

"Friendship?" I asked, with a confused look on my face, taunting him further.

So...he actually wanted to be my friend, even with all the irritable things he was saying.

"Yes," he said.

"You're dreaming."

"I'm dreaming?"

"Sounds to me like you are."

"Scared of friendship?"

"Nope."

"Have you even got any friends?"

"Tonnes."

"I like you."

"Oh really?"

"You're the only one who's ever called me out for my shit," he said, causing me to stay silent and just look at him.

I knew he had a point; I was calling him out on

everything he had said, and he did seem to have a reply for everything.

"I know," I smiled, causing him to lean back in his chair and fold his arms. Oh great, Mr. Insatiable was getting his knickers in a twist.

"How about this?' he started to ask, leaning forward again, still watching me.

"I'm listening," I said, as I reaching forward and grabbed the apple juice, bringing it to my lips.

Sebastian raised one brow, clearly surprised I was willing to hear him out.

"Give me a month?" he asked.

"For what?"

"To convince you."

"To convince me of what?" I asked, leaning forward on the table, intrigued by the situation. What was he offering me here?

"A month to show you that you want me as a friend," he smiled.

"And if I decline?"

"You will regret it."

"That a threat?" I scoffed. This boy had balls alright.

"No, just a fact," he smiled.

Truth was, what did I have to lose?

Fair enough, he seemed cocky, a bit too big for his boot's kind of a guy...but it wouldn't harm me. There was something so homely about him that I did like, even though I didn't know what it was about him. He was a mystery.

I sat there watching him with my squinted eyes as I grabbed another piece of toast and took a bite of it. Sebastian slowly leant forward and snatched it out of my hand.

"That was mine," I frowned, watching the toast thief in front of me smile.

"Mine now," he smiled, as he took a bite out of it.

"Do you like stealing people's things?" I questioned, getting a deep and raspy chuckle from him.

"What are friends for, Adi?" he winked.

Was he now flirting with me, the bastard?

"Giving people nicknames, are we?" I asked, wondering about his agenda.

"Only the people I like," he smiled, causing me to blush and then quickly snap myself out of it.

I knew there was something between us, something I didn't want to lose, but yet I didn't want to tell him that. Maybe it could be a beautiful friendship and I just had to take that leap of faith. Plus, I knew I didn't really have many friends, besides Amelie. I seemed to be the outsider looking in, as people saw me as Hugo's lap dog. I was the girl behind the looking glass and people treated me like I was a fragile flower that would break and go running to Hugo, my 'saviour', my 'protector', when in reality I was a lot stronger than people gave me credit for. They had just never given me the chance, but something was telling me he was.

Holding my hand out towards him I smiled. "You have got yourself a deal," I stated, only to watch him look at it and smile back.

He looked at me hand and smiled. "Friends?" he asked, causing me nod.

"Friends," I agreed. He then leant forward and shook my hand and that smile on his face got bigger and a glimmer of light came to life in his eyes.

"You're stuck with me now," he beamed.

"Am I now?" I asked, smirking at him.

Deep down I didn't care if I was stuck with him, as

long as this feeling I felt stayed. I knew, right then and there, that there was something special about him and that I did indeed need him in my life, a life I knew was going to be an adventure with him in it.

"Get used to me stealing things, Adi. What's yours is mine," he stated, causing me to scoff.

"Two can play at that game," I teased, knowing full well I was forever going to do it back to him.

"Wouldn't have it any other way," he smiled.

This was the start of the perfectly imperfect.

Chapter Eight

Present...

Terror and torment. Future possibilities feeling too close to reality being talked about between everyone. Fragments and snippets of memories we had haunting us, haunting seven minds. A fear to be reckoned with.

It was mostly a rushed day getting everything prepped and ready, making sure everything was right for the night ahead. All we could do was hope for the best. Jack had prepped the van full of equipment, while Jessie set up all her technology. They knew they had to be over prepared just in case, after all we needed this to work and didn't want the chance of a wrong ending. If that was the case, it could mean the end of our survival and freedom. We could forever be trapped in Hell again. The Devil raining fire down on us and sure as hell we would burn.

***

The sun was finally setting on the day, the sky filled with orange, pink and reds. It was beautiful and I had spent the last twenty minutes watching the day turn to night, feeling at peace with the world I could see out of my window, a world full of beauty and grace, wishing for the simplest of lives. There was something about the sunset and the night sky that always made me feel content, it was what drew me to it constantly. The serenity of the moment created a warm environment within my own heart, and I wished I could spend eternity living and feeling this way. An eternity of light dismantling the dark.

The serenity I loved turned to dread, knowing it was time to get myself ready for the event ahead of us, but deep down I wished that I didn't have to.

I got up and walked straight to the mirror, spending the next few minutes doing my hair in a loose curled bun, with two dangling pieces at the front. Something simple but beautiful. I styled my make-up, simple but bold. My eyes winged and golden and my lips blood red, something elegant but not over the top; enough to draw the right attention from the right people.

I walked over to my door and took the dress off the hanger, slipping it on. The dress was elegant, green silk that hung to my figure and flowed all the way to the floor. It had a cut on the left side that went all the way up to the middle of my thigh, showing some skin. The mask I held in my hand was dark green and had some gold flakes on it, something to help disguise me, but something so simple that it wouldn't draw too much attention either.

I knew I had to dress the part, I had to fit in with the crowd and blend into the scenery. The only way to stay off the radar. I just wished deep down that I could just wear it for something special, like the most perfect date with someone, with Sebastian, if I was ever that lucky to go on one with him or for him to want me. I wanted to wear something this beautiful for a memory I could cherish and not a nightmare I had to relive.

I lifted up my dress and tied some ribbon around my right thigh, sliding in a small slim knife, just a backup for extra protection. I also had a gold clutch that held the pen drive and a small gun, something even more extra, just for worse case scenarios. From the few balls I had attended; I knew they never checked bags.

I really didn't want to do this, but I knew I had too, we had to. It was the only option for us to be free. It made me nervous and scared, but I knew I couldn't be any of those things if I wanted it to go right. I knew I had to have courage, strength and ambition to do the job correctly. We had one shot to do this and there wasn't an option for us to go back and correct any mistakes if anything was to happen. A fate I had to deal with.

I took a deep breath and looked at myself in the mirror, a reflection I didn't recognise anymore, a life I used to have. All I could see was the girl who had it all, the girl I lost all those years ago. I was the shell of a girl who no longer lived.

It was simple. Easily done. We just had to simply walk in, get what we needed and leave.

What could possibly go wrong?

All I wanted to do was reassure myself that everything was going to be fine, even with the feeling of my heart breaking and the empty feeling at the pit of my stomach. It was like fear itself was trying to consume me, but I wouldn't let it...I would do my best to fight against the terror.

***

I slowly left my room and walked down the stairs, to see

most of them stood in the kitchen area, waiting. Sebastian turned around and looked at me, his eyes lighting up like a Christmas tree as soon as he saw me.

His eyes looked me up and down, taking in my full appearance. "Wow," he smiled. "You look beautiful."

His words made me instantly smile, there was something about the way he was saying it that made my heart jump out of her chest.

"Don't look too bad yourself," I stated, running my eyes up and down him.

He was in a tailored black suit, that had a dark green tie to match my dress. The suit hugged his body, and he looked so good that I had to bite my lip from saying something inappropriate. He looked like a king, a king without his queen. I couldn't believe that this man in front of me, who looked that good in a suit, thought I was beautiful. Part of me wanted to rip the suit of him instantly, but that would definitely be stepping over the line...But the temptation was real.

He slowly walked over to me and took hold of my hand, lifting it up higher. "Give me a twirl," he stated. I did as instructed and when I came back to face him, his eyes locked on mine and he had the biggest smile on his face, causing me to blush once more. "God, you're out of this world." There was just something about the way he was acting that made me think differently about myself. That he might like me a lot more than I thought. After all, actions speak louder than words.

Taking a look away from Sebastian, before my thoughts became too much, I looked at Jack. Standing there in the same suit as Sebastian, but with a red tie instead, I realised he had been watching our interaction.

"He's right. You do look beautiful, Adeline," Jack said, making me smile at his words.

"And you look very handsome, Jack and you too Arthur," I said, turning to look at Arthur who was wearing a suit for the first time ever in his life. Arthur instantly beamed, loving the fact he got a compliment.

"Thank you! Like they have both said, you look beautiful," he said.

"Thank you," I smiled wider. Taking another look a Jack, I gave him a smirk. "I'm sure Amelie is going to love it. She always did like a man in a suit," I winked. He instantly blushed, probably thinking about Amelie's reaction, now that I had said it.

Out of nowhere, I watched how Jack's eyes flickered away from me and to something behind me and for him to mutter, "Fuck."

Turning to look in the direction Jack was looking in, I saw Amelie walking in. Her dress was deep red, it had a slit just like mine going up her left leg to her thigh, it wasn't as fitting, but was still made of silk and showed off her curves. The colour matched her bold lipstick and her smoky eye look, while her hair was curled, sweeping to the left side of her head. She too looked glamorous, enough for Jack to stand there jaw wide open, looking at her. She looked at Jack and blushed, clearly feeling shy due to his reaction. Anything he said about her appearance always made her cheeks turn that extra shade of crimson, giving her that extra glow that made her shine. Jack walked over to her in an instant and kissed her on her cheek, completely bewitched by her and her beauty. The look in his eyes and the smile on his face said it all. She was his home.

"What do you think?" she asked him, as she stood there biting her lip.

"That I'm the luckiest man alive," he smiled at her, taking a small walk around her to take in her beauty. "I can't wait to take that dress off you later and show you how I feel," he whispered, clearly hoping nobody else would be able to hear him. Only to side eye us and catch us all looking at him, making him aware we did in fact hear every word.

"Jack!" she exclaimed, hitting him lightly in the chest, only for him to laugh.

After a few minutes of everyone standing around, we left the house, heading to the van and slowly one by one got in and settled for the journey ahead. Everyone had some sort of protection on them, in the most discreet of places so it wouldn't be noticed.

***

Sitting there quietly, silent enough to hear a pin drop, while Malcom drove, I took a look around. Jack and Amelie were sat holding hands, looking at each other, adoring one another, being present in each other. Jessie was busy on her computer, relaxed and comfy, just in jeans and a hoodie, with a hot water bottle in her lap, setting up her software for the night and Arthur, being Arthur, was sat in the front next to Malcom as he had called shotgun. While me and Sebastian were sat next to each other, with him holding my hand in his lap, not wanting to let go and with my head resting on his shoulder.

I felt closer to him than normal, like last night had drawn us together and I didn't want to lose that feeling, it was like everything was finally falling into place for us both and that maybe we would finally be able to get our very own happy ever after. There was always that self-doubt in my head, the part of me that made my own skin crawl. It was that part of my mind that would fill my head with

87

worry, pain and torture, my inner demons trying to fight their way free, a war within my own head. A battle I would forever fight. He was the light in the darkest of places that would come forth and pull me from it. If only he knew.

***

After what seemed like a lifetime of driving, we could all see the city centre getting closer and closer. The streets were lit up with bright lamp posts, the colourful lights from shop windows, creating a rainbow of colour. There were seas of cars parked on both sides of the road, people walking around enjoying the city life, enjoying their own normality. The city was just as busy as it was back when most of us attended our very first ball. I could see people in ravishing dresses getting out of cars and being escorted inside on a small red carpet, like they were celebrities in the making, their very own V.I.P experience.

Malcom parked further down the street so we wouldn't be noticed. An extra security blanket to protect us. We all looked at each other again. Everyone was good at that, waiting for someone else to act first, hoping they didn't have to be the first one to point out the truth. We all just wanted that extra minute in our own bubble.

"Ready?" Jack asked us all, getting a nod from each individual.

I took a deep breath as I heard Sebastian slide open the van door and take a step out. This was suddenly far too real for my liking. Sebastian held his hand out towards me, and I slowly got to my feet and accepted his hand to help me get out of the van gracefully, so there was no chance of me falling.

Once out of the van, I turned to see Jack do the same with Amelie, only for Arthur to jump out of the passenger door with a big smile on his face. Arthur had never attended a ball and was loving the idea of it, as when we were in Scarlet, he was far too young to go to them.

Everyone just looked at him, raising their brows.

"What? Got to make an entrance," he stated.

Suddenly, Jessie appeared next to the sliding door, holding a small silver case open that revealed five earpieces, earpieces we could communicate through while we went ahead with our plan. We all then placed them into our ears with apprehensive glances at one another.

"Checking," Jessie spoke, as her voice echoed in our ears twice over.

"They work," Jack replied, leading Jessie to smile at him.

"Let's get to work then," she stated, with a hesitant smile on her face, clearly not wanting this night to go ahead, just like everyone else.

This nightmare was real. All I wanted to do was slay my demons, be rid of them, be free, and be able to have no worries like the ones I had on a daily basis. I always knew we all had our demons, even people living a normal life. It was written in the DNA of everyone, there wasn't one person in the world or universe who never had any doubts or worries, or an inner demon trying to break free. It was the downfall of the human mind, a curse we all faced, but the strength of it was different for everyone.

There was always worse. There was always better.

It was a curse to have dark intentions hidden behind a mask of innocence. A curse that made us all want to disappear when life got too much, too complicated, too scary. Then again, the power of our demons showed us our very own self-control and some control can never be concord, only manipulated into our very own self-worth.

***

Sebastian held his arm out towards me, hinting for me to take hold so he could lead the way. I smiled at him and looped my arm around his. We then started walking across the road towards the entrance, with the other three following not far behind. As we got closer to the entrance I could see two security men, one man on the door with an electronic device in hand and one stood not to far away from him, just watching. The man with the device was taking names and checking them off the list, making sure no unwanted guest would get in. We ended up sliding our mask down as we got closer, making sure we were ready to play our part, to then arrive, causing one of the men to look us up and down with a smug look on his face. "Name," he bluntly spoke.

"Mr and Mrs Sean Fisher," Sebastian replied quickly with a smile.

The man looked back at the device, his finger tapping constantly on the screen, showing his lack of patience... someone clearly hated the job they had tonight.

"Let them in," he said. The other security guard then opened the extravagant doors in front of us, leading the way inside.

Following the red carpet like the yellow brick road, we were led down a small narrow hallway, covered in amazing artwork that I remembered once seeing the first time I ever came, paintings from famous artists that Hugo loved. Nothing seemed to be different, a déjà vu moment for me, reliving my past once more. At the end of the narrow hallway there was a golden arch covered in real diamonds, signalling the entrance to the ball room. As we got closer, I felt the fear I was trying to mask breaking free. I really did need to put on my warrior face and brave it. Lights...camera...action.

As soon as we walked into the ballroom, it took my breath away. I never expected it to look as ravishing as it did or as fancy as it felt. It had been some time since the last time I ever graced the presence of this building and not one part of it besides the layout looked the same. The room itself was that big, it made you feel small. Crystal chandeliers spiralled down from the ceiling above, illuminating the room and creating such beauty, reflecting off people's gowns. There was a bar against one side of the room that was glimmering gold and everything around it was made of clear crystal, stacked with a variety of different spirits. Everyone sparkled, women of all shapes, sizes and backgrounds graced the room, all accompanied with someone on their arm. It was like a true fairy tale ball, creating the same feeling I once felt the first time I attended. Everyone had a glass of champagne in their hand as people talked and socialised, while other people danced to the enchanting classical music playing. Just looking at the scenery made me remember my first ball.

Eight Years Ago...

The room was gigantic, covered in snowflakes that sparkled, all hanging down from the ceiling above and scattered around the room. There were multiple crystal styled mini bars placed around the room and large sculptured naked trees covered in fake, sparkling white snow powder, creating frozen branches. The illuminating fairy lights were dispersed around the room, glimmering down on the people below, it was a true winter wonderland. Hugo had even gone the extra mile in getting ice sculptures carved into giant snowflakes and arctic animals ranging from penguins to polar bears.

Everyone around me wore delicate and glittering dresses that were breathtakingly beautiful, celestial looking.

The whole thing was enchanting, it honestly pulled at the heartstrings.

I turned to look at Hugo, to see a small glimmer of light in his eyes and a smile across his face. He had been watching my reaction the whole time.

"I'm guessing you love it?" he asked me, before I could say anything to him.

"It's beautiful," I beamed, while I spun around, taking in my surroundings and feeling my dress lift off the ground, spinning in the air with me.

"I did it for you. I know you always wanted your own winter wonderland, so I created one," he grinned, making me look at him again.

"You did this for me?" I questioned, surprised by his statement.

"Always for you," he replied.

I instantly pulled him in for a hug because I couldn't believe he had done this all for me. Hugo pulled away from the hug and smiled at someone behind me, causing me to turn and see Sebastian and Amelie.

Amelie had her blonde hair pinned up, with flowers weaved into it and a head piece with a small blue diamond in the middle that matched her beautiful blue a-lined, laced dress, looking ravishing. While in the corner of my eye I could see Sebastian watching me, causing me to feel that unfamiliar feeling inside. As I turned to look at him, I saw him standing there in a dark suit, with a red tie that matched my dress. All I could think about was how good he looked, but I wasn't going to tell him that. My compliments would go straight to his head and fill that ego of his.

"You guys go and enjoy yourselves," Hugo spoke, breaking me out of the trance I had put myself in.

Turning back towards him, Sebastian already had his hand stretched out towards me, waiting for me to take it. Before I knew it, he was dragging me out onto the dance floor, into the sea of twirling people, only to spin me around.

"May I have this dance?" he asked me, bowing slightly, bringing my hand close to his mouth to kiss the top of it. A gentlemanly gesture, causing me to blush.

He wanted to dance with me, yet I had never danced before. Beside the odd boogie in my bedroom and shower....

"You may," I beamed, giving him a curtsy.

A smile appeared across his face as he slowly took hold of both of my hands and lifted them up, sliding them around his neck. He then slid his hands down my arms and down my sides, all the way to my waist, only to pull me closer to him. Our bodies were only inches away from each other as our eyes remained locked completely in the moment.

As we started to dance, I couldn't help but feel an unusual fluttering feeling inside, something new but exciting to me. I looked up at Sebastian to see him looking directly at me, causing me to instantly feel flustered. He couldn't take his eyes off me as I looked up at him through my lashes, only a few inches shorter than him. There was something about him that I couldn't put my finger on, but whatever it was I liked it and wanted to carry on feeling it. I felt myself getting lost in him, his touch, his smell, his smile, and his enchanting eyes. There was just something about him that made me feel safe, loved and at peace. A feeling I didn't know I was missing until now and it sure as hell wasn't going anywhere on my watch. Over my dead body.

"Has anyone told you that you look beautiful tonight?" he asked me, causing me to feel more flustered than I did.

"Did Sebastian just pay me a compliment?" I teased him, only for him to roll his eyes at me.

"Don't get your hopes up," he laughed.

"If someone overheard you, they might think you were flirting with me," I laughed at him.

"Never!" he beamed, causing me to feel even more drawn to him than I already was.

"But thank you."

"No need to thank me. I'm stating the obvious."

"Well, you don't look so bad yourself."

"Now who's flirting," he laughed, causing me to roll my eyes this time at him.

"You are forever going to be insatiable."

"Only with you, only you will ever make me insatiable."

Out of nowhere, I heard a squeal, causing us both to turn towards the noise. In front of us was Jack and Amelie, with Jack chucking her across the dancefloor. He was spinning her around, not in time with the music, but it was making them both smile nevertheless. He then dipped her, making her laugh. That's when I noticed it about them.

"Do you reckon they like each other?" I asked Sebastian, not taking my eyes off them as they carried on dancing and laughing with each other, while we slowly swayed side to side.

"I think they do, but they just don't know it yet," he replied.

I turned to look back at Sebastian, making him smile once more. "Do you ever think anybody in the programme finds love or their soulmate?" I asked him. He frowned, deliberating. I had never heard of any couples or relationships in the programme, besides the occasional hook ups and friends with benefits. It was like they didn't exist, or they were just extremely frowned upon and the reason nobody ever mentioned anything. It was like a heart full of love was a dangerous game.

"I wish I could answer that for you, but I can't," he said.

"I believe it's out there, right under our noses. That it's hiding in clear sight, but we are oblivious to it," I confidently said.

Part of me just hoped it wasn't just a fragment of my poor imagination or a complacent lie I kept telling myself, so I didn't break my own heart.

"Do you really believe we all have a soulmate?" he questioned.

Staring into his eyes and feeling connected to him completely, I replied. "I believe we all have a soulmate, and they are right in front of us."

"Right in front of us," he softly spoke, agreeing with me. "Hopefully we find ours."

"Maybe we already have."

Chapter Nine

Present Day…

"Time to split up," Jack calmly said, snapping me out of my memories and back to the real world.

I looked towards Jack and Amelie as they both diverted right towards the mountain size stack of champagne glasses, while Arthur walked across the room and stood at one end of the bar, while me and Sebastian went to the other end of it.

***

I scanned the room. I could see a small spiralling staircase in the corner that led to the balcony above with silver-coloured curtains tied open against the balcony post. A true royal setting fit for a king. A king of Hell, Satan's kingdom. Hugo had definitely upped his scenery to show off his own wealth. He was a man that was a slave to the money, the power. He was a man who would let it consume him, then again, the man did have a gambling addiction. Money was his means, and it would certainly be his death.

One day was coming for him, the day where he would

piss off the wrong people and a bullet to the head would be the answer and I hoped I was the one pulling the fucking trigger. After all, he had started it and I had to be the one to end it, to hurt him the most. Death caused by the one thing he loved the most...me.

Taking a longer look in the direction of the spiral staircase, I saw a tall man standing there, blocking the way, making it harder for us to get where we needed to go. We needed a plan.

"Two at my side of the bar," Arthur communicated to us, through the comms.

"Two more near the entrance and one near you, Adeline," Amelie said.

Logically, we'd known there would be plenty of security with what happened when we escaped. They were for his protection, a means to survive. It was always going to be a game of survival of the fittest and he sure as hell was going to try to make sure it was him, no matter who he was against. Then again, he had more enemies than just me.

We all looked around making sure we all knew where everyone was stood and where security presented themselves.

"I've got seven cameras, one on the staircase, one on the room you're going for and the rest on the entrance and the ball itself," Jessie spoke softly through the comms. "I can put them on loop when you are ready."

"How do we get the guy on the stairs to move?" Arthur asked, making us aware we needed to cause a distraction and quickly.

In the corner of my eye, I caught a glimpse of Amelie. She turned towards Jack, just for him to quickly look back at her.

'You trust me?" she asked, forgetting the comms could pick up every conversation.

"With my life," he quickly responded.

I watched how she gave Jack a quick kiss on the cheek and turned to walk away, only to head towards the staircase.

"What smart idea do you have now?" Arthur asked, watching her every move.

"I'm going to try and seduce him and get him to leave his post," she responded.

Arthur chuckled. "You really reckon that's going to work Amelie?" he asked her.

"Well, it worked on Jack, didn't it?" she fired back, only for everyone to laugh and take a look at Jack. Who seemed to be smiling and slightly laughing at her comment, while he shook his head. "I've got to at least try. I might not be the prettiest of people, but sometimes a girl offering herself to a man works."

Seduction was one of the many talents any woman could hold. A weakness to most men, but not all. A simple smile, a fluttering of the eyes, a hint of sex. A tempting offer, a small glimmer of hope or potential and you could end up with anything. A simple cat and mouse game, like leaving a lamb out for slaughter, waiting for the fox to pounce and snatch its sweet reward. She was right, she had to try something. She had to play the game.

Before she got close enough, she turned to Jack and blew him a kiss again, which only made him grin ear to ear, reassuring him she was going to be ok. Everyone knew they both trusted each other and wouldn't do anything to jeopardise that, but a little reassurance didn't hurt. Trust, after all, was the most important thing to us all.

We all watched as Amelie approached the man. He

turned and studied her, looking her up and down like she was his prey, his little lamb. Prey we wanted him to see.

As she got closer, she gently placed her hand on the man's arm. "Can I just say that I couldn't take my eyes off you," she smiled, a smile of a million stars, with a giggle to match. Painting a picture of a girl who had potentially had one too many champagne flutes.

No true gentleman would take advantage of an intoxicated woman, then again none of these men were gentlemanly. They were and always would be pigs, sexual predators in the making.

The statement and appearance of a drunken comment, fake as it was, made the man once again look her up and down. He then smirked, clearly letting his own twisted imagination run wild. The look of lust that lingered in his eyes grew, making his smile grow wider and for him to take a small step closer to her. Jackpot.

"Oh really?" he asked.

Amelie's response was to instantly bite her lip, a simple gesture for the man to think his small movement towards her was doing something for her. "I must say I do love a man in uniform," she flirted, as she ran her hand down the man's arm.

"You here alone?" he asked, making her look around like she was searching for someone.

"I'm with my friend, but she disappeared. So, I guess I'll find my own company for the night."

The man's face beamed brighter.

"Would you like to have a drink with me?" she asked, gesturing to the bar on the other side of the room.

"I can't leave my post," he responded,

She sighed and frowned. "That's a shame."

"Told you it wouldn't work," Arthur laughed down the

comms, only to get a sharp glare from Amelie, who knew she had to step it up.

She turned leant forward, close to the man's ear. "I do apologise for being so forward and blunt...but sometimes my dress comes off easier after a few drinks...especially for a man in uniform...like yourself," she whispered.

"I'm going to be sick," Arthur responded quickly, causing Sebastian to spit out his champagne, making me giggle.

Jack however, had his eyes locked on them both watching every movement they both made. We all knew she had to do something to get the man to move and that she wouldn't let anyone do anything to her, but that didn't stop Jack from keeping his eyes on her, making sure she was ok.

The man then simply adjusted his posture, while his smile grew even bigger than before, clearly loving the words she spoke. It was written all over his face, the way he looked at her screamed that he thought she easy, like she was easily his anyway he wanted her.

"One drink?" she asked again, hoping the man would finally take up her offer, so she could get him away from his post.

The man stood there and looked around the room, only to then look back at her, giving her a once over once more. "One drink," he agreed, just for her to go all smiley, pretending she was happy. It was simply a cat and mouse game, where Amelie had successfully dangled the cheese in front of him.

The man then took it upon himself to put his arm around her waist, leading her towards the bar.

"I'm definitely going to be sick," Arthur said, downing

his champagne flute, while Amelie discreetly flipped him off, causing all of us to let out a small laugh.

***

Now that the staircase was left bare, we had a mission to get on with, even when the ball was as enchanting as this one. Time was our enemy, so we had to be quick.

"Now Jessie," I spoke, making it known it was time for her to put the cameras on loop so we could stay undetected. The next step was in motion.

Now was the time for me and Sebastian to do what we needed to do. We started to make our way to the staircase, weaving ourselves through the crowd of dancing guest, while Amelie kept the man distracted.

As we got closer, we both took another look around and then continued to make our way up the stairs and towards the office door, a route I already had sketched out in my head. When we got there, I reached forward and grabbed the handle, only to find it was locked, like we expected.

"What we going to use now to pick the lock?" Sebastian asked.

"You always forget," I smirked at him, as I opened my bag and pulled out a small bobby pin.

Within the programme we had all learnt several skills. Many learnt to pick pocket whilst I learnt to pick locks, especially handy to unlock handcuffs and locked doors. A skill which I was happy to have, especially now.

I crouched down in front of the door and slowly inserted the bobby pin into the lock, wiggling it back and forth, ear pressed towards the door listening for that special...CLICK!

I took a glance at Sebastian with a smirk on my face.

"I'm a girl of many talents."

My comment alone made him chuckle, as it was the words Amelie would use constantly.

As I got back on my feet, Sebastian quickly pushed open the door and walked inside, with me following and shutting the door behind us.

As soon as we were in, I stood there frozen as it had been a long time since I was in this room. I remembered it clear as day and nothing had changed in the slightest. It was as if time was standing still. When I was little Hugo brought me here a few times and every time I came, I would sit on the small purple chair in front of his desk, reading one of the many books he had in his bookcase to the left side of the room, getting lost in my fictional reality while he dealt with business. His desk sat in the middle of the room, two computers and piles of files scattered across it. An organised mess.

Walking over and sitting in the office chair, I grabbed the pen drive and stuck it into the side of the computer. "Jessie now," I said.

"I just need five minutes," she replied. This meant she was now on her way to accessing the server and getting all the data needed, leaving me and Sebastian with no other option than to wait.

Looking to my left, I saw a frame with a photo of me and Hugo, both with massive smiles across our faces. I reached over and grabbed the frame, taking a closer look. I remembered this day like it was yesterday, it was the first week I had spent with Hugo, the first week of feeling I had someone to look up to. Hugo was the perfect father figure, the perfect role model, the perfect everything. He was always buying me toys, dresses, spoiling me rotten. He wanted to give me everything I ever wanted and more,

more than I would ever need. What was there to complain about?

It was a mask, a simple spell to bewitch me from seeing the truth, from seeing reality. It was a charade, a game he was incredibly good at.

I was so consumed by the fakery that I had accepted it with open arms, just because he was the first person to show me love. It was a moment I would always remember and treasure, but a moment that was now part of the nightmares I faced.

Chapter Ten

Seventeen Years Ago...

At the age of eight, I was sat in a darkened gloomy room, a place of abandonment. It was a chamber of eight metal bunk beds.

That was my life. Dark and miserable, damp, and cold. It was a room too small, too confined for even three of us, let alone eight. I would often sit here on the most uncomfortable of beds, feeling every spring in the mattress and hearing every creak of the bed, with the only source of light being three small light beams attached to the wall, that would constantly flicker, like the power was running low, being overrun, or being diverted to a bigger source.

There was only one way out and that was through the locked door. It would forever stay locked until it was time to train, to clean or to eat. Besides that, we were all confined to this room for many hours of the day, doing nothing but talking and sleeping.

Everyone kept to themselves though, afraid if they weren't silent, they would be silenced, so the only sound you could hear, was a slight buzz from the three beamed lights on the wall.

***

The sound of rattling keys made everyone, including me, sit up in our beds and look towards the door. With a click of a lock the door opened, revealing Hugo. He entered slowly, his eyes scanning the room, just to land on me. He took a few strides forward and stopped directly in front of me, arms out in my direction.

Why did he want me?

In all my life, my short life so far, I had never been of any interest before and was just like the rest. One of many, a random child, raised here like everyone else.

Knowing he was the big boss, I reached towards him and let him quickly pick me up and place me on the ground. He then took hold of my hand and led me out of the room.

As soon as we left the room, the door closed behind us and with a twist of a key it was locked again. Hugo carried on walking forward, leading me down the hallway to a set of doors that led to the outside world, away from the compound.

When we were outside, we were met with a long black car and a man holding the car door open for us. The cold air hit me, causing a chill to run through my body. It was the middle of winter, so I felt like if I was to stand here outside in the cold for even a minute more, my whole body would turn to ice, and I would forever be a frozen sculpture. It was making me want to run back inside into the warmth of Hell, the place I had just come from.

I looked up at Hugo, who in turn was looking down at me. He crouched down to my level and his eyes to searched mine.

"How would you like to come and stay with me and a few others?" he asked. I smiled and nodded with joy, longing for warmth and comfort.

Today was going to be the first day of a better life within the programme, a better life for me, a life away from the damp and cold and a future life full of happiness and love.

"How about we take a photo?" he asked me.

I nodded with joy, just to watch Hugo hand his phone to the man holding open the car door, as I turned to face him with a big smile on my face.

"Are you ready?" the man asked, who was fully suited and booted, like a driver would be, with the addition of a loaded gun in a holster on his hip.

"Yes," I smiled.

"Say cheese," he grinned.

"Cheese!" I shouted, as the man before me took the photo.

The man then handed Hugo his phone back with the photo on the screen. A photo that signified the start of my own happy ever after... or so I thought.

Present...

Suddenly, there was a loud bang that snapped me out of my memories, causing me to look in the direction of the noise and see Sebastian standing there with a book at his feet. He must have been looking at the bookshelves, scanning them to see if there was anything interesting there, knocking one off in the process. I watched as he smiled towards me and bent forward, picking the book up, only to slide it back into place, returning it home.

"Guys we have an issue! There are two men walking

towards the stairs, you're going to get caught," Jack warned us.

"Someone needs to stall, cause a distraction," Sebastian quickly said back.

"I have an idea," Jack said, followed with a loud sound of glass smashing.

"What was that?" I asked.

"Jack just tripped someone into the piled high tower of champagne glasses," Arthur responded, chuckling at the scene it must have created.

Jack had done what was needed and made a distraction big enough to disturb people, giving us a little extra time, time we needed. After all, time was precious.

"Guys I'm done, get out of there," Jessie said.

I pulled the device out of the computer and chucked it back into my small bag as fast as I could and got up from the chair, while Sebastian held the door open, only for us both to quickly rush out. I quickly crouched down again with a bobby pin and locked the door, making it look like nobody was here.

"Security are coming up, get out of there, think of something," Jack panicked.

We took a glance over the balcony to see Jack, Arthur, and Amelie glancing at us from down below.

Turning towards Sebastian, I looked directly at him. "Do you trust me?" I asked.

"Yes, why?" he questioned.

The truth was, I had an idea, quick and reckless, but something that nevertheless would fool anyone. It was something he had to be onboard with, but part of me thought he wouldn't be.

"Guys you're running out of time," Jack snapped.

"Kiss me," I blurted out, regretting it the second it left

my mouth, but it was the only way I could see us getting out of this. We needed to become two love-sick people wanting a moment of privacy and sneaking off.

"What?" Sebastian replied, his eyes wide.

"Kiss me!" I shouted. He just stood there looking at me, not moving an inch, like he was frozen in time, making me fully understand I sounded stupid. It was honestly the only thing I could think of without causing trouble.

"Any second now!" Jack pointed out, making it more obvious we were literally moments away from being caught.

"For the love of God, Sebastian! Just kiss m…" I started to shout, but was interrupted by Sebastian pushing me up against a balcony post and him putting his lips on mine, taking me by surprise.

His lips were soft as velvet, tender and warm against mine. I could feel the passion behind the kiss, even though the kiss was forced in the moment. It wasn't how I would have planned my first kiss with Sebastian, but my feelings in that moment were proven to be true. I was in love with him, I needed him, I craved him. All the thoughts I had about him were real. Surely, he wouldn't kiss me like this if he didn't feel the same way? Right?

In the seconds it took, I started to kiss him back, feeling the passion and desire behind the kiss. My arms instantly wrapped around his neck, my fingers slowly resting on the back of his head, entwining into his hair, heating the moment up. I could feel one of his hands cupping my face as we kissed, while the other gripped my waist, holding and pulling me closer to him, while the whole world around us seemed to disappear. In that moment it was just us, getting lost in each other. In a realm of endless possibilities, I never imagined this.

Finally, I now believed that I had found my soulmate, the one person I always wanted to find, the one I once talked about with Sebastian the first time I ever came here, to this event and that we had both found it in each other. A moment I would never forget. I always thought that the way a kiss was described in the book was purely fiction, just a story told to make us dream, but I felt it, I felt the fireworks, the spark, the flame within us. Everything I had once read in a book was coming true for me, the perfect fairy tale kiss I had always dreamt about was finally happening, even under false circumstances.

"You shouldn't be here!" a man shouted, making us pull away from each other.

I couldn't help but look at Sebastian and into his eyes, to see them filled with lust as he stared back at me. I could tell in that moment I wasn't the only one who had felt something and that we needed to talk, there was no way we couldn't talk about this moment.

"Hello?" the man asked, just for us to both turn and face the voice, seeing two security men standing there. "You shouldn't be here," he snapped.

"I'm sorry! Me and my boyfriend just wanted a few minutes alone." I ducked my head in embarrassment, hoping they wouldn't pick up on anything and hoping the plan would work.

"Just go back down and join the others," he said, pointing directly to the stairs, making me realise they had bought it.

Suddenly, I felt Sebastian's hand grab mine, as he interlaced our fingers and lead the way to the stairs. We both glanced at each other and smiled, both of our cheeks rosy as we did, flustered from the moment we had just shared. I couldn't believe we had gotten away with it. Both of us were clearly over the moon from the task at hand, knowing now it was time to go home. We couldn't seem to take our eyes of each other as we made our way to the bottom of the stairs, lost in the moment we had shared. Until, I suddenly bumped into someone, causing my mask to come loose and fall to my feet. I hadn't realised that during our kiss, the ribbon had come undone.

"Adeline?" a male voice asked, causing me to look up at the man in front of me and for me to feel Sebastian's grip on my hand tighten.

My eyes lifted to face the voice. The man before me then pulled his own mask off, revealing a man I wished I would never have to see again.

The man in front of me was the devil himself.

Hugo.

Chapter Eleven

I couldn't believe who I was stood face to face with. He looked the same way he had when I left, just older. He still had his dark hair, his beard that he kept neat and tidy, while his eyes were still as prominently green as I remembered. I could still smell the strong musk of his cologne, the one he always wore. I really couldn't believe who I was in front of, the one person I wished I would never have to see again and all he could do was stand there with a grin on his face.

"Hugo," I hissed, only for him to let out a chuckle.

"You finally come to your senses and come back home to me?" he asked. "I see Sebastian is still by your side like always…like a little lap dog."

He took a glance at Sebastian, who looked ready to fight, just for Sebastian's hand to go straight behind his back, ready to grab the gun he had hidden, a response Hugo was baiting him for.

"I wouldn't do that if I was you," he smirked, as he took another puff of his cigar.

It was only then did I notice the three men behind

Hugo, his own personal security, who all had their hands at their waist, waiting for his command.

"So why have you two come here?" he asked, turning his attention back to me, asking me directly.

"We were just leaving," I hissed again, hoping he could hear the disgust in my voice for being in his presence, let alone breathing the same fucking air.

He sighed, making me realise my answer didn't satisfy him, then again...Who gave a shit?

"You should know that's not going to happen, My Dear," he laughed.

However, I could tell he was impatient and me not coming clean was already bothering him from the clenched jaw and the left eye twitch. He was clearly trying his best to not cause a scene, especially while everyone else was oblivious to what was going on and still enjoying themselves mingling and dancing.

"Just say the word and we will step in," Jack spoke, making me remember Hugo didn't know anyone else was here.

Making sure I wouldn't get caught, I took a sneaky glance around to see Amelie, who had left the presence of the man she was with. She was now stood with her back against the bar watching, while Arthur walked around behind Hugo himself, not too close, but not too far. While Jack was already in clear view waiting and watching. Everyone was ready.

I turned back to look at Hugo to see him just standing there, his eyes watching my every move, like I was a ticking time bomb waiting to go off.

"If you're not going to talk, I'll get you to talk," he said, hoping to get a response out of me, hoping I would explode.

Kayleigh Hilton

I got the hint, but I decided not to say anything, I was doing my best to act like his words didn't bother me, that his words didn't crawl under my skin.

"Nothing?" he teased again. But I remained calm and straight faced, clearly irritating Hugo as I did this. "Fine, grab them," he commanded. His security then stepped forward, reaching for us.

"Now!" I shouted.

The next thing I knew, Amelie had jumped up onto the bar and was jumping on one of the men, wrapping her legs around his neck, only to lean forward and flip him, succeeding in her task. Jack went for another, punching him straight in the face, while Arthur ran forward, dropping to his knees to slide along the floor, taking one of the men down instantly. Sebastian brushed past me, running forward to tackle another, while I quickly grabbed my knife, the one I had tucked away on my right thigh, only to swing it straight towards one of the men by Hugo, cutting the man across the face.

During the commotion, I could hear people from the room start to run and scream, fleeing the scene as more men started to flood in. We were fighting for our lives once again.

The room started to become more and more derelict, things being broken, smashed and destroyed. The perfect scene around us disappearing in seconds into a room of despair. There was broken glass scattered across the floor, while unconscious or dead security men laid there, a scene of foundations cracking, a brutal consequence of being part of the programme, a memory that would forever haunt me further into the life I lived.

In the corner of my eye, I saw a flicker of light, just to quickly jump back and feel the edge of a sharp blade cut my cheek. In that moment, I instantly turned to face whoever had cut me, to be met with a sudden blow that was big enough to knock me off my feet, causing me to instantly crash to the floor. In a moment of haziness, I looked up to see Hugo standing there with a small blade and a tint of red at the end of it, fresh blood dripping to the floor. He had taken me by surprise, it was something I never expected this man do. Never in a million years did I expect him to ever lay a finger on me personally, he had never done it before. I already thought he was from Hell, that he was the Devil reincarnated, but he was so much more than that. He was the flame, destruction, and chaos, all the things Hell was made off.

In the corner of my eye, I saw a gun lying on the floor, not far out of reach. This got me to push myself up and grab the gun, pointing it directly at him as I got to my feet.

He laughed. "I wouldn't do that if I was you."

"And whys that?" I asked, the blood running down my face, dripping off my chin and directly onto my chest.

"Look around," he smirked, looking towards everyone else in the room.

Keeping a strong hold on my gun, I took a glance around me to see Amelie being held against the bar with a knife at her throat, Jack being held by both his arms by two men and Arthur being pinned down, face first to a table. Turning to the other side of me, I could also see Sebastian being pinned to the floor with a gun pointed directly to the back of his head, watching my every move. Check mate.

"So, why are you here?" Hugo asked again, hoping the scene around me would make me speak.

These people, my family, were the one thing he knew I valued, and he was more than happy to use them against me. He knew they were my weakness and the only way he would get answers. He would use my loyalty, my love for them against me.

"Why is it important to you?" I snapped, turning my attention back to him.

"Because you're mine!" he stated, causing me to scoff. "Plus, you have nowhere to go and no one to save you."

"Let them go!" I shouted at him.

"Or what?" he smirked again, taking a step towards me. "Are you going to shoot me? Go ahead! Shoot me, they die if I die." He pointed towards all my friends.

"I have a plan, I just need a few minutes," Jessie said into my ear, giving me a little reassurance. At least she had a plan, but now I had to bide her some time.

"Come willingly and you will all live," he said, like that was the best option for us.

"I'll never come willingly!" I shot back.

"Well, I can kill them and take you. You're the only one I really want, so they mean nothing to me."

"Let them go or I'll shoot!"

"I've already told you what will happen," he hissed, getting more annoyed at my constant threat.

"I wouldn't shoot you," I smiled, taking a deep breath, and placing the gun against my own head. "I'll shoot myself."

Hugo stood there, his left eye twitching more, trying his best to read me, clearly not believing what I was saying or doing.

"No!" Sebastian shouted. I took a small glimpse at him and then back at Hugo.

"You're bluffing," he smirked. "You could never do it."

"Try me!" I threatened, putting my finger closer to the trigger.

His face then dropped, clearly realising that I was

115

telling the truth. He must have known deep down that I would sacrifice myself to save them, especially after seeing the look on Sebastian's face. I watched how Hugo hesitated for a moment, rubbing his face, anger clearly prominent in his features. He clearly felt his control slipping, one thing I knew he hated the most in this world. The lack of control, the fear of his power, his flame dwindling into nothing more than a spark.

He then turned to look at his security and nodded, causing them to let everyone go, while they still pointed their weapons. Seeing his command didn't falter my motives or my control of the situation. I still held the gun to my head, not trusting him for a moment.

Trusting him was like Russian Roulette, he only needed that one chance to strike. He just wanted to bide his time, even if it meant giving me that small spark of potential freedom, only to rip it away from me again. He was, after all, a man of cruel manipulation.

"We walk out of here," I commanded, testing my luck.

He stood still, like one of his popular ice sculptures years ago. He was trying to figure out his next step for handling this situation. He just wanted his power back, because without power...what was he?

"You're not going anywhere," he said, like instant switch had clicked in his head.

"I'll pull the trigger!" I threatened once more, hoping he would understand what was at stake. The price he would pay, my last bargaining chip.

"Pull the trigger, they die!" he threatened back and that's when it hit me.

I hadn't realised what I had set in motion, the chess piece I had played to reach the king, to outplay the player. If I fired the gun, they would die too and if I didn't fire, we all get caught or we all end up dead. I had honestly thought by doing this I was bidding Jessie time, but there was only so much I could do now before he would react on impulse. I was winning the game, but he had just played his piece. I was out of ideas and every way I looked at it, he would win, there was no way out of here, death or capture was the only thing on the cards for us.

"What are you waiting for? Lower the gun! You know it's your only option!" he shouted, a smile plastered across his face, taking in the joy of his win.

As I started to lower the gun, I heard a heavy sigh of relief come down the comms. "Cover your ears," Jessie said, making me think luck was finally on our side again.

With a smirk etched across my face, I looked directly into Hugo's eyes. "I have one more trick," I taunted him, covering my ears. "Now!" I shouted.

A screeching sound so loud it could burst your ear drums came firing out the speakers, causing Hugo and his security to drop to the floor from the pain and for blood to come running out of their ears.

We all started to bolt, sprinting for the exit with our own ears ringing. Every one of us charged down the corridor towards the entrance, only for us to hear a muffled and brief shout. "GET THEM!"

We ran as fast as our legs could take us to find Malcom in the van and Jessie holding the sliding door open. Malcom started the van as we all ran towards it, jumping in one by one, as the van started to pick up speed. Sebastian held his hand out towards me, ready to pull me in as I ran faster to get closer.

I was so close to grabbing hold of him, fingertips just touching, when suddenly there was a noise of gunfire and then a pain shooting through my left shoulder, causing to

117

me to fall to the ground. I had been shot, the blow instantly flooring me.

"No!" I heard Sebastian shout and a sound of screeching tires, signalling the van had come to a complete halt.

I felt dazed and confused, not sure what was happening around me, until I felt like I was floating, realising, and just barely noticing Sebastian was now carrying me. I felt like I was on cloud nine, floating in the clouds, away from all my pain and worries, floating in eternal serenity.

Next thing I knew, I felt myself being put on the floor of the van. Sebastian had come to my rescue and brought me to safety. Feeling the floor beneath me vibrate, I knew the van had started to move again, while gun fire remained prominent, but now coming from both sides.

I was conscious but out of it. I had no idea what was happening, everything was moving too fast around me, too fast for my eyes to catch up. It was like all the moving figures were blending into one, everything muddling together, creating a fog around me. The only thing I could make out clearly was one face...Sebastian. He was knelt over me, his eyes remaining my key focus, the blue eyes that made me feel safe, made me feel like I was home. I could briefly see his hand putting pressure on my wound, yet I couldn't feel any pain. It was like my brain wasn't letting me catch up to the events happening around me, like I was numb to the touch, my body in complete and utter shock.

All I could see was blood, blood that Sebastian was covered in, blood that was all over me and coming out of my shoulder quickly, making me aware that an important artery had clearly been nicked.

"Malcom, she's bleeding out!" Sebastian shouted,

"Arthur, you know what needs to be done, start helping her!" Malcom shouted and the next thing I could see, was Arthur at my side.

I felt myself being lifted up and then dropped, instantly feeling the pain radiate through my body, making me scream out.

"The bullet went through and through," Arthur said. "Keep applying pressure, Sebastian."

I could see the fear in Sebastian's clear blue eyes, seeing that he was doing his best not to break down. Seeing the pain behind his eyes terrified me, made me realise how bad the situation was, how bad I was. I could feel myself getting tired, but I knew I couldn't fall asleep, I had to stay present, be present with him.

"I feel sleepy," I let out, my brain letting me finally say something.

The colour drained from Sebastian's face as he heard my words. "Stay awake! Keep your eyes on me!" Sebastian pleaded.

Just like a magnet, my eyes landed back on him, drawn to him like a greater force was beckoning me to stay. He was my lifeline.

I knew I had to try and fight, fight the darkness that was lingering, beckoning me to follow. I tried my best to focus on his eyes, focus on the colour and how they would pull me into them. I was trying my hardest, but I could feel the darkness coming quick and fast; it wasn't going to be long before it took me, consumed me, and pulled me under.

I watched how his mouth moved, but no words came out, until I heard it. "Arthur, she's bleeding out, do something!" he shouted. It was like the dots in my brain were no longer connecting and the sound was delayed, like a terribly dubbed film with nothing in sync.

"I am!" a voice shouted.

I could tell from the silence around me that the gun fire had stopped, and we were away from it all. We were in the clear.

"She needs blood!" Sebastian shouted once more, his voice bouncing around the van.

"We don't have the equipment in the van, so keep applying pressure, a lot of it!" Arthur shouted back. Sebastian then pushed further down on me and the pain to shoot through me, causing me to scream.

"I'm sorry," he cried, looking down at me, clearly feeling horrified about the pain he was putting me in.

I kept feeling myself slipping in and out of consciousness, the loss of blood was too much for my body to handle and I knew it wouldn't be long till it knocked me out, the darkness calling me. I tried my best to speak, but I couldn't seem to get any words out. My brain was not letting me form any words, like it was shutting down and trying to keep more important things working for me. I kept seeing things, like my life was flashing before my eyes, while my eyes kept opening and closing, like time itself was jumping in fragments and I was missing moments. When my eyes reopened, I could see something massive had changed, but I couldn't ask what was happening due to not being able to form any words.

The next thing I knew, I was being picked up again, feeling light and airy, like I was floating on clouds once again, like a bird flying through the sky, spreading its wings, being free to explore, free from everything around me. My eyes opened for another small moment to see it was Sebastian carrying me, blood all over him, blood smeared on his face. I could hear mumbling voices around me, as blurry figures rushed around. I felt the comfort of a bed, Sebastian laying me down, only to then feel a sharp pinch in my arm, radiating pain around my body once more, as it shocked my body awake, like an electric shock coursing through my veins.

I instantly began drifting once again with Sebastian hanging over me, my own eyes fluttering, fighting to stay open.

"Stay awake," his voice broke, while the tears streamed down his face.

I couldn't hold myself awake much longer, but I tried my best to hang on to Sebastian's voice, hanging onto ever word, but before I knew it, it turned to mumbles; nothing he was saying was making sense, it was just his mouth moving with no words coming out. I tried to focus on his words, putting all the energy I had left to hear him, until a few of them slipped through.

"I love you," he cried.

Before I could even try to form any words and respond to him, making him aware I had heard him, I felt the darkness creeping right over me. I couldn't fight it anymore, all my energy vanished out of my body, while darkness called, beckoning me to the edge, until everything went black, and I was falling.

Chapter Twelve

Sebastian

Three days later, she was still out cold, pale as a ghost, limp, and floppy like a ragdoll, sleeping on the bed in the medical room we had. I sat there in the chair next to her, refusing to move even for a minute, holding onto her hand, hoping, and praying she would wake up.

I would spend every waking hour sat here, watching her, watching for even the slightest movement signalling she was awake. I would spend the nights sleeping in the chair, just so I was the first person she would see when her eyes opened. Her beautiful hazel eyes.

Everything else happening around me was the last thing on my mind. The only thing I wanted was her to wake up with a smile on her face, a smile that would light up the room, just by seeing me sat there waiting for her, no matter how long it took. I knew deep down she would wake up eventually, but time itself was painful. It was tormenting me with every ticking second, minute and hour that was going by with nothing happening, every minute feeling like eternity. Time itself was laughing at me, making me suffer for longer and making the pain and guilt inside grow stronger. I wished I could trade places with her, taking the bullet to make sure she was safe.

There wasn't anything I wouldn't do for her. From the moment I met her, I made it my mission to protect her, be by her side no matter what. I just never knew the importance she would later hold. The stubborn seventeen-year-old with an attitude, calling me out on my bullshit as soon as the first words I spoke came out my mouth. The first time I met her, I knew there was something special about her, but with me being twenty-eight at the time, it wasn't appropriate for me to have a crush on her because she was only just a child. It never felt like that, it was only later down the line when I noticed it was more than just a friendship, it was pure and undeniable chemistry. She was the drug, and I was the addict. I had an addiction to her, and she soon became the reason to breathe.

The programme had rules and boundaries and they would constantly try to demolish the flame people had burning within them, yet it didn't demolish hers. She had a flame so powerful it scorned. It was a fight no one else seemed to have and that's what made her different. She carried herself in such a way that nobody else's flame burned as bright, because all I saw was her.

I was considered Hugo's best male fighter, a leader of the training itself, yet she held the power. Hugo underestimated her, like she underestimated herself. She held the power, and I was a willing victim to it, a willing victim for her to control.

She was forever imprinted on my heart. My heart forever scorned by her flame.

Amelie and Jack entered the room. Just from looking at me, I knew they could see I was worn out, stressed, pale and a ghost of myself, like everything I was, was disappearing in front of them, leaving only the shell of the man I was. I came to life the day I met her and without her the flame I had dwindled, becoming nothing more than a pile of ash.

Amelie approached me and gave me a hug, a hug that I willingly gave back.

"You need to get a proper night's sleep," she said softly, trying to reassure me everything was going to be ok. I knew it would be, but still, it didn't do anything for my guilt.

"I'm not leaving her side," I said, as tears started running down my face once more. I didn't care who saw me crying anymore or if anyone thought I was weak or damaged goods. I was like this because I was in love with her and that was the reason to carry on. Plus, I was too worn out to have the strength anymore to stop them from falling, like all my walls I had built were crumbling with the nightmare I had of losing her coming true, coming to life.

Amelie then walked around the bed back to Jack, who pulled up a chair for her, just for her to sit in it and look at me, clearly seeing the love I had for Adeline.

"She will wake up, we just need to give her time," she reassured me.

"She has to wake up. I need to tell her I love her," I wept, causing Amelie to give me a small smile. "I should have told her the first time she mentioned it and I didn't."

I felt the tears getting heavier, blaming myself for not expressing the truth when she had given me the chance. I was never good at putting my emotions into words,

124

expressing how I felt, guarded by my own self-doubt, my cloud of judgment.

Suddenly, I felt a hand on my shoulder, just to turn around and see Jack standing there, giving me a reassuring gesture. It was a gesture to show me I wasn't alone, and they too wanted the best for Adeline.

"She just needs time to rest, just like you need to rest. Just make sure you go eat and shower at least," Jack spoke, hoping that I might finally listen to him.

"How many times do I have to tell you all? I am not leaving her side!" I shouted, getting annoyed at the people around me, like they weren't listening to me. "I'm not leaving till she wakes up!"

"Ok! Ok! We are just trying to help," Amelie tried her best to calm me down, but she could clearly see I was in agony and everything they were saying wasn't helping the situation, even when they wanted the best for me.

Giving up shouting at them, when they clearly wanted to best for me, I just sat watching Adeline, as Jack walked around to stand behind Amelie, who in turn was watching me. I knew I was in the wrong, but the thought of losing Adeline was eating away at me, causing me to have a short fuse. I took a deep breath and looked at them both, eyes still watering, pain still more than likely present on my face.

"I'm sorry," I said, hoping they could see I meant it. "I didn't mean to shout."

"We get it, don't worry. We fully understand," Amelie reassured me.

I knew deep down I wasn't alone, that everything I felt, they felt too. If the roles were reversed and Jack was sat here with Amelie in the bed, his reaction would be the same. It was a fate nobody wanted, but it was the one we had been dealt. A torturous event for tortured souls.

"Love makes us do many things," Jack mentioned, squeezing Amelie's shoulders. A squeeze that caused her to look up at him with a smile.

"I never got the chance to tell her," I cried, turning to face her again, admitting the truth out loud once more.

It was the truth everyone knew, but nobody said out loud, like they were waiting for us to stop seeing in black and white, only for the colour to come seeping through.

I turned to look at Amelie and Jack to see them both welling up from the words I spoke, knowing I was spilling the truth to people finally, even though it shouldn't be them hearing these words, it should be Adeline hearing it all first.

"I always knew there was something between you both and always hinted at it, but I never knew it was this strong," Amelie revealed, causing me to briefly smile at her. "I promise you Sebastian, you will get to tell her everything and believe me when I say this, she will feel the same way you do...I can see it in the way she looks at you, the way she smiles when you walk into the room and the way you both tease and taunt one another."

Amelie lent forward in the chair. "How about this? We will stop telling you to get sleep and rest, if you promise to eat something?" she proposed.

I sat there just staring at her, thinking about what she had just asked. She was right, but I wasn't going to tell her that, it would go to her head, but I did need to eat, even if it was something small.

"Ok," I agreed with a small smile, knowing they only meant to help me and wasn't doing anything to harm me in anyway.

"Ok," Amelie smiled back at me. "I'll go and make you something and will be back shortly."

Kayleigh Hilton

Amelie then quickly left, just for Jack to then take it upon himself to sit in the chair she had just left, looking at me as he did.

"I'd be the same as you," he stated.

"What do you mean?" I asked him.

"I can tell you now. If it was Amelie in that bed, I'd feel guilty, broken, damaged, not wanting to move from her side, all in the name of love."

"Really?"

"Yes, you have your own roots, ways, your individuality throughout a relationship, but you still find your world in a person. The love you feel makes everything worth it, but in moments like this, it's what cripples you and consumes you, proving the point you knew all along."

"What point?"

"The point of loving someone. Like you knew it already, you feel it already, but the idea of losing the one you love makes you realise you have so much more to lose than you think you do and that idea of loss, it makes you love them more. I love Amelie, with everything I have. I'll be honest, it consumes me more than I let on and I wouldn't want that feeling to stop. The idea of losing her, haunts me…and as horrible as it sounds, I would want to go first, so I don't have to live a life without her or at least go at the same time, so neither of us have to live that life without each other," he explained, as I hung on to every word he spoke, knowing he was telling the truth, that I wasn't going crazy.

We both understood one another, about the love we had for the people in our lives, our other half, our soulmate. The passion and desire we had for our significant other was different, but the same on so many levels, making me feel closer to him, closer than I did before. It was just nice to know we were both devoted and besotted to two women that made our world whole.

Love was many things. It wasn't just lyrics or words written on a page telling us they were the one. It was more than that. It was different for everyone and that was the beauty in it. The beauty of the unknown.

After a few minutes of sitting in silence, Amelie walked in, tray in hand, with a plate filled with cheese toasties, a packet of crisp and a donut. It might not have been the healthiest of foods, but it was the good stuff that I would hopefully enjoy. She walked towards me, resting the tray at the end of the bed. I instantly grabbed a slice and devoured it in seconds.

"Thank you," I mumbled with my mouth full, enjoying the food that was filling the empty void in my stomach.

"Told you," she laughed, causing me to smile.

She then turned to look at Jack to see a smile across his face, both of them happy to see me finally eating for the first time in days.

After watching me devour the second one, Amelie walked over to Jack, only for him to pull her down on his lap and for her to swing her legs across the arm rest. He wrapped his arms around her and engulfed her in a tight hold, likely remembering the heart felt words he had spoken only a few minutes prior to her entering. She looked at him and saw how he had his eyes locked on hers and it was like she knew there was something about the way he was looking at her that was different.

"Did I miss something?" she asked, looking at me to then look at him, "What's been said?"

"Nothing you need to worry about," Jack smiled at her.

Just by looking at her, I could tell she was curious, wanting to know the truth, but biting her tongue and not digging deeper for answers.

"Let me guess, it's a *guy* thing?" she asked him.

"It's a *man* thing," Jack stated.

"As long as you're both fine, that's all I care about," she revealed, causing Jack to give her a quick kiss on the cheek. "I don't think so!" she stated, pulling him forward and giving him a kiss on the cheek too, making him smile more.

It was then I knew for certain, that the one thing we would always have, was love and that was the most powerful thing to hold.

I just had one fear.

If I told her I loved her, I would lose her.

Chapter Thirteen

Adeline

BEEP! BEEP!
The sound of a machine signalling life itself. A heart so fragile but beating, a life not lost, but a world still as chaotic as before.

I felt dazed and groggy as I opened my eyes, everything spinning like I was getting off a playground roundabout, unable to focus. Everything around me was moving too fast for my brain to catch up.

Taking in a deep breath, I closed my eyes and counted to ten, only to reopen my eyes and for things to slowly come into focus. Once focused, I noticed where I was; I was in the medical room we had set up all those years ago.

I slowly pulled myself up, feeling the pain radiating through my body, causing me to let out a small whimper, misjudging the moment, forgetting about what had happened to me.

Taking a glance out of the window, I noticed the darkness. Darkness had fallen and I didn't know how much time had passed. With the scan of the room, I saw one of the two chairs next to the bed being occupied by a peacefully sleeping Sebastian, who had one of his hands resting on the bed close to mine.

I couldn't believe he had stayed by my side all this time. Just by looking at him, I could see how exhausted he looked, making me worry about him and what he must have been going through. From the remains of crumbs on a plate and the fresh scent of strawberry and kiwi filling the room, I knew he had at least eaten something and showered, knowing full well it wouldn't have been an easy task, but a task enforced by the people around him. The thought of them all doing that made me smile, at least someone was making sure he was looking after himself because I knew how stubborn he was. Like me, his stubbornness was his weakness. He ruled with his heart and not his head. A quality I loved and would always love about him.

Sitting there and watching him sleep, I wondered how long he had been there for, knowing full well it was probably the whole time I was out. My heart leapt, knowing I had someone devoted to me, like I was to him. He was my protector, my lifeline, my happiness, my soulmate.

Misjudging my movements, I tried again to lift myself up higher, causing another and more excruciating pain to shoot through me and a loud whimper to leave my lips, making Sebastian shoot up. His actions then caused the plate on his lap to fall, smashing as it hit the ground.

Sebastian's eyes then locked on mine. "You're awake!" he shouted, joy radiating all over his face, like a child in a candy store.

"Sorry, I didn't mean to wake you," I replied, letting out a small smile.

"No, I'm glad you did," he beamed, letting tears of joy run down his face, without a second thought.

His eyes scanned me like they were trying to copy me to his memory. It was like he was trying to imprint me on his mind like a permanent reminder.

The feeling of his hand enclosing over mine sent shivers through me. It was like his touch was electric, like every movement or touch from him against my skin, made the hairs on the back of my neck stand up and my heart skip that extra beat. It was like the beat of my own heart, was a beat of a drum, music to my ears.

I watched how his face went from a smile to fear, his eyes showing his emotions in seconds. The wall I had watched him build over the years had come crashing down, revealing the man behind the mask, the vulnerable and the broken.

"What's wrong?" I asked, as he looked down at our entwined hands.

It was like this was our normality, like it was something we always did.

"I thought I lost you," he cried. The pain in his voice so torturous it broke my heart in two.

I slowly reached forward and placed my hand against his face, just for him to instantly relax into my touch, with his eyes closing. It was like he was savouring my touch, taking in another permanent reminder of the warmth he could feel coming from me, skin to skin becoming one.

"I'm sorry," he said.

"Why are you sorry?" I asked.

His eyes opened and he locked on me. "For crying."

The simplest of answers he could present.

"Don't apologise for crying," I stated without hesitation. "Crying doesn't make you any less of a man,

Sebastian. Showing emotions and not showing it makes you a man, makes you strong and powerful. Everyone has the right to feel vulnerable. Emotions make you human."

I was there to comfort him and support him, through the good, the bad and the ugly. It wasn't forced or pretend, it wasn't a fabrication of lies, it was and always would be the truth. I would support them all, come rain or shine, until we all saw the rainbow seeping through the cracks.

His piercing blue eyes looked at me, clear as day admiring me, while I sat there still feeling a little dazed within myself. I could remember snippets of moments that occurred during that night, small moments that didn't add up, but painted a vague picture of what happened, one by one coming back to me, only to be struck by the words 'I love you!'

The words he spoke hit me like a clap of thunder, striking me instantly and all at once.

I could remember the words clear as day, etched, and imprinted on my mind, like a permanent tattoo in my memory, stuck like glue.

But did I dream it? Was I just hearing things while the darkness took hold of me? Did the darkness want me to doubt myself?

***

Before I could say anything, in the corner of my eye, Jack and Amelie entered the room.

They both instantly smiled as they saw me looking at them. "You're awake!" Amelie shouted, running, and hugging me, causing me to wince. "Sorry."

I let out a small laugh, "It's fine."

Jack then came over and smiled. "Malcom sent me in to check on you. Glad to see your awake."

"How long was I out for?" I asked. They all hesitantly looked at each other and then back to me.

"You've been out of it for three days," Amelie told me. "You had to gain your strength back and rest. So, you need to take it easy."

I slowly tried to turn myself around, just to feel the pain sweeping over me, causing me to wince once more, making me realise why they said I had to take it easy.

"You really are stubborn, Adi. Let me help you," Sebastian chuckled.

I lifted my arms up high enough to wrap my arms around his neck, while he slipped his arms underneath me to lift me up. While he did this, I let out a sharp hiss, indicating the pain I was feeling. I then looked to see a frown sweep over his face, concerned about the fact he had hurt me.

"You didn't hurt me, I'm just sore," I reassured him, making sure he knew that he didn't cause me any harm and that I also didn't blame him for the amount of discomfort I was feeling. After all, he was helping me.

Carrying me in his arms, he walked us out of the room and straight down the hallway, taking me to my room. As he did, I rested my head against him, taking in his scent. The smell of strawberry and kiwi hit me again, which meant it must have been the body wash he had used earlier, something refreshing and soothing that made me think of summer. The feeling of the warm breeze against my skin, the smell of fresh flowers blossoming and swaying in the wind and fresh fruit at a picnic. He was the ultimate summer dream, the one person who took me away from reality and brought me to the land of fairy-tales, like falling down the rabbit hole and ending up in wonderland. A world of colour and crazy possibilities, a world I would forever love to live in.

I felt safe in his arms, I felt at home. It was a feeling I didn't want to disappear. If only time could stand still for just one moment.

***

With a thud of a door, Sebastian entered my room, placing me softly on my bed. He then proceeded to plump the pillows and then tuck me in, making sure I was comfortable.

"Thank you," I beamed.

He stood there at the end of my bed, hands in his pockets, watching me, clearly not knowing what to say or do now I was awake and in front of me.

"Is there anything you need?" he asked.

"No, nothing."

He just looked at me with a small smile on his face. He clearly didn't want to leave my side, but I knew that he knew I had to rest more. The way his eyes looked at me so softly said it all, he didn't want to over crowd me or make me feel uncomfortable.

"I'll let you rest. If you need anything, just shout," he said, as he turned and walked towards the door.

"Wait!" I shouted, making him stop what he was doing and turn towards me.

Butterflies danced in my stomach as I just sat there playing with the sleeves of my jumper, making him pull a puzzled look. "Will you stay with me?" I blurted out, only for a small smile to appear on his face and the light to fill his eyes once more.

"I can stay," he grinned, showing his teeth. I watched how he instantly walked over to the end of my bed without hesitation and grabbed the blanket, turning to walk towards the chair that was at the other side of the room.

"You can sleep here you know?" I said, making him turn to face me again, to see me pointing to the other side of my bed.

"You sure?" he questioned, clearly not wanting to overstep.

His eyes said the opposite, they sparkled with acceptance, like I had offered him the one thing he wanted most.

"I'm sure."

He walked towards me and put the blanket at the end of the bed again, slowly slipping into the other side. After a few seconds, he laid down next to me, while I slowly lowered myself on my right side to face him, making sure to take my time. I gently rested my head against the pillow, to see him watching my every move, taking every second in.

Suddenly, I felt the duvet move, to notice Sebastian lifting it up higher to cover me, making sure I was warm and comfortable, tucking me in for the night. He then moved his hand close to my face, pushing a strand of hair behind my ear, causing me to blush.

Him being here made me feel safe, like being in his company was the safe zone, my own white flag.

"I heard you," I blurted out of the blue.

He gave me a puzzled look. "What did you hear?" he asked.

"I heard what you said that night," I said, rectifying my words so I could make him understand.

"What do you mean?"

I took a moment to watch him, trying to figure out if now would be the right time. But anything could happen at any moment and the fear of losing him played on my mind, especially after the events the other night.

One thing I knew for certain was that I didn't need a knight in shining armour, or a frog that would turn into a prince, all I needed was him. The beautiful and the damned.

"I must admit it's all fuzzy and I don't remember much after being shot, but I remember you saying you love me." Once the words left my lips, I felt the fluttering of butterflies in my stomach once again, nervous about his reaction.

Watching as his eyes widened and how his mouth slowly parted, I could tell I had surprised him. I watched how he pushed himself up onto his arm, scratching the back of his head. He clearly didn't know what to say to me, like he didn't even realise that I had heard him say those three special words.

"I don't know if you meant them or if you were just saying it in the moment, but I just wanted you to know I heard you," I said.

I wanted to believe he had said them because they were true, and I prayed they weren't a fragment of my imagination.

He looked at me and I could sense the pain behind his eyes, the pain of the night in question, like the memory of me getting hurt was on a constant loop, torturing him, a nightmare resurfacing.

He slowly let out a small smile towards me. "I said it cause it's true."

Feeling myself blink rapidly, thinking I was in some sort of dream, I was not expecting him to say anything. It was like time itself had paused and it was just me and him. My heart wanted to jump out of my chest, run around and dance to the beat, while butterflies intensified. Was this what true happiness and love felt like?

"I knew there was something between us. I felt everything you felt, I was just scared to tell you."

The words leaving his mouth made me blink several times, like this moment right now wasn't real, it was all an illusion, I was still in the medical room, out cold, dreaming. "I knew as soon as we kissed, even though it was for a distraction, that I had to tell you how I felt."

Everything felt surreal, I felt like I was floating on cloud nine once again, that the angels had heard my prayers and had granted me my wish, like time itself was finally giving us a chance.

"I feel it too," I said.

He slowly leant closer to me, looking me in the eyes and then at my lips, with me mirroring his actions. He stopped only inches away from my face, both of us clearly feeling the tension between us growing, with the air in the room getting thinner.

"What are you waiting for? Kiss me already," I stated.

His lips touched mine, as he cupped the side of my face. The kiss felt like we belonged together. It was real, it wasn't forced to be a distraction, it was what we both wanted. It was a kiss where we both expressed our true emotions and where I could feel my own getting stronger, especially knowing that we both loved each other. Two imperfect people, perfect for each other and boy, did I love how imperfect we were.

We both parted only inches apart, looking into each other's eyes, both of us having gigantic smiles on our face, while both of us remained flustered.

"Will you hold me?" I asked him.

Without saying a word, he laid down next to me,

letting me rest my head against his chest, with him wrapping his arm carefully around me, slowly rubbing my back.

"Thank you," I spoke, snuggling into him and his touch, hearing his heart beating and feeling the warmth radiating from his body.

"What are you thanking me for?"

"For loving me," I replied, hoping he could hear the happiness in my voice.

"No need to thank me, it's true. I love you," he reassured me, holding me a little tighter.

I reached over and grabbed hold of his hand, the one he had resting on his stomach, only to entwine mine and his together.

"I love you," I said.

"Get some sleep," he spoke softly, as he placed a kiss to the top of my head. "I'm not going anywhere."

I could feel the patterns on my back soothing me, he was trying his best to beckon sleep for me. I closed my eyes listening to the beat of his heart, the feeling of his chest slowly rising and falling beneath me, while I snuggled into him. In his arms I felt safe. I couldn't feel more fulfilled knowing I had the guy of my dreams, my missing piece of the puzzle. A happiness that I had always wanted and now I felt like I finally had it. The start of our happy ending.

I finally had the light that was pulling me out of the darkness.

Finally, I was home.

After all, we were two broken souls being broken together.

We were the wildflowers in a field of roses.

Chapter Fourteen

Amelie

I was submerged under water, a towel placed over my head, water being poured over me, suffocating me. I was drowning out in the open, being waterboarded by the men in front of me. I felt the need to fight, fight for every breath of air, whilst I felt the heavy weight in my chest, the feeling of someone sitting on me, crushing my insides. I was sinking rapidly, the water engulfing me as my lungs burned and screamed for air. The little amount of air I could get felt like I was swallowing razors blades, like it was cutting my throat, making me scream, yet no sound came out.

My head was pounding, blood pumping, as my heart started to slow down dramatically, only to be shocked back awake by the sudden allowance of being able to breathe again. I filled my lungs with air and then began to choke, coughing up the water. I was trapped in a constant loop of torture, a constant loop of being drowned, being allowed to come up for air for only a few small seconds to then be swept back under. I wished it would end. I prayed for the darkness, for it to surround me, take me away, swallow me whole, but it never came. They only let me fade into the darkness, into the void of the unknown, just to then pull me back.

Electrocution, the next big thing they would use against me. The first minor shock would always cause a tingling sensation, something small but noticeable, making me aware of what was coming. The dial was then turned up a notch with every shock they gave me, creating violent spasms in my muscles, in all my limbs, only for me to experience more pain, weakness and numbness, showing me how my body was losing control. The shocks themselves would increase until they created deafening screams, screams that would rip out of me, giving them the satisfaction they craved. The voltage of power they sent to my body would flow through me, current after current, making me violently thrash in the chair they strapped me to, restraints across my chest, my wrist, and my legs, bounding me in place. Every shock would make my hands grip the chair, while a rancid and acrid smell overtook the room, the smell of burning flesh, a smell you wouldn't want to experience again, but yet would forever stay with you. The burns forever being reminders of the torment they were giving me.

The electric shocks themselves would leave my vision blurry, like the whole room around me was crumbling to the ground. All I could see were blurred figures passing by, like the spirits of tortured souls still lingering, while by my body felt paralysed. All my stomach muscles wrenched in pain while the nausea brewed, bile ready to travel up. Sometimes when they turned the dial to the highest setting they could, it would cause a sustained contraction, making me unable to let go of the source, making the pain and the duration of the torment last longer, my muscles and ligaments tearing as the result.

With one electric shock, the normal rhythm of my heart was sent into chaos, causing an arrhythmia, manifesting into a disorganised beat. This caused my heart to stop, for the blood circulating in me to come to a halt, just to then be followed by the loss of consciousness, with death being the outcome. Knowing my heart had stopped, they would place two pads against my chest and using a defibrillator, they would shock my heart back to life, back to a new rhythm, restoring my life, resuming the pain and torture. A repeating nightmare.

***

I shot up from the bed, feeling like the air around me was thin, like I couldn't breathe. Sweat was pouring out of me, I felt clammy like a wet fish.

I felt a slight movement next to me and a hand to instantly touch me, causing me to scream and jump out of bed. I instantly ran straight to the wall and slid down it. I couldn't breathe, I was stuck in my own head, the torments I had endured. I could hear voices in my head, laughter echoing, screams of tortured souls, the voices engulfing me, taking me hostage.

I saw a light flicker on and a man shooting up out of the bed just to come running, running to my rescue. He then crouched down in front of me with his hand reaching out.

"No!" I screamed, hitting his hand away. I stood up and ran to the corner of the room, hoping to hide there and for the shadows to swallow me and take me away. I wanted the darkness to come so I never had to relive this again.

"Amelie, it's me, Jack," the man said, coming closer to me.

"Get away! Get away!" I screamed. My head was spinning, the laughter was getting louder, it was starting to deafen me.

"Babe! Breathe!" the voice spoke, as I sank down the wall, pulling my legs in, wrapping my arms around them, while I rocked back and forth, trying to calm myself down.

The demons were out.

All I could picture were people gathering, all hand in hand with devices and instruments to torture me more, wanting me to endure more suffering, while they got off on my pain. They were overcrowding me, suffocating me, making me feel small.

The figure in front of me crouched down and tried to reach out again, only for me to grab the nearest item I could and chuck it at the man. I watched how it hit the figure, but also how he didn't even flinch. It was like my actions to harm him didn't bother him, even though I could see it would leave a mark.

He tried to reach for me again, causing me to scream louder.

"Don't touch me! Get away! Leave me alone!" I screamed, feeling the tears flooding my face.

Fear was taking over my mind. It was taking over every compulsive moment, every movement, consuming me all in one. The terror was growing stronger, sweeping over me, and dragging me under the rug, taking everything, making me weaker.

I no longer had control. I was broken, crippled and falling. I was giving him power, without him knowing about it. The one thing he craved.

He was winning.

Scarlet

My nightmares had come for me, the voices in my head were becoming too much. I couldn't focus anymore, all I wanted to do was scream. So, I did.

Chapter Fifteen

Adeline

Shooting up from my bed, pain running through me, a scream waking me up, with Sebastian doing the same. We both looked at each other, wondering what was going on, only to hear the scream again, a scream so agonising it made my skin crawl.

As quickly as I could, I got out of bed and ran out my room, wincing from the pain my actions were causing me.

"Be careful," Sebastian spoke, following behind me to the room two doors down from mine, the room Jack and Amelie shared.

I knocked on the door and Jack answered with a worried expression written all over his face and a girl's voice in the background, repeating the same word over and over again. "No, no, no, no, no."

Jack didn't say anything, just stood there in his black boxers looking at us. I pushed him out of the way to see Amelie huddled in the corner of her room, rocking back and forth, tears streaming down her face, cheeks flustered,

4

talking to herself. She looked anxious, paranoid, and stressed, like her whole mind was taking over her and she had lost control. It was one thing we all knew about and had experienced, just not like this.

"What's happened?" I asked Jack, keeping my distance from Amelie, enough to not spook her.

I had never seen her like this. I knew Amelie had once experienced episodes like this before because she had told me, but I'd thought they were rare. Seeing it for myself was a whole new experience.

"She was having a nightmare, so I tried to wake her up. She shot up from the bed and next thing I knew she was chucking herself against the wall," Jack said in a quiet voice. "It's gotten worse since you got shot."

I was the reason she was experiencing this torment worse than ever, the reason she was reliving it. Her mind wasn't staying dormant, it wanted to torture her, all because of a new experience.

"How do we get it to stop?" I asked Jack, hoping he had all the answers, hoping he might be able to calm her down.

"Usually, when I talk to her, she stops. I've tried but it's not working."

I took a few steps towards Amelie. "No! Get away!" she screamed.

I took two steps back but slowly crouch down to her level. She tried to pull herself further into the corner as she rocked back and forth, trying to get away from everyone and everything around her.

"It's ok, nobody is going to hurt you," I spoke softly, hoping my voice was calm enough for her.

I held my hands up so she could see them, like I was surrendering to her, making her know I wasn't going to come any closer to her without her saying so. Her eyes flickered to mine, then to my hands and then to the floor, like her mind was registering things slowly.

"It's me, Adeline. Your friend," I softly spoke again, to see a little flicker of light in her eyes, while she remained unable to make eye contact.

"Adeline?" she asked, still rocking back and forth, eyes still flooding with tears, not looking at me.

"It's me," I replied.

"The voices," she muttered.

"What voices?"

"There in my head, the voices are in my head. His voice is in my head."

I knew she meant Hugo and his men. The men who would drag her away and torture her for hours.

She was put on display like a work of art for everyone to stare and gawk at. She was the walking warning of what was yet to come, a prime example for everyone else and I couldn't stop it.

"Tell me about them?" I asked, hoping that maybe talking about it would calm her down.

"I try...I always try...I try to keep the voices out," she cried. "He's always there, mocking me, laughing at me, telling them to hurt me."

"What can I do to help you, Amelie?" I asked.

"They torment me... he hurt me... they hurt me... they hurt me... I can't fight the voices... they are laughing at me... they... he... the pain..." she stuttered, unable to complete any sentences.

"He can't hurt you. You're safe," I tried to reassure her, not moving, not making any sudden gestures.

"Never safe...never safe... Adeline hurt... Adeline bleed... shots fired..." she stuttered again. "I feel everything...

147

it burns... I'm drowning... suffocating... the darkness folding in."

"What do you feel?" I asked.

"I feel the coldness of the blade running against my skin...his eyes watching me, watching them torment me. I feel the air in my lungs being restricted, the water drowning me, making it difficult to breathe...I feel my body slowly shutting down and the darkness creeping over me," she cried, but it was an improvement.

She was forming sentences instead of broken words, she was putting pieces together, it seemed to be working. I watched how she started to fidget with the sleeves of her jumper and how her breathing had calmed down by a fraction. A small bit of light creeping out of the darkness.

"We are all here for you," I stated, taking a glance at Jack who was stood only a few inches away from me, tears down his own face.

"Who?" she asked, as the rocking started to slow down.

"Me, Adeline, Sebastian and Jack," I said, only for more light to come into her eyes.

"Jack?" she asked, not making eye contact, but perking up at the mention of his name.

"I'm here," Jack said, taking a step closer to her, just to crouch down next to me, not wanting to scare her. His actions seemed to pique Amelie's interest, as she started to quickly glance repeatedly at him, back and forth, watching him, only to eventually lock her eyes on him and for him to let out a weak smile. Jack slowly sat down on the ground, and reached out to her, making sure she was comfortable with his movements, her eyes still locked on him as she carried on rocking back and forth. He shuffled forward, not much, but a little closer to her and just stayed still, watching her.

We watched how the rocking back and forth suddenly stopped and how her breathing remained heavy, while the tears still poured down her face.

After a few minutes, out of nowhere she suddenly bolted, diving straight into his lap and into his arms, with his arms instantly wrapping around her, holding her tightly as she cried. Her head was in the crook of his neck, while he held her close and rocked her back and forth, shushing her, trying to soothe her and calm her down as she tried to return to reality.

"I'm here. Nobody is going to hurt you," Jack spoke softly.

"He hurt me," she cried.

"I know. I'm here, you're safe with me."

Jack tried to soothe her, finally breaking her free from the voices in her head. I was unaware how long we were sat there for, but eventually she was peaceful, she had fallen back to sleep in Jack's arms, finding comfort and support from him. Jack looked towards Sebastian and nudged his head for him to come over. Sebastian then walked over and stood there looking down at Jack.

"Will you just grab her for me, so I can get us off the floor and put her back to bed?" he asked.

Sebastian crouched down and hooked his arms under Amelie, with Jack slowly rolling her into his arms, just for Sebastian to then carry her to the bed and slowly put her down. Jack got to his feet and walked to the other side of the bed, just to slide back in and lift the duvet, tucking Amelie back into bed. He got closer to her, putting the duvet over himself, just for her to instantly snuggle into him, completely out of it, due to the over exertion she had

149

experienced. Jack then slowly started to play with her hair, only for her to get even comfier in his arms and for a weak smile to take over his face. He then slowly looked up and met my gaze.

"Thank you," he quietly spoke.

"No need to thank me," I said.

"I don't understand why nothing was helping."

"Sometimes it happens, it can't be explained. I once had the same issue, but now at least we know what to do in future, if one way doesn't work," Sebastian spoke.

"How do you deal with it?" Jack asked.

Sebastian looked at me. "I never could until...Adi," he spoke, making me let out a weak smile. I was surprised to hear his answer, I didn't realise I was his lifeline, but I felt privileged to be able to help him, to be able to help the man I loved.

"All I want to do is help her," Jack spoke again, looking down at a peaceful Amelie, who was deep in slumber. "I love her."

"She loves you too, Jack," I smiled, getting a weak smile from him as a response. "You do everything right by her and she knows it."

I turned around and walked to the door as Sebastian followed, but I stopped and turned back around to look at Jack.

"Thank you," he said again.

"Get some sleep. If you need us, you know where we are," I smiled, turning back around, and leaving the room, shutting the door firmly behind me, knowing she was safe and that she had the best person at her side.

The one person she needed.

Her Jack.

***

Walking back into my room, I climbed back into bed straight away, pain prominent in my shoulder. I was definitely not taking it easy. Sebastian followed me, sliding back into the other side, watching me.

"What?" I asked, as he turned away from me, shaking his head.

"Nothing," he smiled.

I slowly lowered myself down, getting comfy, turning to face Sebastian who had his back rested against the headboard, while he looked down at me.

"You never told me," I spoke, only to see his brows furrow.

"Told you what?" he asked.

"I didn't know I made things better for you."

"You always do." He smiled again, pushing himself down, to only be inches away from me. "You're the light at the end of the tunnel, pulling me from the darkness, guiding me."

"I'm nothing special," I stated.

A deep chuckled rippled from him. "On the contrary, you are more special than you think," he said, just to then kiss me, causing us both to smile into the kiss. After a few seconds he pulled away, pulling me closer to him as he laid down. "Without you, I'd be suffering in silence."

"Without you I wouldn't be free," I added, feeling him pulling me in tighter.

"And with that we can finally fly."

Chapter Sixteen

T he next day was just a day of relaxing. Taking it easy, enjoying each other's company. Sebastian had spent the day taking care of me, even when I insisted he go and do things he wanted to do, his excuse was him telling me I was his priority, so he stayed.

The day was spent cuddling on the sofa, watching shitty movies, eating junk, chucking popcorn at each other, trying our best at getting it in each other's mouth. Amelie, Jack, Arthur, and Jessie eventually joined us, with Amelie apologising for the events of the night, with both of us telling her not to worry and that it happens. Nobody could blame her for what she went through, and I couldn't imagine what it was like; we lived two opposite lives in the programme, and I got the better of the two.

Amelie and Jack spent the day baking, in the most entertaining way possible. She had chucked a small amount of flour at Jack, only for him to start chasing her around the counter, flour everywhere. Jack then caught up to her, just for them both to tumble to the floor. I watched how they just laughed at each other, just for Jack to then lean down and kiss her, while they both remained covered head to toe in flour.

Malcom, throughout the day kept making sure I took my pain medication, while he also checked my wound by cleaning and redressing it, making sure there was no sign of infection.

Malcom's passion was medicine, and it was also his main focus within Scarlet, due to his obsession with science and how the human body works. From all the knowledge he had, he kept making me do exercises to slowly build my strength up, no matter how much pain I felt, due to knowing it would lead to a faster recovery. Malcom was also different to the rest, he never once treated me like I was made of glass, like he didn't need to walk on eggshells around me or treat me like a damsel in distress. Unlike the others, he had all his ducks in a row and was treating me like I was just the stubborn half-wit idiot I was and for that I was eternally grateful. Even if it meant cursing him out for making me do the exercises.

By the time I checked the clock, it was half nine and dark outside; the day had passed quickly, and everyone had gone to bed, while Sebastian had gone to do something, leaving me on the sofa. I slowly got up from the sofa, grabbing the blanket as I went and walked out the back door, straight into the garden to just sit on the grass and look up.

Sitting outside, looking at the starry night sky, always seemed to make me forget. It was something I would always do when I was in the programme; go to the roof with a blanket and look up, forgetting all my pain, worries and fears, feeling safe and content.

There was a faint breeze to the night, not enough to leave me freezing cold, but not warm enough to sit there with nothing wrapped around me, hence the blanket I brought with me to wrap myself in. I watched the trees slowly dance in the wind, hearing the rustling leaves and the faint sound of owls singing their own tune. The stars themselves shimmered in the night, scattering like glitter through the sky, as I laid down on my back.

Moments like this were Heaven, silent times taking in my surroundings, being able to wonder about many things, feeling free and full of hope. All the things I worried about were free from my mind. I always wished that the magic of shooting stars was real because every time I saw one, I would wish that my life was different. I wanted a life full of contentment and happiness with the people around me, being free to go on dates, have fun with friends and build a life for myself. I wanted to explore, learn new skills, go to theme parks, and have those romantic moments of going to the beach, going skinny dipping in the sea, and going on romantic meals at the most expensive restaurants we could find, just to experience it, experience it with him, Sebastian. I could see it clear as day, both of us eating spaghetti just like "Lady and The Tramp", getting lost in the time we spent together, creating a future that we both truly wanted. Truth was, I was just happy I had them around me, even in all the chaos and destruction, they were my family, a family I would do anything for, till my dying breath.

***

In the corner of my eye, I saw a figure walking towards me, only to see Sebastian appear.

"I wondered where you went," he smiled, as he sat down next to me.

"Just needed a breather," I smiled back and as I did, he

laid down on his back next to me, looking at the sky above.

"Didn't realise you still did this," he said.

"I always do it, helps me forget. Plus, I usually do it when everyone's asleep so I can have a moment to myself."

"I can go back in if you want to be alone."

"You can stay," I said, turning to look at him. "I don't mind." I then turned my head back to look at the stars once again, still continuing to find peace in it.

"Why do you do this?" he asked.

"To forget, to get a moment of serenity. I find comfort in it, even in the worst moments of my life, I find myself here. The stars seem to find a way to help me control my own mind, my body, my soul and just feel free from everything. I find the beauty in it. It reminds me of myself, space in general. I'm one in a million, my life, like everyone else's, is different. We expand ourselves, we learn, we adapt, we change, we try to be like everyone else, when we are all just part of a chain of existence and when we get to the end of it, our light fades," I explained. I then took a moment and closed my eyes for a second, taking in a deep breath before continuing. "A glow stick has to break in order for it to glow, but the glow doesn't last forever. Once the glow fades, the glow stick remains broken, and we just continue on." It was a quote I once saw somewhere and it stuck to me like glue, making me realise we are all broken in our own way, but we can still shine.

I took a glance towards Sebastian to see him studying me, clinging on to my words. I knew in that moment my honesty was compelling and pulling him in, just for expressing my views on the world around me.

"Do you ever wonder who our real parents are?" he asked, out of the blue.

"All the time," I said, even though I hated to admit it.

It was always a question that burned in my mind, an unspoken truth I wish I knew.

"Do you blame them for putting us here?"

"No, I don't," I replied. "I believe they did what they thought was best for us and for them. I bet he manipulated them around the truth, promising them good things would happen for us. Do you blame them?"

"I don't know, but I do wonder who they are."

"I don't think I would want to find out because I know who my family are. You guys are my family."

I then felt Sebastian grab hold of my hand, just to feel him drawing patterns on my palm.

"I agree, we are a family, but also..." he hesitated and turned to look at me, causing me to face him. "Might sound soppy. I believe you're my future."

"When did Sebastian get so soppy," I teased, causing him to laugh. "If people heard you say that they might think you're flirting with me."

"So be it!" he laughed. I slowly leant forward and kissed him, instantly feeling him kiss me back and cup the side of my face, both of us melting into the kiss.

I eventually pulled away and looked at him. "To think we almost didn't become friends," I laughed.

"You're the one that didn't want to be friends!"

"You called me psychotic or did you forget?"

"Hey! You called me insatiable!"

"Well, you were full of yourself," I teased.

"Someone had to set you straight," he smiled, propping himself on his arm, looking down at me, while he played with my hair. "You know, you were the first person to ever call me out on my bullshit. The first person I truly felt connected to and actually wanted to be around."

"You filled a void I didn't know I had," I smiled towards him.

I then sat up, pulling myself out of his grasp, only to look up, feeling emotional about everything and before I knew it, I had tears falling down my face. I then felt a hand on my thigh, causing me to see Sebastian comforting me.

"Why are you upset?" he asked, trying to make sure I was ok.

I sat there in silence, knowing it was going to be painful to be honest to him. It's one thing I always promised to myself, to be honest to him, no matter how painful the words may be.

"I feel like I'm drowning," I stated, as more tears fell down my face.

Sebastian moved closer, only to try and bring me into a hug, just for me to shake my head and him to stop. If he was to hug me, I would break, and I wouldn't be able to get all the words out.

"I feel like I'm drowning on the inside, being consumed, and suffocated by my emotions. I feel like I'm always looking down on myself and hating everything I see, wishing I was different and wondering what I did wrong to end up with a life like this…I'm tired of hanging by a thread, but then again, I'm a survivor, it's what's programmed into me, into all of us…I try so hard to hold on to all my emotions, keeping them all under lock and key and keeping myself stable…but I'm not…I'm broken, I'm damaged…I'm finding it so hard to carry on doing it…I know I'm not the only one who has it. You and Amelie had it worse than me and I know I was better off…but I feel completely broken inside, like everything is my fault…I hate myself and there's nothing I can do to change it. Every time I get upset; I lose control."

Honesty seemed to be coursing through my veins, becoming too much for me to handle, the reason for the sudden outburst of emotions. My walls were falling and crumbling to the ground, turning to ash and smoke.

I felt a shift next to me again and then Sebastian putting his arm around me. I let my head sink onto his shoulder, into the crook of his neck, just to feel him rest his head on top of mine. He reached over with his other hand to hold mine, which I willingly let him do. He was trying his best to comfort me, doing anything he possibly could for me and for that I was grateful.

"There is no shame in breaking down. Isn't that what you told me?" he softly asked.

"I know," I sighed, letting myself feel the comfort he was trying to provide me.

"The deeper we fall, the weaker we feel, the stronger we come out of it," he soothed.

"When did you get so wise?" I asked.

"Well...I met this most amazing woman a few years ago and she changed me for the better...she's the wise one and she knows what to say to make everyone feel better...plus, she is the strongest person I know," he stated. "But don't tell her I said those things though. It might go to her head."

"She sounds like an amazing person," I smiled, pulling out of his embrace, to look up at him.

"She is...she doesn't realise it yet," he smiled back at me. He then reached forward and wiped my tears away, the ones that were staining my cheeks, causing me to let out another smile. Smiling around him was contagious.

"Oh really?" I asked, taunting him, making him chuckle.

"Really!" he shot back, causing me to roll my eyes at

him. "Hey!" he exclaimed, making me laugh again.

I looked towards him again, holding on to his hand tighter. "Can you promise me one thing?" I asked.

"Anything"

"Don't hurt me," I said.

"I promise," he agreed. "I love you."

"And I love you," I beamed, as he leant forward to kiss me.

"You will forever have my heart."

"And you will forever have mine."

This time when he kissed me again the world around us seemed to disappear. It was a kiss that made me feel like I was in Heaven and the universe itself was pushing us together, like the stars in the sky had aligned and that our love was eternal, a love that would run along time itself, forever floating in space.

"Just say the word and we'll take on the world, side by side, together as one. Always," he said.

"Always."

And with that, the stars in the sky were the unanswered dreams in the world, the fallen ones being granted...and finally I could say, one of mine had fallen.

Chapter Seventeen

Two weeks had passed since the ball and my injury. I had finally gotten my happiness and had spent my time being loved, by the man I loved. Timeless moments spent in each other's company, loving every second of every minute of the day, as time flew by. I felt like I belonged in the world, that I had finally found my place and role in it, feeling like I was no longer the girl watching from the outside looking in.

I finally had my partner in crime, my last piece of the puzzle, my penguin.

***

I woke up in my bed, feeling warm and toasty. Sunlight was creeping in through the curtains and the smell of coffee filled the air, like it always did. I didn't want to move as my head rested against Sebastian's chest, while his arms remained tightly wrapped around me, holding me close.

I slowly lifted myself up and looked at him, admiring him as he slept. He looked peaceful, like he had no care in the world, which was something he had been for the last two weeks. His nightmares had flown away, and I was the light that guided him out of the darkness and burned the demons away. I was his haven, his safe place, his home, and he was mine.

His skin glowed in the sunlight, as I carried on staring at his beauty, while a strand of hair dangled down. I slowly lifted my hand and pushed the small strand of dangling hair out of his face and admired him more, just to feel him stir and watch his eyes open, instantly smiling at me. He then quickly grabbed my pillow and hid under it, causing me to laugh.

"Hey!" I exclaimed, causing him to chuckle.

As quick as he covered his face, I pulled the pillow he was hiding behind away, to see him smiling as our eyes locked. He then quickly leant forward and kissed me, taking me by surprise, only to be greeted with a kiss back and a smile against his lips. He slowly turned me around, so I was now on my back, with him hovering above me, without breaking the kiss. My hands started roaming his torso as the kiss started to get more passionate. He pulled away and kissed my neck, making my breathing heavier, making the air in the room seem like it was getting thinner by the minute, only to feel him stop.

"You sure?" he asked, hinting at what could be just around the corner, causing me to smile and pull him down to kiss him again. He stopped and pulled away slightly. "I want to hear you say it, Adi."

"I'm sure," I spoke, making him smile at me.

"Promise me, if you want to stop you will tell me?" he asked, only for me to let out a small giggle in response.

"I promise."

My words were followed by a kiss, the kiss being rougher and more heated than before. I felt one of his

161

hands at my side, while the other one got pinned above my head as he slowly kissed down my neck, leading to many wild and pleasurable adventures ahead. A moment in time I could forever get lost in.

***

The morning itself was spent rolling around in bed, showing each other how much we loved one another. There was passion, heat, suspense, and love during our time together, during the connection shared.

We both laid there hot, sweaty, and breathing heavy. Sebastian turned to look at me, propping himself up on his arm as he did, reaching over and pushing a strand of my hair behind my ear, like he always did.

"I love you," he spoke, causing me to grin ear to ear, with my rosy cheeks still present from our interaction only seconds ago.

"I love you," I gushed, causing him to smile back at me. "Today's the day we get back to our mission."

As soon as the words left my mouth I was met with a frown, making him pull away. I got out of bed myself, just to quickly chuck some clothes on. When I turned around, he was sat on the edge of the bed, his feet on the floor, just staring at his hands.

"What's wrong?" I asked him, walking around to his side of the bed. As I stood in front of him, he pulled me down onto his lap, making me straddle him. He then wrapped his arms around my waist and rested his forehead against my chest.

"I'm just worried," he spoke, "I'm worried something bad will happen. That you could get killed or badly injured again or caught."

I slowly pulled back, lifting his chin and planted a

small kiss against his lips. "I promise you; I will always find you," I reassured him, hoping to soothe him with my words.

"What if they catch us and make us forget?" he asked.

I knew that deep down this was his recurring nightmare, one of us being taken and being made to forget the other, or even worse, one of us being killed.

"I could never forget you; I love you," I stated, words as true as they could ever be.

"What if we do forget?" he asked again.

"I'd find my way back to you," I said, making sure he knew I would do anything I could to be back in his arms.

"I'd find my way back to you... the fear of losing you, would make me remember," his voice broke, clearly feeling overwhelmed with emotion.

I kissed him again, a kiss that was to comfort him and to show him how much his words meant to me. He pulled away and weakly smiled, taking in the moment, keeping his arms wrapped around my waist, as I kept mine loosely around his neck.

"We better go down or they will come hunting for us," I spoke, causing him to laugh. He knew it was true, if we didn't head down soon, the others would come running in and invade our moment; they had been doing that a lot recently.

Before I knew it, he flipped me over onto my back, onto the bed once more, causing me to let out a squeal. He leant forward and kissed me, both of us melting into the kiss, only for it to turn more heated, until he pulled away from me, leaving me with a frown on my face.

"No fair," I huffed, causing him to let out a chuckle.

He then walked towards the bathroom and closed the door behind him, leaving me on the bed. I then turned and got out of bed myself, only to walk across the room and pick up the dirty clothes, chucking them into the washing basket next to my door. I then sat back down at the end of my bed, waiting for him.

After a few minutes, he came out of the bathroom. His hair was freshly washed, specks of water slowly running down the side of his head, while he stood freshly dressed, seeing me sat there.

He then walked towards me, holding his hand out. "Come on," he beckoned. I then took his hand and followed him out my room, down the stairs and into the kitchen.

***

As soon as we entered the kitchen, I saw Malcom and Arthur sat on the sofa, Jessie sat on a stool and Amelie standing there eating cereal behind the counter.

"Fine, I'll teach you," Malcom said to Arthur, with the other two just listening in on the conversation before them.

"Teach him what?" I asked.

"He wants me to teach him how to mix chemicals," Malcom spoke, which was another speciality of his.

"I want to be able to poison my enemies," Arthur mockingly laughed, mimicking an evil villain. Jessie rolled her eyes.

"It would be a handy trick," Sebastian put his penny in.

"See! Even Sebastian thinks it's a good idea!" Arthur pointed out to Malcom.

Malcom just sat there, rubbing his temples. He was always arguing with Arthur about things because Arthur wanted to learn twenty things at once, not one at a time, which was never a good outcome. Malcom knew how to do many things; he was probably the most skilled out of all of us. Mixing chemicals and being a medic was his main duty, according to him anyways.

"I said it was handy, not a good idea," Sebastian expressed, as he poured himself a cup of coffee.

In this house we sure did drink a lot of coffee, it seemed to be the only source of energy for everyone. It was our addiction, our one thing we only ever had in the programme too.

Hearing the sound of footsteps, I turned around to see the twins, Hannah, and Luke entering, with Jack not far behind them. Hannah and Luke walked over to the sofa sitting themselves down next to Arthur and Malcom, while Jack made his way over to Amelie, just to stand behind her, hugging her from behind, while giving her a kiss on the cheek.

"I love you," he said, causing her to blush.

"I love you too," Amelie replied, giving him a quick kiss on the lips. She then proceeded to lift up her spoon and feed him a mouthful of cereal, to then be returned with another kiss to the cheek.

I took another look around me, seeing everyone smiling, laughing, enjoying each other's company. Seeing this made me feel guilty, guilty inside for everything that was happening. It was worse than ever before, I felt like a ticking time bomb waiting to go off, causing destruction and chaos all around me, like everything was my fault, it was my destruction, and I was taking them down with me, taking them down the rabbit hole.

"So, what supplies do you guys need?" Hannah asked.

Everyone looked towards her and realised this chat needed to happen now, a chat long overdue and one we needed to get to the bottom off. We hadn't sacrificed ourselves and done what we needed to by attending the ball for no reason. We had to take them down, burn the programme to the ground. Not only was Hugo saving children, he was torturing them the way he had Amelie and the rest. All the programme did was rid you of a normal life. It just made me remember the moment I found out the truth, the truth of what was waiting for everyone there.

Six years Ago...

Sitting in the chair, flicking through one of the many books in his office, I waited for him. Hugo had told me to be here for two, but it was now half past, and he was late. Being late wasn't something new, he always was, the man never had a sense of time, everything always seemed to run over.

Chucking the book on the desk in front of me, fed up with waiting, I got to my feet. Slowly pacing around the desk, I slid my fingers across the surface until I ended up next to his chair. Taking a seat, my eyes scanned his side, just for me to simply look down at the set of draws and open the top one. I wasn't someone to snoop, but he was taking his time and curiosity was getting the better of me.

Casually looking at the draw's contents, all I could see was stationary, a bottle of whiskey and a small brown box. Looking at the box, I opened it to see a silver key, a key I presumed that would unlock the cabinets at the other side of the room.

Giving into my hunch, I got up from the chair and walked over to the grey cabinets to slide the key into the lock, only to turn it and for it to open. I was right.

Opening the top cabinet, I saw a number of files, all named and assigned with a number; the number that was tattooed on our ribs.

I picked up the first file with the title, 'Thomas:

Number 1306', just to open it up and be met with a mugshot styled photo of him and a pile of paperwork. Thomas has ash blonde hair and deep hazel brown eyes, with a scar that went from his left eyebrow all the way down to the middle of his cheek.

Scanning the paperwork, it told me he specialised in combat and machinery. It told me his date of arrival, September 1989, age: six weeks. The rest of the paperwork included the missions he went one, the reports Thomas had given and the people he had met along the way. On the next page, the word 'ASSASSINATED' in bold red letters grabbed my attention.

"What the?" I said out loud to myself, surprised to see he was no longer with us. Someone had killed him?

Wanting to find out what had happened, I skimmed over the last few details on his last mission to see everything had run smoothly. "If everything went fine...how was he assassinated?" I asked myself.

Looking at the last part of the page, I saw something that was signed off by Hugo himself.

'Thomas is a risk. Solution: execution, bullet to the head. Executioner: Eleanor, 1697. Official story: mission gone wrong. Details TBC.

Hugo'

"What? No this can't be true," I said again out loud. "Hugo wouldn't kill his own people; this is a joke clearly."

Slamming the file shut, thinking I was clearly reading things untrue, I put the file on top of the cabinet and grabbed the next one titled, 'Eleanor: Number 1697.' Quickly flicking through her folder to get to the latest report, the words 'ASSASSINATED' appeared again, with another brief description signed off by Hugo, the same as the one in Thomas's folder.

"What the fuck?" I said louder to myself.

Chucking her file on top of the previous, I grabbed the next and the next, reading the same thing over and over again, with yet another brief description signed off by Hugo.

'Maxwell: Number 1456' - ASSASSINATED.

'Aaron: number 1444' - ASSASSINATED.

'Emily: number 6793' – ASSASSINATED.

***

Picking up all the files on the top of the cabinet, just to throw them back in and slam the draw shut, I rested both my hands against it and looked to the floor. My heart was racing, my breathing heavy, I felt my own heart break. The man who I had treasured, the man I loved like a father, the man who raised me like his own, was killing his own people, killing people who had done nothing but be loyal to him.

Feeling the rage within me build, I snapped and slammed the cabinet, over and over again. He had betrayed everyone's trust; he had betrayed us all. He had others do his bidding, just to get another to do the same, a never-ending cycle and it was only a matter of time before he did it to someone I knew and loved to pieces.

The terror inside me suddenly heightened, as my heart continued to pound away in my chest. Just the other day, Amelie had told me she was going on a mission that would take her away for a long period of time. What if Hugo was going to kill her?

Hitting my hand again against the cabinet, the anger, the betrayal consumed me. The one person who had taught me everything, my protector, was nothing but a monster, a hypocrite. He was killing people for his own benefit, his own personal gain, his own pleasure, and I wanted no part of it. Yes, I had killed people before, a lot more than I wanted to admit to, but they were bad people, not good people, they deserved it, but these people didn't. They did what they were told to do, they did what he wanted them to do, protecting him, protecting the world from the bad guys, when in reality he was one of them all along.

Snapping me out of my rage, I heard voices echoing down the hall. Shit. They were coming.

Quickly picking up the key, I locked the cabinet and bolted across the room. I then grabbed the box and placed the key inside, just to chuck it back into the draw and slam it shut. They were going to be here any second. Hurrying quickly around the desk, I dived back into my seat and grabbed the book of the desk, opening it at a random page. The office door then opened, and I looked up from the book, acting like I was just reading. I watched how Hugo and Nick entered, both instantly smiling at me as they did.

"Sorry I'm late," Hugo said.

"It's fine," I weakly smiled, as I tried to swallow my thoughts and act calm, trying to act like I didn't know anything.

If he knew that I knew his secret, would I be next?

Present...

When that day came about, I remembered running to tell Amelie everything I had learnt. I remember the words coming out my mouth and Amelie not being surprised by what I was saying, due to everything she had experienced. As much as I wished I could have stopped the torture she endured, everything I tried to do would end up with me locked in my own room, unable to get out. Which was the reason we had to watch the programme turn to ashes, by being the flame that was going to make the place burn.

"Well, we will probably need some more knives, kind of lost a few two weeks ago," Arthur said, snapping me back out of my own memories.

Luke then pulled out his phone, typing away, making a list of supplies he knew we needed, making sure he had everything properly planned and noted, so he didn't get anything wrong.

Sebastian then walked over to the sofa and sat down on the last free part, with me following him, only to sit on the arm rest. It didn't last long, he quickly grabbed me, pulling me down onto his lap, just to twist me around so my legs went across him. He then wrapped one of his arms around my waist, holding me close, just for me to turn and see Hannah watching us.

"Since when did this happen?" Hannah questioned, pointing to us both, with a smile across her face.

"Two weeks ago," Amelie answered before I could, not giving me the chance.

"Finally!" Luke shouted, raising both hands in the air with excitement. Everyone looked at him and burst out laughing. "Well, I'm happy for you both."

"Thank you," I smiled towards him, only to turn slightly to see Sebastian looking at me, making me blush.

We honestly couldn't get enough of each other. The way he looked at me, made me feel like the only girl in the room, like nothing else mattered, like he only ever would have eyes for me. It was the love I had always dreamt of, a love that consumed me. It took over me completely, making me feel like the world was our oyster and nothing could ever break that or get in our way. I was thankful, thankful for every rainy day, every problem, and every mistake we had made because it had led us to this moment. The perfectly imperfect.

"I looked through the drive," Jessie said, breaking the small silence that had just fallen. "There are two compounds, the one where we came from and another one on the other end of the city in the countryside," Jessie informed us, making us break our gaze on one another to look at her. "The new one seems to be their new headquarters. It seems to be where everything is based. The other just seems to be for data or something."

"So, we're going in blind?" Malcom asked, looking towards Jessie.

"No, she has seen the blueprints," Amelie answered, just before Jessie got a chance to, as she walked around the counter, sitting herself on a stool, only for Jack to do the same, but to sit down in front of her on the floor, resting his back against Amelie's legs and for her to start playing with his hair.

"Jessie showed us the blueprints. There are eight floors and three buildings all connected together. Six floors and two basement levels. In the basement there seems to be several labs and a chamber of some sort," Jack explained, trying his best to highlight what there was in the new compound.

"So where do all the recruits stay?" Arthur asked.

"They seem to be in a building behind the compound, building three. First two floors of that building appear to be the floors for babies and children and the rest are quarters for all the adults. It seems like they have a lot more people now," Jessie explained.

Hearing they had more people made me realise more children had been taken, more children had been sold to them. They were being put through hell and being manipulated by him. A fate worse than death.

"We can't just go charging in, we can't kill the children!" Arthur snapped.

He looked disappointed, like the thought of us going in and fighting was going to end in children and innocent lives being taken.

"The plan is to go after Hugo and if anyone steps in our way and comes for us, we take them down," Jessie said. "We are not going to go in and kill children Arthur, you should know that."

"Hopefully, when we are there, people join our side. If they do, we might be able to set something up for the children and young ones to be moved and taken somewhere safe, if not we will have to sort that when we come to it," Malcom reassured him.

Everyone wanted the safest option for them and for the innocent lives that were still trapped in Scarlet. We wanted everyone to get their fresh start, even if it meant setting up a sanctuary and helping them, as long as we saved others.

"Jack has asked us to come in with two large buses to hopefully help collect and transport them all. Only when the coast is clear," Hannah said, revealing plans that had been previously talked about beforehand.

"So, either way the children go unharmed?" Arthur questioned once more, trying to get the reassurance he needed.

"Yes," Jack replied.

"I'm going to be coming in with you all. I can hack the cameras locally and will have a miniature device on me to do this. *Nobody* is being left behind," Jessie said.

"One thing we need to tell you all," Jack said, making everyone look at him.

"What is it?" Malcom asked.

Jessie let out a cough, making all eyes land on her as she hesitated to speak. "There was a file on the device, about people they have there. There seems to be a list of eleven names that are being locked away. Eleven who escaped the same time as us, who have been recaptured and locked away on the basement levels, being experimented on. They are keeping them there and going through the process of clearing the slate." She looked hurt at the words, a reflection of the pain she once endured during this process, many times over.

"Clearing the slate?" Arthur asked, confused at the statement.

Every one of us sat there, not saying a word, while eyes moved around the room, glancing at each other. All we wanted was to save him from the pain, the pain of what it was all about, we didn't want him to worry or be afraid. After all, he was only twelve when we escaped and hadn't experienced much.

"It means to wipe you of your memories," Sebastian explained, taking a quick look at Arthur to see a surprised look on his face.

"They can do that?" Arthur asked.

"Yes..." Sebastian hesitated. "I've had it done a few times. The more it happens, the less chance you have of remembering anything at all. It's temporary at first, but the more it happens, the harder it is to remember."

I held him tighter, with him returning the gesture, bringing me closer to him.

"It also means when you do remember, it haunts you and I've been suffering ever since. It may not be every day, but it's still always there," Amelie added.

Only a few of them had experienced it, experienced

173

having their mind altered, let alone being tortured.

"So, if we get caught, we get our memories erased?" Arthur questioned, still looking for reassurance.

"Yes," Malcom said. "When it happens, it's a challenge to help someone get their memories back, but the more it happens, the harder it gets. Until it's impossible."

Arthur sat there in shock, evidently not knowing what to say, listening to everyone explain it to him. He had a look around the room to see everyone had a worrying look on their face, realising it was a real-life nightmare and everyone feared it, even the ones who hadn't had it done to them.

"I'd rather die," Arthur finally spoke up. "Is there any chance you can create a cyanide capsule?" he asked Malcom.

Every one of us looked at Arthur in surprise, not knowing what to say or how to really react to his quick-thinking response. Cyanide meant instant death, no chance of survival, no chance of being free, but an ending. It meant to be free, free from pain, free from torment, free from life itself. Complete darkness.

All of us looked at Malcom, seeing the pain in his eyes, a knowing look that explained to us he had once thought about it himself.

"I can," Malcom sighed.

The look in his eyes told me he might have once thought about it before, that he had once made one for himself and he didn't want anyone to know about it.

"I'd rather go out on my own than have my mind wiped," Arthur enforced, making it known he was confident in his words and his wishes, a fate he would rather face.

Nobody said a word, nobody knew what to say. Cyanide was the last option in my own personal preference and Arthur had the high chance of remembering, but yet wanted an option that would mean the worst thing possible.

"I am not going to let you take one, Arthur," Jack enforced. "You will easily remember, others won't."

"I might only be eighteen and the baby of the group, but it is my choice and that is what I choose. I don't want to have to go through the pain, the torment, or the fear of reliving my torture. I have been around you all for the last six years and I have seen the effect it has on every single one of you. I am not putting myself through that. I don't want to live my life in fear!" Arthur expressed, getting emotional over his explanation.

Over the silence that fell, Jack broke it. "If that is what you wish, nobody will stand in your way."

"I'll take one too," Jessie said. "I'm not being controlled by them again; I've had my mind erased a lot more than Sebastian. If I'm caught and they do it again, I won't come back from it this time."

Hearing that they both wanted that way out as an option made me feel like my own heart was being ripped out of my chest. Suicide by cyanide wasn't what I wanted for anyone, let alone myself, but I couldn't force someone to change their mind either.

"If that is what you wish, I'll make a few. You will have the option to take one or not to take one, the choice will be yours. I'll support you all no matter what you all decide," Malcom offered. He would do anything he could for all of us, no matter the cost, like we all would for one another.

I knew I couldn't, wouldn't take one, but at least I knew I had the option if I changed my mind. I could tell by the expression on Sebastian's face that he was unsure of what he wanted to do, depending on the outcome. The idea of it was hell itself, it was like your deepest and darkest fears coming to the surface, living them in real time, over and over again. Like the world around us suddenly got darker with no way out, not even a torch light could light the way to safety and that was something we all had to just deal with. Like me, he knew if he was caught that it would be extremely difficult to get his memories back, but he wouldn't want to leave me. I could see that he was debating it, the light in his eyes flickering as he tried to make a choice.

"I'd come for you if you got caught. I would come and rescue you. However, if you feel like you would rather have one of them as a backup, as much as it would break my heart and I'd be devastated..." I paused, feeling my own heart crumble at the words I spoke. "I won't stop you and I'll support your decision."

Instead of saying something, he kissed me, taking me by surprise, but making me smile into the kiss, as a tear slipped out and slowly ran down my face. The kiss made my heart feel like it was being mended back together again by him, fixing the hole I had just created by my own words.

"Now that is love," Hannah said, making us look at her.

Hannah smiled at us, clearly happy for us. However, her eyes to portrayed sadness, due to knowing what was coming and the possibility of us losing each other, like time itself wasn't giving us a fair chance.

"I don't want one," Sebastian spoke, taking a look at me and wiping the tear that had fallen away. He then caressed my cheek with his thumb. "I believe the love we share would make me remember."

Hearing these words made my eyes water, made my heart cry. He believed in me, believed in us, believed we would forever mend each other, saving each other from ourselves.

Suddenly, without any warning, an alarm started to screech throughout the house, sending every one of us to our feet. We all looked at each other, not knowing what was happening. We had never heard the alarm go off once since living here, it was something new for us, something unheard off, a warning.

Was it a false alarm?

Jessie darted across the room, straight for the computer, only for everyone to see the colour from her face disappear, like she had seen a ghost. She turned and faced us, looking scared to death, every one of us worried by her expression.

"They found us."

Chapter Eighteen

The words coming out of Jessie's mouth became a nightmare in seconds. Time itself came to a halt as fear ran through all of us, every fibre of our being. Bedtime stories once told to children to scare them, making them fear the darkness, coming real for us all. Everything we had dreaded since leaving was back, the hope we had built lost in seconds. An ending was coming, sooner than planned.

Everyone bolted, grabbing any weapon we could find to defend ourselves. We had kept things hidden in every nook and cranny of the house in preparation for an event like this, just in case of this happening.

Before Jessie could say anything else, the power went out, leaving us blinded, leaving us in the dark, leaving us not knowing what was waiting on the outside. It was the middle of winter so darkness was coming earlier, soon enough we would be consumed by it, with nothing lighting our way out.

"They could be anywhere!" Jessie shouted, slamming her keyboard repeatedly, with keys flying off in all directions, showing the anger that was raging through her.

The power hadn't come back on in the seconds it would take the backup generator to kick in, making us all realise that they must have taken that out too. We were doomed.

We all then stood against the walls, away from windows and the doors, preparing for the intruders to break ground. Every second of waiting was an extra second closer to death, to destruction.

"We fight, get out and we run," Amelie whispered, everyone nodding in agreement.

Amelie and Jack had their favourite knives at the ready, spinning them in their hands, ready to gut people like fishes if it came to it. Everyone else carried their own weapon of choice, prepared and ready to fight for their lives, willing to do anything to make sure everyone got out.

"We will get you two out of this," I stated, looking directly at Hannah and Luke.

They both looked at each other and then looked at us. "We have been in many of these situations before," Luke said.

"We are ready to stand by your side and fight, we are your friends," Hannah added, pulling out a gun from behind her. "We are always ready."

They were warriors in the making. In that moment, I finally understood, they weren't just friends, they were part of our family and we protected our family.

I stood there knowing deep down I wasn't ready for this, I wasn't even back to my full strength, but I knew I had to do this, for them, for their safety. I had to be ready to sacrifice everything to protect the people I loved.

Out of nowhere, gun fire hit the house, glass doors, windows shattering everywhere, causing everyone to duck to the ground in seconds. I watched how everything was getting destroyed around us and how the feathers from the pillows were floating through the air, floating to the ground, a beautiful picture in the worst of scenarios. The pictures on the walls, the lamps, the lights around us were cracking under the pressure of the bullets, glass scattering into tiny fragments, with all of us trying shield our faces from the sharp, broken pieces. Sebastian looked towards me, I could faintly see him looking at me, while I tried my best to protect my face. He suddenly got closer to me and grabbed me, protecting me from all the glass and bullets, making sure I was safe.

As soon as the gun fire stopped, we looked at each other.

"I love you," he spoke, kissing me quickly, with me returning the gesture.

"I love you," I weakly smiled back at him. It was a moment needed, just to make sure that we had said something to each other, just in case of any misfortune coming our way. It was one thing we could hold on to. Our love was eternal.

Arthur, Jack and Jessie all quickly disappeared out the room, going to check the rest of the house. Before anyone else could follow, we heard fighting, causing Malcom, Hannah, and Luke to run forward. I stood up quickly, hoping to take a glance around the corner to look outside the house, until I saw a knife fly past me, striking a man down, a man who was about to make his way through the door. Turning to look in the direction the knife came from, I saw Amelie, who just stood there with a smile on her face.

"Bullseye!" she grinned.

"Good shot!" Sebastian rejoiced, clearly surprised about her aim and take down.

"Jack's been training me, it was my weakest skill," she winked at him, while she spun the other knife in her hand.

Amelie then started to creep around the room, getting ready to take a look in the hallway, only for all of us to see Arthur being chucked past the gap before she could look. Before any of us could jump in and help him, we watched how he got up from the floor and readjusted himself with a smile towards us. He then turned back around and charged back down the hallway like nothing had happened. That boy was something else.

Out of nowhere, a man appeared at the door shooting, just missing Sebastian and me, to then be elbowed in the face by Amelie. The guy swung his gun towards her, only for her to kick it out of his hands and for Sebastian to fire his gun, shooting the man to the ground.

"I had him," Amelie reassured him.

He rolled his eyes. "You're very welcome," he sarcastically replied.

Two men then appeared next to me, coming through the shattered glass door, the glass cracking more under their feet. They started shooting towards Amelie, just for her to dive behind the counter. I bolted for one of the men, knocking his feet from right under him, to then pounce on top of the man, punching him over and over again, knocking him out cold. Sebastian tried his best to shoot the other, missing my head by a fraction, causing me to turn and look at him.

"Really?" I asked.

"Sorry," he replied, shrugging his shoulders.

"Aim better," I laughed.

Before Sebastian shot again, Amelie was on the other man's back, slitting his throat in the process, the blood spurting from his neck, covering herself in his blood. The man then dropped to the ground, leaving Amelie standing there looking at us. We both just stared at her; we had never seen her do that before.

"What?" she asked, confused by the expressions written on our faces.

We didn't say anything just looked at her.

"Not like you two haven't killed anyone," she shot back at us. "Don't judge! Would you rather he shot you both?" She did have a point; we could be dead. I shook my head at her. "There you go then."

Amelie quickly raised both her hands to her face just to wipe the blood away from her eyes, for us to suddenly hear a loud scream coming from the hallway. I bolted to my feet as fast as I could, running through the door to see Hannah being pinned to the wall by a man. I ran forward, jumping on the man's back, putting my arm around his neck; trying my best to restrict his breathing, hoping to turn his lights out. The man let go of Hannah and charged backwards, running me into the wall, over and over again, hoping to get me off him. The man soon seemed to realise his efforts of running me into the wall were useless by quickly changing his motives. He tried to reach down to pick something up in the hopes of striking me with it, but as he tried, the man suddenly started to get weaker and before he could even reach anything, he went unconscious, falling to the ground.

As the man dropped, I rushed over to Hannah, grabbing her hand, helping her up off the floor, while she tried her best to fill her lungs back up with air.

"Thank you," she croaked, as she continued coughing.

"Anytime," I smiled.

We then heard a tumble coming from the stairs, only to see a male figure with blue hair rolling down them, making us both run towards him, to Luke. Hannah darted towards him as he laid there at the bottom of the stairs, blood drenching his shirt. We quickly realised that he had been shot, just for Hannah to drop to her knees.

"Luke!" she screamed.

Just from the look in his eyes, I knew deep down he wasn't going to survive this, he knew he wasn't going to survive, his injury was fatal. Luke then started to cough, and blood splattered upwards, making us aware he didn't have long left.

"Safe house! Get them... to... the... safe... house," he barely got out, reaching up and gripping Hannah's collar.

"I will," she cried, as she cupped the side of his face.

"I... love... you...Hannah," he stuttered, as his breathing started to become shallower.

"I love you brother. Until we meet again," she sobbed, causing him to let out a weak smile. She leant forward, pressing her lips to his forehead. "Rest now."

There was a moment of silence, while they both just looked at each other, until Hannah started to sing a small little lullaby. "The stars they shine, the moon that glowed, the wolf that howled and made it known. The trees they swayed, the fireflies that flew, we made a wish and then we knew. Time has come, time has gone, let's close our eyes and start anew."

As soon as the last word left her mouth, his grip disappeared, the life behind his eyes faded, his soul disappeared from his body. He was dead. His soul had gone to join the stars above and shine brighter than ever before.

"No!" Hannah screamed, leaning over her brothers' dead body.

The scream itself was agonising, ripping my heart out. The pain she must have felt was crippling. The one person she had in her life, the one person who had forever stood by her side, was gone.

Hannah took a second and sat up, wiping her face. The tears that fell soon disappeared as rage swept over her. She turned to look up the stairs, where we both could hear a noise coming from, as she grabbed the gun that was led next to her brothers' body.

"They're going to pay!" she seethed.

Before I could even say anything, Hannah, with all her rage, bolted up the stairs, disappearing from view, only for me to hear a gun fire and then see a man falling, after being chucked over the banister. He instantly landed in front of me, just for me to hear the snap of his neck the moment he hit the ground. I looked up to see Hannah leaning over the banister, her face red with rage.

"Let's go and kill these son of a bitches," she hissed through her teeth.

She was pissed, she wanted vengeance, we all did. They were going to pay, pay for her brother's death, meaning anything and everything was up for the taking. This was now a fight she was determined to win; she wasn't going to stop till they were all dead. She wanted justice for her brother and so did I.

Out of nowhere Jack and Arthur appeared at the top of the stairs next to Hannah, breathing heavily, looking down at the man below them and then at Hannah.

"Girl, you got moves!" Arthur spoke in clear shock. "You single?" he asked, with a cheeky grin on his face.

"Really?" Jack looked at him.

"What?" Arthur responded, shocked at Jack's comment, like he was asking the most innocent question.

"Not the time," Jack spoke again, rolling his eyes.

"Not my gender type either," Hannah muttered at the

same time, causing Jack and Arthur to look at her in shock.

"There are more outside," Jack said, changing the topic, just for me to look out the window and see a small glimpse of flashlights heading towards the house.

Great, there were more coming, and we still couldn't even determine how many we would have to fight.

A scream echoed the house, it was a scream that was coming from the kitchen, just for the fear in Jack's eyes to light up. It was Amelie. They all bolted down the stairs, only for Jack to charge past me, causing me to follow. We ran straight into the kitchen to see Amelie on the floor, her arm slashed to pieces, blood soaking her and a man above her, a gun pressed against her temple.

Jack charged at the man that was standing over her, but the man punched Jack in the face, knocking him to the ground. I went to charge at him, but he held up a switch, causing me to come to a halt.

"I wouldn't do that if I was you," he laughed, as his finger pressed against it, ready to let go of it at any moment. "The house is rigged."

I tried my best to study the switch, looking at it more closely, to acknowledge it was a dead man's switch and that the house must have been covered in explosives, meaning one slight move of the man's finger and it would be game over and there was no coming back from that.

Everyone stood frozen in place, not knowing what to do. I looked around the room, looking for Sebastian, only to not see him, making me anxious. The man in the middle of the room stood there smiling, looking directly at me, his eyes running up and down, making me feel sick to my stomach. He was watching me like I was prey, like I was fresh meat, like he was an animal on the hunt, waiting to attack.

"If you come with us, you will all live," he rejoiced,

happy with how things were going for him, like he held the fate of us all. Which he did. One false move and we were done, we were rubble, piles of ash on the ground or a burnt corpses lying in the flames.

"I'm not going anywhere!" I shouted at the man, causing him to chuckle, knowing full well I would more than likely end up coming with him. In this scenario I really had no other option.

In the corner of my eye, I saw Hannah lifting her gun, but the man noticed this and faced her. "I wouldn't," he snickered, shaking the dead man's switch again.

Hannah then lowered the gun, but as she did, another gun went off from somewhere else, causing us to look at the door and see Malcom and a bullet going straight through the man's torso. I watched as the man went falling to the ground, it was like everything around me was going in slow motion as I charged towards him. I wasn't going to reach him in time to quickly take the switch.

Out of nowhere, Sebastian appeared and grabbed the man's hand, holding his finger down on the trigger, forcing the man's hand to come apart from the device as his body hit the floor. Everyone stayed frozen, glued to the spot they were standing in, hoping, praying, thinking the house was going to explode, only to be presented with silence. I looked around me to see Sebastian breathing heavily, laid there on the ground with his finger on the button.

We all sighed, letting out a breath, a breath none of us realised we were holding. Crisis averted. For now.

I quickly ran towards Sebastian, making sure he was ok, while Jack went to help Amelie, ripping his shirt to wrap the fabric around her arm, acting as a tourniquet, making sure the bleeding would stop for the time being, until we had time to see to it properly.

"Are you okay?" I asked Sebastian, as he pushed himself off the floor onto his knees. I couldn't seem to see any injuries, wounds, or bullet holes.

"I'm fine," he breathed out, looking down at his hand, realising what he had just done. He looked back up at me, resting his forehead against mine. "Are you ok?" he asked me.

"I'm fine, but we lost Luke."

"We need to get as far as possible before he lets that button go," Malcom spoke, causing everyone to look at him. "Do you reckon you could hold it till then?"

All eyes turned back to Sebastian, our lives were in his hands, he couldn't let it slip, let it falter, not until we got to the safe zone.

"I'll make sure that I do," Sebastian made it clear. He knew, we all knew he had to, if he let it go too soon, we could be caught up in the explosion.

Malcom came walking over, taking a look at the device in Sebastian's hand, studying it, seeing if anything could be done, as this was the field he was highly trained in.

I heard him sigh as he scratched the back of his head, looking defeated. "I can't defuse the device, soon as there isn't any pressure it will go," Malcom sighed, disappointed in himself.

"We need to go. Split up and meet at Hannah's," Jack enforced.

Her house was our second safe house, always had been, always would be, but we had never imagined we would have to use it, until now.

"No matter what happens, we meet at mine," Hannah made it clear, making everyone aware what the goal was. That was our ending.

Before we could make a move, a red dot came through

187

the window, landing on Sebastian's hand. Me and Malcom instantly noticed it, only for me to look in the direction it was coming from and for Malcom to shout "Move!"

Just before any of us could move, a bullet hit Sebastian's hand, causing him to release his finger from the device and for everything around us to fly in every direction as the house burned and came crumbling down, with everything around me turning black.

***

Coming to, I opened my eyes with everything around me blurry, my ears ringing, muffling everything. I was laid in rubble, smoke, fire, ash, clumps of rocks, wood and house parts surrounding me. I pulled myself up coughing, head pounding. I instantly touched my head and pulled my hand away, seeing it was covered in blood. I pulled myself to my feet, feeling all the aches and pains from being chucked during the explosion. I shook my head, trying my best to restore my vision, making all the blurry images come into focus.

I looked around me to see all the memories, our home, crumbled around me, everything we had was gone, nothing more than ash scattered on the ground. I tried to look around, searching, hoping to see someone, anyone, but I came up empty handed.

"Sebastian!" I shouted, looking for him, looking for anybody.

I couldn't see anyone anywhere, nothing but rubble, rock, fire, until a rock in the short distance started moving. I moved as quickly as I could across the rubble and with all the strength I could master, I moved the rock, helping whoever it was underneath push the rock away, to reveal Jack. My heart instantly sank a little, part of me wished it was Sebastian, but I was still over the moon to see my friend, to see that he had survived.

I held my hand out towards him, helping him to his feet.

"We need to find the others," Jack said, throwing a panicked look around. He was clearly worried about Amelie, just like I was about Sebastian, but still wanting to find the others.

"I'll check over there," I pointed to the left, causing Jack to nod.

"Shout me if you find anyone and if you need help, be careful," he said as he gave me a quick hug, a sign he was happy that I was alive. "I need to find Amelie."

I pulled away and watched how he went hunting, pushing everything he could out of the way, hoping for any sign of life, for any sign of her.

I started to search myself, moving everything I could out of the way searching for anyone. "Sebastian! Amelie! Malcom!" I shouted.

I needed Sebastian, I needed to know he was alive. I didn't want to leave here without knowing that. I would stay here until I found something, anything, even a body.

A small distance away from me, I saw a hand covered in blood, waving. With all the strength I had, I ran over, moving rocks and everything I possibly could to help who it was. I finally moved the last piece to see Arthur. He was covered in ash and didn't seem to have any injuries, besides a small graze to his chin. The lucky bugger was unharmed.

I offered my hand to him, to help him up, but he shook his head, pulling himself up as he did.

"Glad you're ok," he said towards me, giving me a quick hug.

"And you," I replied. "I can't find anyone, not even Sebastian. Jack's also looking."

I was worried, nobody was replying, he wasn't replying.

"I'll help you find the others. We'll find Sebastian," he reassured me, giving my hand a squeeze.

We both carried on searching, shouting, calling out for people, until I saw Arthur fall to the ground. That's when I noticed them. More people were arriving, making me look more closely at Arthur, to realise he had been shot with a tranquilizer, knocking him out cold.

I then saw a dark figure heading towards me, aiming a tranquilizer at me, causing me to duck, just to avoid being hit by one myself. I knew I had to run, even though I needed to help the others.

I picked up my feet and ran, but before I could get anywhere, I felt a sharp pain in my lower back and crashed to the floor. I reached around and grabbed the tranquilizer, pulling it out, flipping myself over in the process, staring up to see the night sky was finally starting to set in. I started to feel heavy, something weighing me down, my vision faltering, becoming fuzzier by the second. I could make out a brief, tall figure stood above me, looking down at me. I tried my best to focus, focus on the man hovering above me, only for the man to crouch down next to me and come into full view. Nick.

Nick was a man loyal to Hugo, a man two years older than me, a sheep following the herd. He never did see eye to eye with me when I was there and was always trying his best to suck up to the boss. I was in trouble because Nick would do anything he could for Hugo. No matter who you were, no matter your age or circumstances, you were collateral damage. He had killed thousands, maybe even millions, he had once killed innocent children, in the most brutal and monstrous ways possible, poor misfortunate souls. Innocent lives lost, like a sickening game he played, a list he had tallied on his wrist.

I felt my body turning to stone, becoming paralysed, unable to move, my muscles screaming. The shot was working quickly, and Nick could see that I recognised him.

He reached forward, watching me, brushing a piece of hair behind my ear, with a smug look on his face. He was taking pleasure out of my misfortune.

"It is always lovely for dear friends to be reunited, Princess," he smirked, seeing the fear and anger in my eyes, knowing full well what I was thinking about him.

"You...you won't..." I stuttered, trying to speak, not being able to form all the right words as my brain started to shut down.

"Get away with this?" he finished my sentence, causing his smirk to grow. "Too late sweetheart, the fun is just about to begin." He paused, watching the tranquilizer taking over me, binding his time.

He slowly ran his hands down the side of my face, knowing I couldn't move from his touch, making me feel disgusted. "You get some sleep, Princess. I will see you shortly," he beamed, knowing full well he couldn't wait to get his hands on me. I saw him look up and ahead of him. "Grab the others!" he shouted, only to look down at me again. "Night, night, Princess," he laughed, as my eyes slowly started to flutter and close. Not only did Nick then disappear into the darkness, he came to live within my nightmares.

Chapter Nineteen

D reaming. Floating on cloud nine. Feeling at peace. I was floating through the sky, flying with birds, the sun shining, sun-kissed skin. It was a dream from the fairy tales, a happy ever after with anything I wanted being granted.

Next thing I knew, I was in a field of flowers. A field of rainbow hues being kissed by sunlight, with a light breeze in the air, making them sway and my hair lightly float.

Hearing a rustle, I turned around to see Sebastian stood there in an unbuttoned white t-shirt and burgundy pants, to then realise I was in my favourite daisy dress, with flowers in my hair.

Was this Heaven?

"Sebastian, where are we?" I asked. "Is this heaven?"

He took a step towards me and rested his hand against my cheek. "You need to wake up now, Adi," he smiled.

"What you taking about?" I asked.

"Wake up and find me...open your eyes, Adi," he softly spoke, keeping his eyes locked on mine. "Open your eyes, everything will be fine."

***

"Adeline! Adeline! Wake up! Wake up!" a male voice beckoned, calling me away from the clouds, calling me home.

I felt a touch, someone shaking me, over and over, just for my eyes to flutter open and a foggy figure to appear in front of me, an angel beckoning me to my life on land.

A sharp pain came flooding through, a pounding in my head, causing me to put my hand on the front of my temple. I tried to focus my eyes and let the figure before me come into view.

"Here," Arthur offered, holding his hand out towards me, helping me to sit up and put my back against the brick wall.

I had a look around me, taking in my surroundings. Cold concrete walls, floors, and metal bars, trapped like a zoo animal in a public display. In the corner of the cell there seemed to be a leak, dripping water into a bucket, making me realise the disarray that surrounded me, a disarray I was now enclosed in.

I shifted my weight and heard a rattle, causing me to look down at my ankle. My ankle was enclosed in a thick, grey shackle. It stretched from my ankle to an attachment in the wall, like I was an animal changed up ready for slaughter.

I turned to look at Arthur, who was sat next to me, noticing he too had a shackle, he too was trapped. I then had another look around me, just to see two other people, sat in the next cell, huddled in a corner. I tried to focus on the figures, my eyes still remaining a little fuzzy, until I could make out who they were.

"Rose? Donald?" I asked. Both of them looking at me, moving closer to the bars.

"Adeline!" Rose shouted, looking a little happier to see a friendly face, given the circumstances.

Rose was a girl who tried to escape with us six years ago. She was a darker skinned girl, with big curls and a curvy look, but from what I could see, she now looked like skin and bone, worn away, evidence of starvation and malnutrition. Scarlet was the same as it ever was.

Next to her was Donald. Donald was a tall lad, probably the tallest person at the programme I knew. His hair was red, ginger locks, covered in dirt. He too looked like skin and bone. His freckles stood out as they covered him head to toe as his complexion had faded to a faint white, grey even, a ghost of himself, a deathly colour.

"I thought you got out?" Rose asked me, causing me to let out a small scoff.

"They found us. How come you're here?" I questioned her.

"They found us," she frowned, breaking eye contact with me.

"You escaped?" I asked, surprised.

Something in me was over the moon, excited to hear that there was a possibility of more people being free, being able to escape. Part of me felt broken, knowing full well that they would be on the run until they were found or killed. A life I wished nobody had to experience.

"We escaped the same time as you did, but we got caught four months ago. We thought everyone else was dead," Rose stopped for a moment and looked at Donald again, who wasn't saying anything. "There were four of us," she carried on, taking hold of Donald's hand before looking back at me. "Think there's only three of us left though." She looked like she didn't really want to talk about the subject, but I could tell she also felt like she needed to. "Larna was with us and so was Audrey, but they killed Audrey right in front of us." A tear then slid down her cheek.

"They took Larna away and we haven't seen her since," Donald added, his voice barely a whisper, still not looking up at any of us.

They had lost someone, like we had lost Luke. There only seemed to be me and Arthur, making me fear the worst about everyone else. Was it only me and Arthur who got caught? Did anyone else survive?

"I'm sorry, this is all my fault", I apologised, putting my head against the wall, closing my eyes. "He wanted me back and if I came back willingly, he would have left you all."

The thought of people suffering, being slaughtered like animals, just for his amusement got under my skin. Everyone around me had to mourn for the life they wanted to live, a life I had put them in, a curse I had forced upon them all.

"It's not your fault, he's after everyone who escaped," Rose reassured me. "There's more of us out there, supposed to be another fifteen on the run." Her words giving me hope.

"Really?" I asked, surprised at the number of people who had got out. "Bet Hugo is pissed."

"We've all been looking for you. You started it all. We all wanted to follow you and we plan to if we ever get out," Rose explained, making me see the bigger picture.

They all thought I was a hero when I was far from it. Everyone wanted to support me, follow me, only because I wanted out, only because I had set them free. I wasn't the saviour; I was the damned.

Arthur sat there watching Donald and suddenly got a curious look on his face. "Donald...what are those marks on your arm?" he asked.

We all looked towards Donald to see needle marks and bruises all over him, like they had been taking blood, injecting him with substances unknown, experimenting. He just sat there silently, pale as a ghost, lifeless, tracing his finger over them all, looking like a skeleton.

"They were doing experiments...on me." His voice sounded shaky, barely audible.

"What experiments?" Arthur asked.

"They took my blood several times, injected me with chemicals, not sure what for," he said softly.

"Have you seen anyone else?" I asked, hoping Sebastian was alive.

"I haven't seen anyone else," Rose said, a frown upon her face.

I was worried, I didn't want to think about the possibility of Sebastian laying under a pile of rubble, nobody finding him, his body decaying, rotting away, being mauled by animals, snacked on, insects crawling all over him. I felt sick but I couldn't stop picturing it. His eyes glazed over, his skin turning grey, bite marks scattered all over his body with chunks missing, rotting away with nobody but me and the others caring or mourning him. His dead corpse screaming at me, crying out to me, blaming me, no life left in him, his soul disappearing and never coming back. It was an image that made me cry, made my heart crumble, haunted my mind.

Arthur noticed me crying, instantly pulling me in for a hug. "I'm sure they're alive," he tried to comfort me.

"I hope so too," I sobbed.

They were his family too and all we wanted was the best for them, even if it meant I had to shove the nightmares of bodies down in my head and picture them all running around happily in a field of flowers.

We all then suddenly heard a bang and some shuffling, just for a man in a white lab coat to appear at the cell doors, with two other men beside him.

"Get them two," he said, pointing directly at me and Arthur.

One of the men then stepped forward to unlock the cell, only to then walk over to us and unshackle us. He then grabbed hold of us, dragging me out of the cell first.

"Get off me!" I screamed repeatedly, trying to fight my way free, only for them to hold onto me tighter, tight enough to leave bruises.

They dragged me down a dark and barley lit hallway. Lights flickered, a lack of power down here in the basement, making it a living nightmare. It was cold and musty with a damp smell lingering in the air, newspapers scattered around, with a trail of glass from a broken door window, showing me trouble was brewing. The place itself had been neglected, making me realise it was a place for forgotten souls and once you were down here, imprisoned by them, they didn't care. You were now part of the trash and what did they do to trash?

They let it wither.

They then dragged me into the room with the broken window and chucked me down into a rusted metal chair, strapping my ankles and my wrists to it, making it unbelievably hard for me to escape. The straps were tight, cutting their way into my skin, the more I moved. The more I tried to get myself free they cut into me, breaking my skin, causing me to bleed.

I sat there silently as the men left. All I could see were medical machines. Some machines I recognised, but others, I wasn't sure about. They were torture devices at the ready, intended to make one spill their secrets. There were

197

broken cabinets full of drugs against a wall, making me think of doctors, making me think of people poking and prodding their victims with weird and painful instruments leading to illness and death.

The man in the white lab coat from mere seconds ago appeared in front of me, taking the chair opposite me in front of the cabinets, with a clipboard and pen at hand. He was a tall man with brown hair, glasses, roughly mid-thirties. I took a closer look at him, my eyes looking him up and down taking in his full appearance, only to see the bottom of his coat had bloodstains all over it.

"Adeline?" he asked, a strong American accent coming through as he spoke.

I just looked at him, keeping my mouth shut, refusing to speak. I wasn't going to give him anything, even if it meant the fate of others before me, was going to be my own.

"Silent treatment?" he asked again, still getting no response. "Well, my name is Dr Roberts, or you can call me, Sam."

I could read him as clear as day. He was trying to come in and be the sweet, innocent doctor that you could trust with everything. He wanted to use his charm, his charisma to make you feel like he could be trusted, just like 'Ted Bundy'. He wanted to manipulate the situation in his favour, wanted to take control, he was a man made from Satan's very own cloth.

"Will you speak to me if I say we have Sebastian?" he asked with a smug look on his face, dangling the one thing I wanted most in front of me, enticing me to talk.

The smirk that presented on his face meant he could read me, read the faint light of hope that came into my eyes, using my own tricks against me. He knew he had my attention. He had won.

"Fine," I hissed, causing him to let out a chuckle. He had got what he wanted, me. "Where is Sebastian? What do you want? Where am I?" I asked, anger and disgust radiating in my voice.

"You're at the new compound, back at Scarlet. We are in the basement, and you have been out for at least a day or...*two*," he explained.

The one place I wished I would never step foot in again, I was there, strapped to a chair, unable to get out of it. Trapped.

"What are you going to do with me?" I asked again, staring at the man in front of me.

"With you? Nothing. With the others? Well, that depends on how you behave." He looked down at his clipboard and back at me. He wanted answers too.

"Keep them out of it!" I hissed.

He chuckled. "Comply and I will," he smiled. "You've been hiding for six years?"

"Yes."

"How many of you?"

"How many did you get?" I asked, not wanting to give away the truth. It was the one thing I wouldn't do, betray the ones who may have gotten free. They didn't need him coming after them too, the less he knew, the safer they would be.

"I'm the one asking the questions" he shot back, getting annoyed at me.

"Answer me, I'll answer you."

"Fine. Four," he answered. Either three had gotten away or three were dead.

"Yep, four," I lied.

"Their names?"

"You already have that. Next question." I wasn't going to answer, I didn't want to expose the others, just in case they did get free. I planned to be blunt and vague, as much as I could possibly be. I wasn't going to expose any secrets to him, no matter how hard he tried.

He rolled his eyes at my response. "Ok then."

I will personally slit your throat Sam, keep your eyes open.

"Next question," I shot at him, making him aware I was getting annoyed with the twenty-question bullshit of a game.

"Why did you leave?" he asked.

"This place is evil," I spat towards him, part of it landing on his face.

I could see he was getting flustered, flustered in rage from my actions as he wiped his face. I was getting under his skin.

"Do that again and your friends will pay!" he threatened, still trying to stay calm and collected, when he was truly losing it.

After all, we were all chess pieces on a board and I planned to make it one less, him being the first.

"Fine. Hugo's a monster. He may have raised me, but I want him dead and for him to rot."

He picked up his pen, scribbling down some notes on his pathetic clipboard, like it was some sort of importance knowing my feelings towards this place.

"We're the good guys. Don't you see? We take all the unwanted children in and make them important. If it wasn't for us, they would all be dead or being brought up in horrible situations."

"I'd rather die before being part of Scarlet again," I seethed.

The flicker of emotion in his eyes made me realise he could tell I was telling the truth, causing him to chuckle once more. "Well, you'll be back to your normal self before too long," he laughed.

"What do you mean?"

"Well, when I'm done with you, the brainwashing begins," he taunted, causing my face to drop.

They were going to wipe me of my memories, make me forget, make me forget everything. They were going to reboot me, restart me, make me Hugo's lap dog again, a fate worse than death.

"Don't worry, the same will happen for your friends too," he promised me.

I could see he was extremely pleased with himself, flaunting everything in front of me, getting the reaction he wanted, scratching that itch.

"Right. Now you have answered my questions, we are going to put you in another cell for the time being." He smiled as he got up from his chair and walked towards the exit.

"I can't wait for the day I can tear you, limb from limb and I promise you now...Sam! You will get what's coming to you," I threatened him, making him stop in his tracks and face me.

He stood there, watching me, only to then proceed and walk towards me, leaning in close, only inches away.

He lifted his hand and ran his thumb across my bottom lip, watching his own actions, smile on his face. "That pretty little mouth of yours darling can talk," he chuckled.

I leant forward, mouth open and bit him hard enough

to draw blood, causing him to hiss and strike me across my face. I then started laughing at the top of my lungs as he took a step back away from me.

"You will pay for that, you *vicious* bitch," he threatened.

I just sat there, laughing at him, spitting his blood out of my mouth, watching him with a creepy smirk across my face. "I'll have the last laugh," I mocked him, as he walked out of the exit, disappearing down the hallway.

You have met your match Sam. Just you wait.

***

After a few minutes of silence, the two men from before came in, one unlocking my right wrist, right ankle, giving me leverage. I swung my fist at the man, knocking him to the ground, while I kicked the other.

With the distraction I had caused, I quickly grabbed a small, sharp object from the table, only a few inches away from me, slipping it into the top of my shorts as they both got up from the ground. One came close to me, slapping me across the face, a blow so hard, so fast and brutal it made me hazy.

I felt the other man unlock my other wrist, then my other ankle. I was floating once again, dazed by the blow as my body was dragged down the same hallway as before and into a different grey coloured room with more cells than before.

Suddenly, I felt the ground of cold, broken tile, with my ankle being dragged and shackled into a new chain, a new cell. I didn't move, the blow still making me feel weak, unable to even muster the strength to turn around or pull myself up, leaving me led on the wet floor.

I laid there facing the wall, hearing shackles, hearing

movement from the other cells around me, signalling I wasn't alone.

"Arthur, where did they take her?" a voice echoed, sounding oddly familiar.

"They just dragged her to another room, while they dragged me here," Arthur said.

I slowly pulled myself up, dragging myself along the cell, the shackle around my ankle being longer than the first, but weighing me down. I moved down the cell until I could see a hole in the wall, just to look through it and see a familiar face.

"Sebastian?" I asked.

He turned towards me, his eyes lighting up from the sound of my voice. "Adeline!" he shouted, quickly shuffling himself to the parting, reaching his hand through, caressing my scolded face and busted lip.

"I thought you were dead," I cried, placing my hand over his, letting my emotions take over. "I kept thinking about you. You were dead, your body decaying in front of me."

"I'm here," he weakly smiled, tears of happiness running down his face.

The one thing I prayed for, wished for was him, to know he was safe.

Another star of mine had fallen. A wish being granted by his presence.

I pulled away from the bars, taking a glance behind Sebastian, to see Jack sat there, his face-stained red from crying. "Jack?" I asked, causing him to look at me, giving me a weak smile.

"Hi Adeline." His voice cracked as he spoke.

I could see the pain, the heart wrenching pain behind his eyes, written all over his face.

"So, it's me, you, Sebastian and Arthur they got?" I

asked, trying to confirm the four Sam had mentioned only minutes ago.

"It is," Sebastian replied.

"The others?" I asked, causing him to frown and to take a look at Jack, whose face faced the ground.

"We don't know if they are alive or dead," Jack said.

I couldn't help but picture it, her body decaying, mummifying, her pink hair covered in ash, insects crawling out of her mouth, her eyes vacant, only for her to wake up and scream at me.

"Did you find her? Before we got taken?" I asked Jack, shaking the image of her corpse out of my mind.

"No. I saw Arthur go down, then you and then I got hit," he spoke. "But before it knocked me out, I saw them dragging Sebastian out of the rubble and then I woke up here."

Leaving the lives of Amelie, Hannah, Jessie, and Malcom in the unknown.

All I could see was a picture of home. The sunlight rays hitting the rainbow hues of congregated flowers, with the fresh smell of blossom in the air and how it suddenly changed.

From sunlight and hope to a decaying body in a field of rotting flowers.

Chapter Twenty

Everyone sat there in silence, not saying anything. There was nothing but the sound of water leaking, the sound of air echoing down the halls. They had vacated, left us in the lurch, left us to think about our fates, about what was to come, the terrors they would inflict.

In the silence that consumed us, I couldn't stop thinking of her, of Amelie. Amelie had been with me through everything. She was my sister, the first person I truly had in my life. She came into my life all of a sudden and she stayed, and I couldn't help but think about the first moment I met her all those years ago.

Seventeen Years Ago…

Skipping along the corridor, enjoying my free roaming time, I sucked a lollipop; cherry flavoured, my favourite. Skipping along, humming to myself, I heard a sound coming from the little training room, making me stop. It was the training room for years seven to eleven to train in and it sounded like someone was going through a rough time.

Scarlet

Creeping up to the door, I leant towards it, pressing my ear flat against the surface, hoping to hear what was going on.

"You need to train better or there are going to be consequences," Hugo said, a voice I recognised clear as day.

"I'm trying," a young female voice said.

"Try harder!" Hugo said with some aggression. I then heard the sound of someone being slapped and a thud like they had fallen to the ground, just to be followed by a small whimper.

Pushing open the door ever so slightly, I slid my way in, hiding behind one of the small punching bags. Poking my head out, I saw Hugo with two of his men and a young blonde girl who looked around my age. She was on the red mat wearing black leggings and a pastel pink top, but no socks. Looking at her hands, I saw she was wearing boxing gloves and that in front of her was another punching bag, with Mr. Wong, our trainer, behind it, holding the bag in place.

"Like I told you, little one. You need to strike the bag harder and with precision," Mr. Wong said.

The little girl then went to hit the bag again, only to punch the bag a few times and for Hugo to shake his head. One of the men then stepped forward and back handed the girl, just for me to hide my face behind the punching bag, not wanting to see what was happening.

"You will learn to do things correctly," I heard Hugo say, not wanting to look around the bag. "How are her archery skills?" I heard him ask, poking my head out once again.

Mr. Wong sighed and his shoulders slumped. "Questionable."

SMACK!

One of Hugo's men smacking the girl again, hard enough she fell to the floor with a thud. Why was he letting them do this to her?

"Stupid child, you've had plenty of time to learn all of this! We don't like slackers!" Hugo shouted at her, just for her to whimper again. "How about her combat skills?" he asked once more.

I watched how Mr. Wong then scratched the back of his head and looked to the ground, clearly telling Hugo everything he needed to know.

Watching as one of his men stepped forward and raised his hand again, my instincts kicked in and I ran across the room to stand in front of the girl, just for the man's hand to catch me around the face. My breath caught sharply as I felt a tear fall, just for me to let a whimper slip and for Hugo to drop to his knees in front of me to check me over, looking at the mark the man had just left across my face.

Hugo then looked at the man in question with his jaw tensed, while his nostrils flared. "Get! Out!" he shouted, just for the man to silently nod and scurry across the room, leaving it quickly.

Hugo then took one deep breath and closed his eyes, just to open them and look at me with a concerned look on his face. He then took hold of both my hands and sighed. "Are you ok? I'm so sorry he hurt you, Adeline."

"I'm fine," I said softly, just for him to instantly pull me in for a hug and quickly break it, pulling away.

He then looked at me with a questionable look. "Why did you do that? Why did you stand in front of her?" he asked.

"She's my friend. I protect my friend," I lied to him.

I watched how Hugo's mouth gaped and how he cocked his head to the side.

"Amelie is your friend?" he asked, and I nodded. "Well, your friend is falling behind and needs the extra help. That is why he hit her because naughty children get punished, but you, my dear Adeline are a good girl and good girls get presents."

"I'll help her," I smiled. "Then she too can get presents."

Hugo then looked at Mr. Wong, just for him to shrug and Hugo to sigh. "Fine, just this once. However, if it happens again, you are both in trouble. Do you understand?" he asked me, just for me to nod profusely. "The things I do for you, my sweet Adeline," he said as he slowly caressed the mark on my face. He then stood up and looked back down at us both with a frown. "Tidy up and then go to your rooms," he said.

Without even waiting for a 'yes sir', he turned away and walked towards the door, just to be followed by Mr. Wong and the other man, leaving me and Amelie alone in the training room.

After the door shut, I turned towards the girl and held my hand out towards her. She looked at me hesitantly and sat up, pulling her boxing gloves off, just to then take my hand, letting me help her to her feet.

Once on her feet, she took two steps back. "Why did you do that?" she asked.

I shrugged. "I guess I didn't want the man to hurt you," I said. She then weakly smiled at me. "Does it hurt?" I asked, pointing to the handprint across her cheek.

She slowly lifted her hand and rested it against the mark, letting out a hiss. "It's sore," she said.

"I'm sorry he did that," I said.

"It isn't your fault, I was naughty. He was right, I need

to learn. It's not the first time and I've had it worse." My mouth suddenly fell open. "Guessing it's the first time you have heard about this?" she asked. I nodded.

"I didn't know," I said with a frown, just to then smile showing my teeth and for her to furrow her brows at me.

"What?" she asked.

"I will help you, so then we both get presents," I said, just for her to look surprised.

"Really?" she asked.

"Really!"

She then held her hand out towards me. "I'm Amelie."

"Adeline," I said, shaking her hand with another smile on my face.

"I guess, after all, you didn't lie to him."

"What do you mean?" I asked her.

She let out a small laugh. "That I'm your friend."

Hearing the words, I started to feel giddy inside, like I was suddenly full of sugar, all because I had made my first ever friend. I finally had a friend; a best friend and she was called Amelie.

Present...

"You're bleeding!" a voice shouted, snapping me out of memory lane to see Sebastian looking down at my side, causing me to look down and see the red stain on my jumper.

As if I could forget the sharp object I grabbed before I got hit in the face.

"I almost forgot," I said, pulling out the sharp object I had hidden to see it had nicked my skin. Which actually didn't hurt. "I grabbed this when they unchained me from the chair, to help unlock the chains. It's thin and sharp, so it might be useful to pick the lock."

Perking up from hearing an escape plan, Jack looked up and directly at me, just for a little bit of light to enter his eyes. "We need to get out of here and find the others."

"We need a plan first," Arthur enforced, making sure everyone knew we couldn't just go on autopilot, which would most likely be the case anyways.

The possibility of death lingered in the cells. Everyone had to be certain if this was the path they wanted to take, we wanted to take. Did we want to just forfeit and let our last six years be erased? Did we want to fight and be free? Would we ever find the others? Was everyone alive?

Questions and questions went through my head, and I couldn't help but think of the worst-case scenarios, especially when we were in a place completely unknown, different to where we grew up in. This time would be different because we didn't have control of the situation, all we had was endless possibilities of what could happen, what we wanted to happen and what we didn't know.

Suddenly, we all heard a scream, causing us all to look up and see two men dragging a girl in. She was thrashing like a fish in their grip, trying to fight the hold they had on her, but the way they held her made it damn right impossible for her to get free.

The girl in question had prominent red locks, locks that travelled all the way down to her hip, while her eyes were prominent green, like nature had taken over them. She seemed to have a little colour to her, like her skin had been sun-kissed ever so lightly. Scanning her up and down, I could make out the bruises, bruises that told me she might have been experimented on. She was covered in them, black and blue marks scattered on her, in the gaps of skin that weren't covered in tattoos, meaning she too had once escaped, long enough to cover her body in black and grey artwork that covered her head to toe.

Quickly slipping the sharp object back in the side of my shorts, I sat with my back against the bars as the two men opened the cell I was in, just to chuck the girl in and chain her up like another animal.

The girl then spat at one of the men, only for him to slap her around her face, causing her to grin. "That felt good baby, hit me again," she winked.

Out of nowhere, she then swiped her leg under his, causing him to tumble and land on his back, just to then lunge herself on top of him, scratching away at his face with everything she had until the other man pulled a gun and pointed it towards her.

"Stop or I'll shoot!" he shouted. She then turned her head ever so slightly and made eye contact with the man holding the gun and smirked. "Get off him or I'll shoot," the man warned again.

"I think I've made my point. I got a few marks in," she laughed, as she slid of the man.

While she remained laughing, the man on the floor dragged himself out, while the other man lowered his gun, shutting the cell and locking it behind him. He then crouched down and helped the man up, just for them to then disappear out of the room.

All eyes then locked on her, just for her to look at us all.

"What?" she demanded, with one eyebrow raised as she grinned.

Nobody said anything and she rolled her eyes at the silence.

"Cat got your tongue?" she asked. "Names Larna," she smiled, holding her hand out towards me.

I hesitated but shook the girl's hand. "Names Adeline," I hesitantly smiled back.

"Hugo's bitch?" she scoffed.

"Definitely not," I replied quickly.

"But you are the one Hugo adores?" she gleamed, fluttering her eyelids as she pretended to be in awe of my presence, causing me to huff at the comment.

"Yep, that's me," I said coldly.

"I want that man dead," she said bluntly. "I need to get out of this fucking place and free my friends."

"Rose and Donald?" Arthur asked.

Her eyes lit up at the sound of their names and turned to him. "Have you seen them?" she questioned.

"I was in a cell next to them not too long ago," he replied. "I don't know why they moved me."

"Well, we are the next ones to get our brains fried," she laughed, "just a waiting game now."

"Anyone ever told you that you're bat shit crazy?" Arthur asked.

"All the best people are," Larna grinned towards Arthur. "Mad as a hatter!" she laughed, making everyone go silent again, causing her to let out another sigh. "When life gives you lemons, you're supposed to make lemonade, but fuck that! I want lemon margaritas."

Hearing this made me snort a laugh, causing her to look at me with a grin.

"Anyone got a plan to get out of this nightmare?" she asked. I reached down and pulled out the object to show her. "Smart girl! I like you," she grinned wider.

"Could pick the locks?" I suggested.

"Pick the locks and when someone comes, stab them in the neck," Larna cheered, overjoyed with the idea of attacking some.

"That's the only way to think about it," Jack said.

Larna then turned her attention back to me and held her hand out, signalling she wanted the object and I happily obliged. She then took the object and instantly stuck it into the lock of the shackles, wiggling it around just for the shackle to come loose. Once done, she then handed me the object, just for me to do the same thing and then pass it on to Sebastian.

As soon as everyone was unshackled, Jack tried his luck with the cell lock, only for it to not work. The lock itself was too narrow.

Sitting there for what felt like hours, we remained in the dim lights, in the coldness of the cell, neglected. We knew it was going to be a challenge, that we needed to risk everything, but deep down we knew it could be done. After all, we had escaped once before.

Chapter Twenty-One

Six Years Ago...

All of us gathered in the training room. Not just Sebastian, Arthur, Amelie, Jack, Jessie, and Malcom but others too. We had an army, a pack, forty or more of us ready to fight, ready for our freedom, a life outside these walls.

The training room itself had lots of colourful mats, weights, weapons lining the walls, an option for any weapon to practise with, this being the perfect supply of ammunition for us to use against them. This room was where I grew up, learning, developing my skills, training to become the person I was today, even if everything was a lie. I knew it was going to be a fight for survival, which we all knew deep down had to be done, but still the fear of thousands of possibilities ran through my mind.

We all went and grabbed what we needed. Many of us had guns, knives, bows and arrows at the ready, our personal weapon of choice, our lifeline.

I wish it was different, that everything I learnt was a

lie, that he wasn't the man I now thought he was. I wanted him to be the saviour, but in reality he was Satan.

Sebastian dragged a chair across the room and stood on it, standing tall above us all. Everyone turned to face him, turned to hear the command, to hear how it was about to go down.

"You ready?" Sebastian shouted, raising a fist in the air, for all the rest of them to raise their weapons in silence.

This was going to be a bloodbath, this was going to be war, we all knew it; it was us or them.

Sebastian took a step down, walking over to me, taking my hand in his.

"You ready?" he asked, getting a nod as a response.

I wasn't ready, but I had to be. The motions had been set. The plan was in place. We had to fight. We had to run. We had to get out.

"Let's get out of here," I said, holding the knives in my hand, ready to attack.

"I'm with you till the end," he smiled, giving my arm a quick squeeze.

"And I, you," I smiled back.

Sebastian turned towards Amelie, both locking eyes and that's when I knew it was about to start. "Do it!" Sebastian shouted, causing a blonde Amelie to walk over to the fire alarm and pull it.

***

The alarms started blazing around us, lights flashing red, a war brewing and finally starting. The alarms were screaming, signalling everyone to evacuate. I knew by now we would have cameras on us, monitoring us, we were now on show and Hugo would be watching.

Sebastian opened the training room door, taking a

look around, probably seeing others walking fast down the hallway. We all left, one by one, to see people with weapons coming towards us. He had sent them, sent them to come and rally us up, take us down, make us suffer.

We all started to sprint and fire our weapons, shooting everyone coming for us. They all knew the truth and still stood by him, making them just as guilty. Arms and legs were swinging, knocking people to the ground, a massive attack in progress. A fight for our lives, our freedom.

Soon as I made my exit, a man came charging towards me. My instincts kicked in and I lifted my knives, just to then swing my left hand towards him. The knife slashed the man's face, causing him to reach up and touch it and then look at his hand to see blood on it. While he was distracted by his minor injury, I raised my leg and with all my force, kicked the man in the stomach, sending him straight into the wall.

Others then started to help, punching, knocking others out cold. I could hear screams, screams that echoed down the hall, screams that got louder the further I followed the others to get out. The screams were coming from the fallen, the broken, the beaten, the ones being butchered behind me, making me want to race back and help. I should go back and help them, but I couldn't, we all knew we couldn't, we had talked about it. Everyone was told the same; you run, you fight, you get free.

I could hear radios, speakers going mad calling out CODE RED. Code red meant we were under attack, trouble was coming, but we were the trouble. As soon as we pulled the alarm, it was coming, he was coming, he knew. People would be radioing others, asking for help, for back up. I couldn't help but see people dropping like flies to the floor, either badly hurt or dead, with other's being recaptured, sedated, and taken away.

Suddenly, I felt myself being grabbed, being pinned to the wall by my throat and the knives being knocked out of my hands. The man before me was strong. I tried my best to kick and punch him, but he wasn't budging. I tried grasping at his hands, clawing away, scratching him, trying to pry his hands away from my throat as I felt the air getting tighter, being more restricted. My time running out.

Out of the blue, I saw a blonde set of hair behind the man and a gun pointed at the back of his head.

"Let! Her! Go!" Amelie spoke, causing the man to freeze.

She pushed it further forward, so it rested against him, causing the man to do what he was told. His grip around my throat loosened, letting my lungs fill with the air I needed.

As soon as he let go, she smacked him around the back of his head with the gun, just for his body to drop to the floor as she had knocked him out cold.

Taking a look at Amelie, I saw she had cuts across her face and a busted lip, but yet a smile remained on her face.

"You ok?" she asked, checking me out, making sure I wasn't seriously injured.

I stood there coughing, getting the air back into my lungs, nodding at her.

"Yeah...I'm good...thank you," I spoke between breaths, getting a bigger smile from Amelie.

Amelie held up a gun towards me, offering it to me, just for me to instantly accept, I needed another weapon.

Behind Amelie, I saw a man fast approaching, only to raise the gun and shoot, getting him directly in the chest.

Amelie turned around, looked down at the man and then back at me.

"Thanks," she laughed.

"Let's get to it, shall we?" I gestured to the door, wanting to get out now more than ever.

We both ran to the door and through it, to see Jack and the others at the other end of the hall, fighting, punching their way through. We caught up to them quickly and carried on moving forward, seeing the exit before us. We ran with all our might, flying through the exit straight into the courtyard, seeing the gates not that far away from us.

"Jessie! Go hot-wire that van!" Jack shouted, pointing with his head to one of the many vans parked up as he held Arthur, the young boy in his arms.

Jessie ran over to the van and smashed the driver's side window with a stone she had picked up. She then reached in and opened the door, cutting her hand on the shattered glass as she did and quickly got in. I could see people gathering around us, guns firing, hitting the side of the van, just missing us. God they have awful aim. Lucky for us they did though.

Quickly seeing a knife coming towards us, I ducked, just to then turn and see Amelie not paying attention. Before I could even shout anything, Jack quickly put Arthur down and darted towards her. He slammed her against one of the vans, taking her by surprise, as the knife went flying past them.

"You ok?" he asked her, as they both stood there breathing heavy.

"Thank you for saving me," she beamed, staring at him, their faces only inches away from one another.

He then took a step back from her with an awkward smile on his face. "No problem! I couldn't let you get hurt."

She just looked at him, not being able to take her eyes off him.

Out of the blue, she stepped forward, crashing her lips to his, taking him by surprise. After a few seconds, he grabbed her, kissing her back, only for her to then pull away from him, remaining inches apart.

"The number of times I've wanted to do that and never done it," she spoke, with a grin on her face.

His eyes opened wide, and his mouth briefly gaped as he heard her confession. "Really?"

"Really!" she grinned.

"I've been wanting to do that to you," he smiled, relieved to hear they both felt the same way.

"As much as I am happy for you both, we have trouble," I said, just for the engine to come alive.

Noticing more trouble was coming behind me, everyone ran forward, jumping into the van, as Amelie took over the driver's seat and got ready to drive us to safety, away from this hell. I was about to get in, until guns started firing, causing me to duck.

"STOP!" a man yelled, causing the gun fire to cease.

I quickly got to my feet and turned around, facing the direction of the voice I heard, only to see him. Hugo.

Hugo was stood there, in the middle of a group of men and women, men and women who had their guns pointed directly at me, at us.

"Don't go!" he shouted towards me, taking a few steps forward. He then stopped and gave me a pleading look.

"I'm leaving!" I shouted, pointing my own gun towards him, towards them.

"We can fix this!"

"You can't fix anything! You're the bad guy!" I screamed at him, feeling a few tears run down my face.

All I could feel was heartache, pain, rage, and wrath. Everything I had known all my life had been a lie and the man I grew up loving like a father, wasn't the man I thought he was.

"I can't lose you!" he shouted; begging for me to come back.

"You're a monster! You can't be trusted!" I screamed again. "You do as you please, you take and never give anything back!"

"I'm not the monster your making me out to be!" he shouted.

"You are the embodiment of evil!"

The sentence itself seemed to hit Hugo hard, the words striking him like a bullet, shattering his heart into a million pieces. I was the one person he loved with all his heart, the one person he would do anything for, and I was now one of many who looked at him in the worst way possible.

"Don't leave me! We can run this together! Father and daughter, side by side!"

"You are not my father! You are dead to me!" I screamed, pure anger and betrayal in my voice.

I watched how he turned to his people, signalling them to lower their guns. He was letting me leave.

Why was he letting me? It wasn't like him to let me do anything.

"I'll find you if it's the last thing I do!" he shouted.

I turned around and jumped into the passenger seat without hesitation, only to turn and look at him once more. I was unnerved, he wasn't even trying to get me, but for now I just had to focus on the simple truth; we were nearly free.

"Happy hunting!" I shouted, with a smirk on my face, slamming the door shut.

Amelie put the van in gear, just to then slam her foot down. The van then picked up speed as she drove us towards the closed gate.

"Hold on!" she shouted to us all, just for us all to then brace ourselves as we went crashing through the closed gates, breaking them instantly. Once through, I looked into the wing mirror, watching my home fade into the distance. He was watching me, watching us disappear into the night and deep down I knew it wasn't the end. It was only the beginning.

Chapter Twenty-Two

Present...

The sound of rattling keys, the sound of change loose in a pocket echoed down the halls. I snapped my eyes open to watch, to wait for whoever it was to appear. After a few minutes, two men appeared, keys in hand, watching us, studying me and Larna.

"Which one is she?" one of the men asked the other, pointing to us both.

"Seriously you don't know what she looks like?" the other man asked, looking at the other like he was brainless and then back to us. "Then again...I don't know either. I've only ever heard the stories about her. All I know is that she is his favourite." That's when everyone turned to look at me, giving me away, slapping a target on my back. "Well, from their reaction it's her," he said, pointing towards me.

"Why does he want her?" the brainless one asked.

"He wants to talk to her and alter her mind set," he chuckled.

Shuffling myself further away from them cell door, I

felt my heart start to beat out of my chest. They wanted me first, I was the target, I was next in line. They wanted to brainwash me, they wanted to take my memories, they wanted me to forget, but they wanted answers first.

The brainless one stepped forward and took the keys out of his pocket, just to scan them.

In the corner of my eye, I could see Larna wetting her lips as she watched the man, while her hand wrapped around the sharp object, waiting to pounce. The man soon found the key and unlocked the cage we were trapped in. He then pulled the cell door open and took a few steps inside, while we both sat there and waited. He walked towards me and knelt down, while the other man followed him in, watching everything the man in front was doing.

Not even a second passed before Larna quickly stood up and launched herself at the second man, just to plunge the sharp object into his jugular and pull it out, causing the blood to spray and cover her. Before I could do anything, Larna was on the other man's back, doing the same thing she did to the first one, but this time the blood sprayed all over me, covering me head to toe. As the dead man dropped to the floor, I looked up and saw Larna smiling with lust in her eyes. She had loved every minute of killing the men, especially the spraying of blood.

With both my hands I wiped my face, only to catch Larna staring at me. "What?" I asked.

"When we get out of here, can I have that?" Larna asked, pointing to my blood coated jumper.

"Why?" I asked.

The way her eyes stayed full of lust said it all. "I love blood, especially the blood of my enemies," she grinned.

Everyone looked at her, not saying anything to her

comment, as Larna scanned everyone and smirked. "What?" she questioned.

"You're mental," Arthur stated, for Larna's eyes to land on him.

"Babe, I'm a psycho," she laughed.

Turning back to look at me, she offered me her hand, which I willingly accepted. As I got to my feet, I let go of her hand and looked down to see the keys next to the man who was in front of me. Stepping over his dead body, I knelt down and picked up the keys just to then walk past Larna and out of the cell. Scanning the keys as I walked out and in front of the other cell, I tried each key, searching for the correct one. On the second to last key, the lock finally clicked, causing everyone to stand up as I opened the cell door.

As the cell door opened, Sebastian came running through it, pulling me into his arms, not caring about the blood that was transferring over to him. He then pulled away from me and kissed me quickly, which I happily returned.

Pulling away ever so slightly, he rested his hands gently on each side of my face. "I honestly thought I lost you," he spoke softly, resting his forehead against mine.

Feeling a small tear escape, I briefly pulled back and looked into his eyes. "Never," I grinned, as he wiped the tear away. He then kissed my forehead and pulled me back into his arms.

The fact I almost lost him, tore my world apart. He kept me grounded, made me feel secure, he saved me from turning into a shell of my former self and for that I would be forever grateful.

"Wait, what's that?" Arthur asked, causing me and Sebastian to pull apart and for everyone to look in the direction he was pointing, only for us to see it was Larna's exposed side. He was pointing to a mark on her ribs, an area of skin where everyone else had numbers tattooed and imprinted.

Larna looked down at the mark and laughed. "Oh, I got a torch lighter and burnt it off. I unbranded myself."

Cocking his head to the side, he blinked a few times, taken back like the rest of us by the fact she had gotten a torch lighter and burnt it off. "Did it hurt?" Arthur asked.

"I loved the pain," she smirked, leaving Arthur standing there, wide eyed, looking at her. "I want no part in this place and it was always a constant reminder. Now I'm just me, just Larna and before you say it, Pretty boy," she said, making eye contact with Arthur. "I'm bat shit crazy."

"Let's get back on track," Jack said, grabbing the keys from my hand.

"We need to get Rose and Donald; I'm not leaving them behind," Larna made clear.

All of us nodded in agreement. We didn't want to leave anyone behind. They too would walk free.

Trying to move things on quicker, Jack walked past us and into the cell where the bodies of the men Larna killed laid in pools of their own blood. He then crouched down and grabbed the two guns and the taser from the floor, only to walk back out and hand one gun to Sebastian and the taser to me.

"Guessing you're happy with your sharp object?" Jack turned to Larna, pointing to the object in her hand, causing her to smile.

"As long as I can slit a few throats, I'm happy," she beamed.

"What about me? What can I use?" Arthur asked, empty handed.

Larna took two steps towards Arthur. "Stay behind me, Pretty Boy," Larna smirked, as she reached her bloody hand forward, rubbing his cheek, smearing the blood along his face, with a wide smile on hers. Arthur blushed, clearly enchanted by her, making Larna laugh a little more. "Got to keep that pretty face intact."

Jack took this as his moment to walk past us all, peeking his head around the door; making sure the coast was clear. "All clear," he confirmed.

Everyone followed him, letting him lead the way. We started to walk down the gloomy, grey corridor to the doors at the end, peeking our heads around it once more. Jack signalled it was all clear again, only to take a step forward, everyone still following him. The next corridor was the same, but with the addition of three rooms attached to it. Jack looked around the first door and walked in, everyone still following him as we went along. I recognised it straight away, it was the room me and Arthur were in at the beginning when we first woke up, the one they dragged us out of.

I quickly ran forward to grab the keys off Jack, running towards the cells. I could see Rose and Donald just sitting there, staring, wondering what was going on.

"We've come to get you out," I reassured them, as I jumbled with the keys, switching between them all, figuring out which one would fit the lock.

The cell door finally opened, making me run in, jumbling with the keys once again, trying to find the one to unchain them, to then release them from the shackles.

"Are you both going to be able to walk and fight?" I asked, looking at them both.

"I'll fight and do whatever it takes," Donald responded.

He seemed to be more alert than he did before, as if

the possibility of freedom had ignited something in him.

"Same here," Rose agreed.

Helping them both to their feet, Rose suddenly spotted Larna and bolted towards her, with Donald doing the same. They instantly both engulfed her in hug, just for her to hug them back. After a brief moment, they both pulled back and noticed the blood she was covered in.

"What happened?" Rose asked.

"My passion for blood," she laughed, causing Rose to shake her head with a smile.

Taking a look around the small room again, I looked at the cabinets and the desk, just to walk towards them, searching for anything we could use to protect ourselves. After a quick nosey, I ended up finding two knives and a few sharp objects, only to hand them to the others, making sure everyone had something. We all then watched how Larna picked up a sharp pencil, to instantly place it behind her ear and then notice us.

"What? I like sharp and pointy things," she smiled innocently.

"A pencil?" Jack asked.

"Trust me, you will see." She winked at him.

She then walked past us all and took a look out of the door, just to signal the coast was still clear. As we all walked down the corridor, a few men walked around the corner, causing Larna to lunge at them, stabbing one of them over and over again. The others started to reach for their guns, but the boys raised theirs first, shooting them down, stopping them from firing.

However, before one was shot, he hit the alarm on the wall, setting off a code red alarm like the first time we escaped. Now we were in trouble. He would know.

Everyone bent down quickly, grabbing the weapons

of the fallen, handing them out. Jack then started to lead the way down more corridors with nobody in sight, while the alarms were still going off, lights flashing red.

When we finally reached the next door, we all rushed through to find ourselves at the bottom of a staircase, knowing we had to go up. We all ran forward, taking as many steps as we could at a time, making our way up as we heard voices of men and women coming from above. They all started to come into view, only for Jack to fire his gun, shooting down many in our way. As Jack and Sebastian pressed on, a man lunged for Larna, wrapping his hands around her throat as he chucked her to the ground and got on top of her.

Larna had a smile radiating across her face as the man did this, making his brows furrow, confused by her expression.

"Choke me harder baby, it turns me on," she breathed out. The man in question, surprised by her remark, released his grip ever so slightly.

She then took her chance and raised her leg, hitting him right between the legs. The man instantly rolled off her, while his hands went down to his crotch as he hissed in pain. She then took the pencil from behind her ear and jumped on top of the man, just to jam it straight through his right eye. Arthur just stood there, looking at her, watching her, as she carried a smile of pure pleasure on her face. Pulling the pencil out, Larna looked up and caught Arthur watching her, causing her to wink and for me to shake my head.

"Do you ever speak?" she asked him, not getting a word out of him, only to roll her eyes. "Not that I should have to explain myself to you, Pretty Boy. They killed people I loved, they took enjoyment from torturing me, from experimenting on me, so I find enjoyment in them, in killing them, in ending it all and chucking them into the darkness. Karma's a bitch."

Hearing a clatter from above, I looked up to see Jack holding on to the railing for dear life. Me and Larna ran up quickly and grabbed hold of him, helping him over the banister.

"Thank you," Jack said quickly, letting out long breath.

"Let's get back to our killing spree," Larna grinned.

Looking further up, I could see Sebastian and the others trying to get to the ground floor, trying to fight their way through the people coming down the stairs. As we got further up, one of the women lunged for me, only for me to quicky taser her and for her to drop to the floor. The man behind her then lunged for Jack, but he quickly grabbed him and sent him flying over the banister, falling to his death. That was one way to get people out the way.

As we got the ground floor, the door automatically swung open, with every single one of us charging through, running to the exit, only to come to an abrupt stop.

Taking a quick look around me it looked like a normal office reception with multiple desks and computers. The only difference was there were files scattered all over the floor, pieces of paper flying through the air, chaos everywhere. There were polished floors, walls, elevator doors and two glass staircases that led up to the next floor. It gave off a false reality, as false as the plants they had in the lobby. In the centre of all chaos, with men and women around him, holding their weapons, Hugo stood there waiting. He had waited for us, waited for me and the only way out was to go through him.

Chapter Twenty-Three

The sound of the alarm filled the room, while we stood there surrounded, we were trapped. Everything we had done, everything we had just spent the last few minutes doing had come down to this, us versus them.

The way he looked at me said it all, he wasn't going to back down this time. He was going to fight. Well, get them to fight for him more like. Looking at the people around him, it made me realise he had spent the last six years making major upgrades to his people, putting more protocols in place and more structure. We must have triggered something for him when we escaped the first time. It was like we had shown him his weaknesses, his breakable points in the programme and he must have corrected them, made them stronger, making them unbreakable. We had saved his company by breaking free. We had made him stronger.

Us escaping six years ago was now our disadvantage, we had cracked the foundations of the programme, just for him to rebuild, rebrand, regroup. He had leverage, he had

Kayleigh Hilton

numbers, he had weapons and we had nothing but us and the loose items we collected.

Hugo, one.

Us, zero.

The only way to stop the larger problem was by aiming at the source, aiming at him. After all, what was the saying?

Oh, yeah!

To cut the head off the snake.

***

"Another great escape?" Hugo laughed, smoking on his cigar, eyes scanning me up and down, taking in my bloody appearance.

I wondered if he cared, if he was scanning me to see if I had been injured, like I was frail, like he may have to 'save' me.

"Why would I want to stay?" I asked.

"Stay and you all will live, leave and I'll kill them all," he said again, with a massive smug look on his face. The same words he threatened me with at the ball.

They all had their guns pointing at us, ready to fire. One step, one wrong word and it was game over. He could look at them and it would turn into a blood bath, turn into countless bodies on the ground.

I took a look around to see there were more people than I could ever imagine watching us, watching me, ready to fight us. I could see the worry behind all my friends faces, knowing we all feared the unknown, the mystery before us. I couldn't ask them to pay the price anymore, the stakes were too high, it had gone way too far. It wasn't fair to them, they never asked to fight for their freedom. The cost they would pay just for him to have me was too much. I

231

couldn't breathe, I couldn't see a way forward anymore, I couldn't ask them to do this for me.

"Why am I so special?" I asked him. He raised his eyebrows. He clearly never expected me to ask such a question, expecting me to remain left in the dark, never knowing the truth, leaving me blindsided.

"You're my second in command, my successor, my one and only. Should I go on?" he explained.

He saw me as his property, his lifeline, when in reality we weren't blood related, we had no connection. All I was to him was the puppet and all he wanted to do is have me by the strings. All he wanted was control.

"You're nothing to me!" I spat at him, rage filling my voice.

"I will be everything to you. Once we sort that head of yours out."

"I will never be yours; I will remember everything! Again, and again!" I hissed.

"I can tell you now, you will be," he said, determination laced in his words.

Nobody said a word, everyone just stood in silence, as the sound of the alarms stopped.

The man before me made me feel disgusted to even walk the planet, there wasn't any part of his DNA where the term good laced it. I wished I could have an ounce of love to give him, something that could turn his black heart back to gold, but it was something I knew would never happen. I had spent years believing the man before me could have been saved, but now I truly knew that nothing in this world would change him.

In the mist of the silence that now surrounded us, the sound of two guns being fired took the room by storm, nobody expected it, nobody knew what was happening.

The silence was disturbed, the voices drowned out, by a simple act. A few men that surrounded Hugo dropped to the floor, instant kills, instant death, not enough time to get a reaction from them. Everyone around me took it as a sign to fight, to go forth, punching, kicking, shooting and for Larna to start stabbing people.

I turned my head and looked above to see two people I once worked with, side by side, their weapons pointing towards Hugo and his men. Watching them both fire, I focused on the man with the pink hair. I was surprised to see who it was. It was Jonas.

Jonas was a technology genius, just like Jessie, he was also Amelie's twin brother, the one we all thought had died during the escape, one of the fallen we spent the last six years mourning and he was stood there smiling at me with a gun in his hand after all these years. He was alive.

Taking a look at the person next to him, I noticed it was Elizabeth. She too was firing her gun at everyone she could, coming to the rescue, saving us from this nightmare.

Elizabeth was a tall woman with long brown plaited hair, who was roughly the same age as Jack and who was also Jack's second in command. She was someone who would step up, take charge and help. She was also someone who had tried to escape with us six years ago but had been recaptured during the escape.

I didn't know what to feel or how to feel. I didn't realise there were people hiding in the shadows waiting to break free once again, but it did make me think that maybe luck was on our side after all.

Feeling a set of hands suddenly grab me, my instant reflexes kicked in as I pushed the taser into the man's chest, just to watch him drop to the floor. Turning around and seeing another man come for me, I punched him in the face, causing him to grab hold of his nose as the blood poured. In a second of being blinded and focused on the man in front of me, I felt an arm wrap around me, while a hand covered my mouth. The man who I had punched, snatched the taser out of my hand and proceeded to use it against me, causing me to scream and go weak in the man's arm.

Everything around me happened in a blur, as I saw both men get punched, just for me to drop to the floor and for Sebastian to appear in front of me, coming to my rescue.

"Jack! Arthur! Get her out of here!" he shouted.

I felt myself being grabbed and chucked over Jack's shoulder, just to see Sebastian in front of me, as Jack walked us away. With the little strength I had, I tried to break but I couldn't. I knew what they were doing and that wasn't going to be an option. While Jack carried me out, I was forced to watch the scenes in front of me take place. I watched how Sebastian got rugby tackled to the ground and pinned to the floor by two men, as Jack sped up, taking me away from this hell.

"No!" I screamed. "Sebastian!"

Jack kept a tight grip on me, even though I thrashed in his arms, but with the little strength that I had, he was too strong for me, so I couldn't break free from his grip. I had to go back for him, I couldn't leave him. He knew this was going to happen, he was sacrificing himself to save me.

"Let me go! Let me go!" I screamed. "We can't leave him!"

I kept my eyes on him, while his where locked on me, watching me, watching me crumble. He was watching me cry, watching how his actions ripped my heart out of my chest, how he was breaking me, but yet saving me all in one. Nothing in the world mattered, not the war, not the programme, the only thing that mattered was him.

"No!" I screamed again, as the tears ran down my face. I couldn't leave him, I couldn't. I needed him, I needed to save him, but they wouldn't let me. "Sebastian!" I screamed as loud as I could, trying to break free of the hold I was in, watching the glass doors before me close, leaving him imprisoned inside.

His eyes were still locked on mine the further I got dragged away, only to see him mouth 'I love you' to me.

Before I knew it, I was being chucked into a van, a van that Elizabeth had started. Once the doors shut, they let me go. I rushed to the back window to see the building getting further from me and to see them pick Sebastian up, dragging him away, with his eyes watching us fade into the distance.

I started crying heavier, my hand resting on the window, while everything I wanted disappeared from view. My home, my safety, my treasure…was being left behind.

My heart too.

Chapter Twenty-Four

T he sound of silence, with only the engine filling the void. I didn't know how long we had been travelling for, but it felt like an eternity.

I felt numb, numb to touch, numb to voices, numb to love.

The feeling of smashed glass being twisted at the bottom of my heart.

My heart was empty, my heart was stone. I was a sinking ship being engulfed by the water and drowning. I was drowning in my own sorrows, my own self-pity, my own love.

Nothing made sense anymore. What was love without the one you wanted it from?

The world was a dark place, selfish and cruel. Every little bit of light that entered my life was dismantled; the flame was burnt out.

***

Turning around and looking at the others, I saw Jack and Arthur not being able to make eye contact with me, while

Rose and Donald were sat there with their eyes closed as the rested. Elizabeth and Jonas were sat in the front, driving us to the safe house, while Larna was just being Larna, admiring the blood on her clothes with a massive grin on her face.

"How could you leave him?" I shouted, disgust, betrayal and hate laced in my words, causing Jack to look at me. The vulnerability in his eyes said it all, I wasn't the only one in pain.

"Sebastian told us if anything was to happen, we were to get you out and leave him. I followed his instructions," Jack quietly spoke, regret trailing in his voice.

"We could have saved him! It's all your fault!" I screamed at him, just to reach forward and shove him over and over again, causing wandering eyes to watch us and look away, not wanting to get involved.

"He told us to do it! So, we did it!" Jack shouted back. "Don't you think I would have if I could?"

That's when I stopped shoving him. I could see the pain behind his eyes, the torment and loss of control. He too was breaking, his own foundations crumbling inside. He wanted his friend, his brother here.

Just like me, his heart felt poisoned by the consequences of the fate we lived. We both clearly felt guilty inside, guilty for taking it out on one another. I felt guilty for blaming him, making him feel like he was the bad guy.

Vulnerable, that was how we both felt.

Vulnerability was like handing a friend, a lover, a family member a loaded gun that was pointed at your heart, just hoping, praying they wouldn't pull the trigger. Sebastian had pulled the trigger unintentionally.

To save us, save me, he had sacrificed himself. A single bullet from my valentine.

A hole only he could fix by being with me, side by side, skin to skin.

***

Without even thinking, I quickly launched myself towards him, only to pull him into my arms, into a warm embrace. Within seconds, he had engulfed me in his, grabbing onto me with dear life, like I was a lifebuoy keeping him from drowning.

"I'm sorry, I'm so sorry," he cried, holding on to me with everything he had.

"I'm sorry too," I cried, not letting him go. Just letting us both fall into the empty void that was consuming us, while we travelled into the unknown.

***

I never looked at the clock, never took in the time. I let the void carry me, a voice in my head of constant negative energy. The voice constantly created a tsunami of events that kept me drowning, dragging me away from the shore, away from safety.

Jack was now driving, and I was in the passenger seat, staring into the outside world, while the world darkened around us. We had been driving for several hours, which in reality was a peaceful thing to know. It means we wouldn't be found.

The rain was falling, streaming down my window, even the world around me was crying for the souls we had left behind. I didn't know when I had stopped crying, I just knew I was now running on empty, my own body shutting down, cracking under the pressure. All I knew was we were heading to Hannah's safe house, a place we hoped we would find others waiting. A place of sanctuary.

We had already switched vehicles by ditching the van and hot wiring a car. We had to keep are tracks hidden so they couldn't find us again, ever again.

With me and Jack awake, everyone else was sleeping peacefully, piled in the back, tucked up together, but I couldn't sleep. I had tried so many times to shut my eyes, switch off, let myself reboot, my brain alive but broken. By closing my eyes, all I saw was him, his face, his mouth mouthing the words 'I love you'.

"He's stubborn," Jack said, causing me to break out of my own doom, my own mind to look at him. "He's always been stubborn. Even if we went back, we would be wrong for doing it and we both know it."

***

Sebastian was a guy who never held himself high up in the world, when he should have. To me, his touch was electric, his voice was a song, a melody I could forever get lost in and his heart was my haven. His selflessness was a quality that shined like the stars, while his love was like a warm hug you could forever feel embracing you.

As much as we all loved him in our own way, he was a stubborn prick. He was a guy who wouldn't falter from doing the right thing, even if it meant he suffered. We couldn't hate him, we couldn't be angry, we couldn't be upset at his actions, all we could be was grateful. Grateful for the sacrifice, the love, the hope he gave us.

"You're right," I weakly spoke.

With heavy slamming of both his fists against the steering wheel, losing control of his anger as he continued to drive, he angrily spoke, "I'm the oldest, it should have been me!"

"He knew it had to be him," I reassured him, as I took

a glance in his direction. "He knew you needed to find the truth about Amelie."

With a quick lingering glance towards me, his eyes spoke more than words possibly could. They screamed of sorrow and love, with that little glimpse of hope. He was hoping for the light to come back, the hope that was hanging from a thin rope.

"He really does love you; you know?" Jack said.

It was something I already knew, but the reassurance was still weirdly needed.

"I know... and I really love him. It's the reason he did what he did. He would sacrifice everything for me and for that he is my hero, but at the same time he is still stubborn as anything."

"You are right on that one," he agreed with a weak smile and a faint chuckle.

"We will get him back," I spoke to myself out loud, reassuring myself about it.

"We will," he agreed, just for me to stare back out the window.

Staring out of the window, I couldn't help but get lost in the scenery around us, a scene of wealth and luxury passing by. It was a sea of houses that screamed the rich and a scenery where dreams lay, and we were on the outside looking in. The houses to me were a little girl's dream. I could imagine a little girl playing with her dolls, all spaced out on the grass with her very own 'Barbie Dreamhouse'. She would be running around in her endless collection of princess dresses, while she would throw her very own teddy bear's picnic. I could see how her life would be growing up and all the amazing adventures she would go on, the life experience she would get while having fun. It was a life we all wanted.

But I was Alice looking through the looking glass.

***

"This is all because of me," I randomly blurted out, knowing full well it was the truth.

"This isn't your fault," Jack tried to reassure me.

"I was, am, his centre of attention. All of this is because he wants me and by him wanting me…it puts you all in danger and I'm not worth it."

"None of this is your fault. If we didn't care for you or want to be around…we wouldn't be. No matter what, Adeline, you're part of our family and we will never have a normal life. We grew up in a programme, we became assassins…I think the life we have is beyond normal and I wouldn't change it because I have all of you and I have…or had… Amelie," Jack expressed, his words slipping on Amelie's name.

She had to be out there, Amelie wouldn't let anything like that take her down, but I still couldn't help thinking about the field of flowers.

"I just don't want any of you to suffer and by knowing me, that's all you're going to be doing," I hated to admit, but it was truth, the truth I had always felt. "Sebastian is going to end up suffering the consequences, being stuck there, no way out, alone…all because of me."

"Love makes us do many things."

"Loving me is going to get him killed and I couldn't live with myself if something was to happen because of me."

The idea of him suffering, becoming another tortured and corrupted soul destroyed me. The chill in the air, the feeling of insects crawling all over my skin, the feeling of a broken heart…that was my life now I knew where he was,

241

and it was never going to sit right.

"We will get him out of there and we will all survive this," Jack tried his best to reassure me, knowing how broken I felt inside.

***

If only words could fix everything.

Chapter Twenty-Five

T he house itself was a mansion, bold, bright, and expensive and dead centre in a land of luxury. The small lights I could see barely lit up the driveway in the starry night sky, but they led the way to our new haven. All I could hear was the trees rustling in the wind and the owl's singing as we got closer to our new home as I looked out the open window.

As we pulled up outside the house, I could see golden looking doors, with lots of plants scattered around, making it more homely. It was a welcoming sight, a feeling of security and warmth, something we had lost being reinstated.

Turning in my seat, I saw the others sleeping, all huddled up close together, only to reach through the gap and put my hand on Arthur's shoulder, gently shaking him awake. "We're here," I spoke, only for Arthur to slowly flutter his eyes open and look at me.

He then started waking the others.

"Are we in the right place?" Larna asked, looking at the beautiful house next to us.

"I think so?" Jack replied, unsure in his own response.

We all then got out of the car and walked straight towards the door and knocked three times. Jack looked up and pointed to the corner of the door, directly at a camera. The camera moved, looking at us all, like it was scanning us one by one. After a few seconds, the little red ring in the camera turned green, like it was accepting us, granting us entry, just for the doors to click and open, revealing a marbled entrance and a grand staircase.

We all slowly walked in, not believing what was in front of us. There were two sets of marbled staircases at each side of the room leading to a balcony, with a large golden chandelier hanging in the middle of the room, glistening across the marbled table that sat below it. There were vases that looked like they were made of gold, filled with the most beautiful and expensive bouquets of flowers I had ever seen. This place was a palace. Fit for a king or queen.

Suddenly, I heard fast footsteps, like someone was running, to catch a blaze of pink hair to appear around the corner. Amelie. She ran without stopping, jumping into Jack's arms, taking him by surprise. He instantly went crashing down as his legs gave way, with Amelie on top of him, both hitting the floor. Jack instantly started crying happy tears, as he held her tightly, like this moment wasn't real and if he was to let go, she would disappear.

"I thought I lost you!" he cried, his own heart crying with happiness.

It was like she had instantly filled the void he was missing, the void he had created with his own imagination.

She pulled away without saying anything and kissed him, a kiss full of passion, fire and love. Two people broken by separation, being fixed instantly by being in each other's presence once again. This moment was theirs, their happiness shining, but my own heart was breaking.

"I thought I lost you!" she cried back at him, looking at him as they both sat up still holding each other.

"I thought you were dead!" he cried more, realising his nightmare wasn't real and his very own star had fallen, his wish being granted

Everyone else suddenly came running in, only to run up to everyone and embrace them. There was Jessie, Malcom, and Hannah; they had all survived the house collapsing and made it to safety. I honestly couldn't believe what I was seeing.

After a few minutes on the floor, Amelie got up, pulling Jack with her. She then caught something in the corner of her eye and looked towards it, giving it her full attention.

"Jonas?" she asked.

"Amelie!" he shouted, only for them to run into each other's arms.

"I thought you were dead!" she cried, still hugging, and squeezing the life out of her unidentical twin brother.

"I thought you were dead too," he cried. They both pulled away and looked at each other, while Amelie's hands rested on his face, taking in his full appearance.

"I can't believe it's really you," she sobbed, hugging him once more.

A heartfelt reunion, happiness, and laughter. All our hearts becoming whole again, but my heart wasn't here, it was missing.

"Where's Sebastian?" Malcom asked, looking around. His eyes then landed on me and I shook my head.

The light behind his eyes soon faded, just for him to charge across the room and pull me into his arms. A hug I willingly reciprocated.

245

"He's alive, but they have him," Jack said, just for everyone's eyes to fall on him.

"What happened?" Malcom asked, as he pulled away and looked down at me, with both his hands resting on each arm, just for me to lock eyes with him and a small tear to fall. A tear I didn't know I still had in me.

"How about you all get cleaned up and we can talk about it shortly. You all look like you have had a long day," Hannah interrupted, before anyone could say anything.

Nobody said a word, just nodded in agreement. It then led to Hannah showing us all where we could shower, sleep, and change into a fresh set of clothes. It made me realise that she had faith in the fact we would show up and that we weren't part of the rubble. They had all been prepared for our return, they all had hope.

Faith was the only thing that could never be destroyed, the one thing he could never destroy and deep down in that twisted soul of his, I knew he knew that, but it wouldn't stop him from trying. To him, where there was faith, there was a broken structure, hairline fractures in the foundation waiting to crack at any given moment.

***

After freshening up and a few hours kip of tossing and turning, I walked into the living room to see satin painted walls, expensive paintings, and a collection of medieval weapons in a grand cabinet display, torture devices at the ready and it wasn't just few. Hannah seemed to be a collector of medieval possessions, like she was addicted to history. The room also had countless comfy chairs, all spread out in the middle of the room with everyone seated. Everyone was admiring the room we were in, amazed by the place Hannah and Luke had been living all these years.

Hannah had put a variety of food out on the table, bottles of water and fizzy drinks, just for everyone to dive in, stuffing their faces, grabbing anything and everything, enjoying the food melting in their mouth and the fresh taste of something warm filling their bellies.

Me, on the other hand, couldn't eat. The feeling of something, someone missing, was making me sick to my stomach. I felt like if I was to take the smallest of bites out of something, I would be throwing it back up in seconds. I also felt like I didn't deserve to eat while he was more than likely being starved, turning into nothing but skin and bone.

Why should I be treated while he suffers?

I deserved nothing special, no special treatment...he should be here, not me.

Life seemed to have a way of being a continuous cat and mouse game, an endless cycle of negativity. There were still a few chess pieces on the board, and I was going to have to make my move to knock them down, fight my way through, until I hit the king.

I needed checkmate.

***

"I forgot what food actually tasted like," Donald mumbled, snapping me out of my own head to see he had his mouth full.

"This is heaven!" Rose beamed, as she sat there enjoying every bite.

Jack and Amelie stayed attached at the hip, snuggled together on the sofa. He kept kissing her on the forehead, not wanting to let her go. He had clearly thought the worst had happened to her, but now he was full of pure happiness. Just by looking at him, I could see the light in his eyes from having the one thing he wanted the most in the world in front of him, but yet from the side glance he kept giving me, I could sense the pain he felt. The pain over the fact he had the girl he loved in his arms, and I didn't have him, that I didn't have Sebastian with me. It was written all over his face, clear as day for me to notice and I didn't want that for him, I wanted him to take in every minute he had with her, with the one person he loved most in this world because if I was him, I would. I could also see the light in her eyes, that she was over the moon that he was safe with her again, he was home.

Silence remained the thing most noticeable in the room of people, it seemed to be like nobody wanted or could say a word, like they didn't want to be the first one to start the conversation. I already knew it was going to be pretty much a black and white conversation. What happened? Where is he? Can we go and save him?

The simple questions that would be asked and needed to be answered. They couldn't be left in the dark because without truth, where is the trust?

***

Larna let out a sigh, causing everyone to look at her. "We just going to sit here and do nothing? Or are we going to talk about it?" she asked, rolling her eyes at the situation before her.

"What happened?" Amelie asked, the concern written all over her face.

"They asked me questions. They asked me about us and then they wanted to brainwash us," I said, not making eye contact with anyone, trying to remain somewhere in my own bubble.

"Then we broke out," Jack finished for me, knowing I didn't have the strength to say much more.

I hesitated for a moment, feeling tears running down my face. "Sebastian... sacrificed himself for me to escape," I sobbed, feeling my own torment consuming me once more. The heartbreak I felt coming back to me was catastrophic, a chronic pain that overwhelmed me and consumed me entirely.

Before I knew it, arms surrounded me, pulling me towards the source, only for me to see it was Jack. He had run over the second I broke, to take me in his arms and give me a quick kiss on the top of my head as I sat there crying in his arms.

"I'm sorry," he whispered, making me hold onto him more.

He knew what I was feeling, what I was wishing for and all he wanted to do was to take my pain away. I knew he had felt this, he had felt it with Amelie, and it was a pain that was worse than death. I'd rather my life ended than feel this type of pain, like my heart had been snapped into two and I could no longer breathe.

Sad and lonely, a fate worse than death. I missed him.

"We need to save him," I cried.

"Maybe we can," Jonas said from his seat, causing everyone to look at him, including myself.

"What do you mean?" Malcom asked.

"Well, before we came to your rescue, I downloaded all the data to this," he smiled, holding out a small device. "This has everything about the building, access to their cameras and also data we can use to our advantage. This can give us a live view of what's happening in the building. Since Jessie left six years ago, they made me head of security. Jokes on them though because I made a bug and that bug is extremely hidden in their server and can't be unwritten, so it gives me all the access I need and is completely untraceable."

Within seconds, Hannah got up and ran out of the room, only to return, laptop in hand. She handed it to Jonas who instantly flipped the screen and got to work. It was like he was the flower and we all swarmed to him like bees, to be consumed by what he was doing.

Within minutes, he had the camera footage on screen and then clicked on one camera in particular. The camera he clicked on revealed Sebastian was still alive, but the sight before me wasn't something to be happy about. There on the screen was Sebastian, tied to a chair, like the one I was tied to when Dr Sam bloody Roberts was questioning me, with the restraints cutting into my skin. He too was strapped to the point he would be left with bruises.

Next to enter the live camera footage was Dr Sam Roberts, he had some sort of needle with him that was filled with some random yellow liquid, just to stick the needle in Sebastian's arm. I watched how he put a guard in his mouth, something to protect his teeth and pulled his head back further, strapping a brace over his neck so he couldn't move. Sebastian was trying his best to fight against the restraints, not caring they were cutting into him, making him bleed and that's when I knew what was coming. It was a fate he knew himself was coming, a fate he had experienced many times before.

I could see the fear in his eyes as this was all happening around him and how he suddenly let out a few tears. He suddenly stopped fighting and blinked a few times, just to then close his eyes and fall still, he was accepting his fate. He was making himself come to terms with his reality, that there was no light, no saving grace coming to his rescue, that this was it, he was in hell.

I knew in that moment what he was thinking about. He was thinking of me, his family and what he was going to lose. He feared forgetting the love people had for him and what he had for us, for me. In our moments confined together, he had admitted to me the truth, the truth of what went through his head before traumatic events.

If it was me, my last thought would be my family and him. I would think of those deep blue eyes and how they consumed me, how he made me feel safe, made me feel whole. I couldn't imagine what it would be like to wake up not knowing what was happening and who I was. Truth was, I didn't know how much of his memory would be taken.

Would he only lose the last six years? Or would it be me entirely?

***

We all stood there, eyes locked to the screen, watching helplessly as they attached a metal device to his head, the wires coming from it being connected to machines around him. I took a look towards Amelie, only to see the expression on her face, the expression that confirmed they were going to make him forget. They were going to strip him of his memories, his lifeline, his only hope and leave an empty shell.

I turned my attention back to the screen to see Sam walk to the other side of the room and slip some goggles on. I watched how he turned to face a screen, pressing buttons repeatedly, preparing for the torture. He seemed to have no soul, no heart, no sense of respect, he followed the herd.

He turned back around and faced Sebastian again. "Ten... nine... eight... seven... six..." he started to speak.

251

It wasn't going to be long before he wouldn't be mine anymore.

"Five... four... three."

Numbers ticking down, the feeling of sick brewing in my stomach. Nothing could prepare me for what I was going to see.

"Two...one."

The numbers finally stopped and what I saw terrified me. On the count of one, he flipped the switch, sending a voltage of power through the wires. Sebastian screamed, but they were muffled by the guard in his mouth. His body started to convulse under the pressure of the electrocution, sending his limbs into spasm and his eyes to shoot open, making them look like they were going to bulge out and burst. Sam stood there switching it on and off repeatedly, making Sebastian suffer.

I couldn't take it anymore and turned away from the screen, taking a few steps back, just to drop to the floor crying. I couldn't believe what I was seeing, the pain he was experiencing...all to save me. I felt dead inside, felt like my whole life was being destroyed before my eyes because the man I loved the most in this world was going through that.

I kept picturing the moments we shared, the kisses we gave and received, the warmth he had when he embraced me in his arms, the scent of fresh berries in the spring. I kept picturing him. I was fighting through my memories of us, searching for peace, hope, love, but Sebastian was going to have hollowness, fragments of the past gone. To look into anyone else's eyes right now, would be too much. All I would be able to see was going to reflect him, everyone was going to have him on their mind. They say the past will always guide you to do better and become better, but the past was going to haunt me. I would forever remain remembering us and our love and to him, I would forever be the ash, the flame that was once lit burning out and forgotten about.

I was damaged, broken, a shell, I was trash. I had so much to say to him and yet I had no one to say it to, it was like the monsters in my head were screaming so damn loud I couldn't focus.

The tears poured down my face, as the rage, the pain and the torment filled me, until I couldn't hold it in anymore. I screamed, letting out all of my emotions. An agonising scream. It was a scream of a thousand lifetimes, so powerful it could shatter glass, a scream for the fallen.

Everyone's eyes lingered on me as the scream crippled me, until I sat there silently. The tears they stopped, but the pain stayed, like something within me just switched. I could feel my face change instantly. I wasn't crying anymore, I had no tears falling, all I had was the face of pure hatred and evil coming to life, like I had simply turned the switch off, turned off my humanity and all I could see was red. Nothing else mattered in the world, not how I felt, not how broken my heart was, but only the anger that consumed me, consumed every single cell and fibre of my wellbeing.

I felt myself look towards them all, only to see them watching me speechless.

I felt the creep of a wicked grin spread across my face, only for them to finally see what was happening. The girl Hugo knew was vanishing, the girl he wanted, gone. I finally knew what I had to do, what the plan was, what we all had to do, with Sebastian being the answer. We had to rid the world of Hugo.

He wanted a war and that's what he was going to get.

We were going to cut the head of the snake.

Bring. It. On.

Chapter Twenty-Six

Heaven and Hell combining and combusting into flames. It couldn't be heard, but it was felt. The goodness I wanted in the world, being replaced by the evil flame of Hugo. Hugo was going to pay for everything, all the tortured souls, all the marks he had left, all the children and lives sacrificed to fill his pockets with wealth. I was going to make him regret his life, his choices and for picking me as his 'one and only'.

***

I sat there in the garden, staring up at the sky, after taking myself away from it all. The sunrise was beautiful, a peaceful serenity, a wave of colours mixing together, nature at its best. I could feel the warm breeze surrounding me as I heard the birds sing and watched how the bees found the most enchanting of flowers to feed on. I couldn't enjoy the experience, enjoy being free again, being able to witness such beauty before me, when I knew he wasn't there by my side. Something that I would always find comfort and serenity in, wasn't the same. This was meant to clear my mind, but now it just made my mind jump through more hoops.

I heard a set of sliding doors, footsteps coming from behind, making me turn around to see Jack and Amelie coming towards me.

"Mind if we join you?" Amelie asked. I nodded my head and looked back to the sunrise.

They both took a seat next to me, watching the sunrise before us. Taking it in, sitting in silence, being there if I needed them.

I had already thought about how to get Sebastian back, but it was a plan nobody would like. I knew no matter which way we went about it; the ending would be the same. No matter what, it was something I had to do, but I just hoped they would accept it.

Nothing would ever be the same, even if we got him out. We would have to get him to remember, get him back, to fill the void that he was missing. I knew he would know somethings, but I didn't know what he would know. One thing I did know was that his feelings towards me wouldn't be the same.

He was a fresh slate, a new start, a new possibility of danger.

I had to make him remember.

***

Getting to my feet, I started to pace back and forth, fighting with the idea of telling them about my plan.

"I know a way to get him back...but nobody is going to like the idea," I explained, stopping in my tracks to turn and face them.

"What's your plan?" Jack asked, shading his eyes from the sun.

"To get someone on the inside..." I hesitated, knowing this wasn't going to end well. "I want to willingly surrender."

As soon as the words left my lips, Jack was on his feet, charging towards me, getting in my face. "Are you stupid? You can't do that!" he shouted.

I shoved him. "What other option do we have? Tell me!" I screamed at him.

"Sebastian sacrificed himself to get you out!"

"Don't you think I know that? I'm the reason he is in there in the first place!"

"Surrendering yourself is not going to do shit!" he shouted again, as both his fists clenched at his sides.

"We have to do something!" I shouted back at him, as I threw my hands up in the air.

"Surrendering isn't the answer!"

"What is?" I asked, seeing as he had all the answers.

"I don't know," he said, as he wiped his hand over his face.

"See you don't have any *fucking* idea!" I shouted.

"Least I'm not stupid enough to think surrendering is going to solve anything!" he shouted.

I prodded his chest with my finger. "You left him there, not me!"

He swatted my hand away. "I didn't have a choice! He told me to!"

"We all have a *fucking* choice! If you really cared, you would have got him out! Some friend you are!"

"I didn't have a choice!"

"He needs us! Even if there is the slightest chance that we can save him, get him out and put a stop to this, we take it! No matter the cost!"

"He did it for you!" he carried on shouting, pointing at me as he did.

"I didn't ask him to!"

"You didn't have to!"

"Shut the *fuck* up! Both of you!" Amelie shouted, causing us both to look at her.

She stood there looking between us both, seeing the redness of our faces, hearing our heavy breathing, a screaming match coming to an end.

"Screaming at each other isn't going to do anything. This is what Hugo wants," she said.

I took a few steps back away from Jack, taking a moment too cool myself down. I knew my surrender was the only way. I knew Jack wasn't going to accept it; I knew none of them would have.

I turned back around to look at them. "Hear me out?" I asked them both, hoping they would listen.

"We are not doing your stupid *fucking* plan!" Jack shouted.

"Jack shut up and listen to her," Amelie implored.

"You're supposed to be on my side!"

"I am but listen to her...please?" Amelie asked him, walking towards him and squeezing his hand, trying to cool him down and see reason.

"Fine!" he huffed, not looking happy about it. "Talk," he sighed, looking at me. "I promise I won't interrupt."

"By surrendering, we get an inside man. Someone who can get to him and find things out. If I go in willingly, Hugo will want to talk to me and he will listen to me, he will also not do anything to me directly. Yes, he will want to rewire my brain, but that's only if he catches me. I know if I go in and hand myself to him, he will want to talk. It could buy everyone time to get in and go from there," I explained.

"What are you going to do? Just turn up at the front door and be like, 'Hey I've come home'?" he laughed, mimicking a version of me who would turn up and wave at the front door, willingly surrendering.

"No need to be a dick," I said, rolling my eyes at him. "Look, I know how to get in touch with him. If we have a burner phone, I can call him and offer myself willingly and when they send patrols, we take a few out and some of you can dress up as them. I'm sure Jonas and Jessie between them can make proper passes, that way we have a way in," I explained, only to see him raise one of his eyebrows. He hadn't realised I had thought about this properly.

With a heavy sigh, he ran one of his hands in his hair and across his face. He then looked at me again. "Fine, on one condition. We go in together, me and you, and the rest either go as guards or stay behind?" he asked.

"You can't go in willingly, Jack; Hugo knows you too well and you will be directly taken to be wiped and we both know that."

"No, you don't."

"Listen to yourself Jack!" I shouted at him. "You used to be one of his first commands. If Hugo notices you personally, its game over!"

"I'll do it," Amelie offered, causing us both to turn to look at her.

"No way in hell will you be going!" Jack shouted, as he walked closer to her.

"You can't keep me hidden every single time!"

"You're not going!"

"Watch me!" she snapped.

"I don't want to lose you!"

"If you love me, you will let me do this," she said softly, cupping his face with both her hands. "You need to trust me. Hugo doesn't like me, but we both know if I go with

258

her, he won't touch me until he gets her on his side because he knows he won't win her back."

"I think I need to go in alone," I disagreed. "I know for a fact if anyone else surrenders, no matter who you are, you will be taken and made to forget."

"That's not happening!" Jack shouted, walking up to me again, red in the face.

"You are all going in, but you're still going to be dressed as them. Technically I'm not going in on my own," I said.

Jack sighed. "I really don't like this," he spoke, rubbing his hands over his face again.

"Like it or not, agree or disagree, I'm doing it. You're either with me or not, the choice is yours," I stated, knowing full well he didn't like the plan, but he had to be on board because he knew I would do it anyways, no matter what people thought.

I wasn't going to let any of them stop me. I no longer cared if I was being stubborn or selfish, Sebastian was selfless in sacrificing himself, so I was going to be selfish and risk everything to get him back.

"Fine! We will do it your way," he surrendered, knowing there was no other option. "I really don't like this though."

"Neither do I, but it's our only option."

"You're just as stubborn as him" he huffed, shaking his head.

"So are you."

We both just stood there, looking at each, until he walked up to me, pulling me in for a hug, with me instantly returning the gesture. "I'm sorry for shouting," he apologised.

"I'm sorry, I didn't mean anything I said."

"No need to be, we both said things in the heat of the moment," he agreed, as he pulled away from the hug. "Let's go and tell the others," he said as he turned around and walked towards the doors, disappearing inside.

Amelie waited, just looking at me. "We will get him back," she smiled weakly.

"What if we're too late? What if we can't get him to remember?" I asked, tears brewing at my eyes, threatening to spill.

"We will solve that when it comes to it, we will get him back," she tried her best to reassure me.

I knew deep down that there were endless possibilities, possibilities I didn't want to think about, but the one in a million chance was coming and I knew it had to be the right one. His time was running out, the fact his mind had been wiped meant it was going to be a challenge, a challenge that would be worth the risk and a challenge it was going to be.

He will remember.

He had to.

***

Me and Amelie headed inside, joining the others in the living room, only to enter a screaming match.

"That is the worst idea ever!" Larna screamed.

"It's the only option we have!" Jack shouted back. "I don't like it either, but do you have anything better?"

"No," she sighed, backing down from the fight.

"Is this really the best option?" Malcom asked me.

I just sighed and looked down to the ground, knowing nobody wanted to go back. "Yes," I answered, as I looked back up to see people pacing the room, while others just sat there with their faces in their hands.

It was like I had chucked the weight of the world on them, which I had; I had chucked the weight of their lives on them. I wasn't going to force anyone into doing what I had planned, it would be a freedom to pick the path they wanted to take, a freedom Hugo had already stolen from us, but a freedom that I was giving back to them.

"You all have a choice here. If there is any of you that would rather run and leave and never go back, then please do it. Nobody will look at you badly for doing so and if anyone wants to stay and help, well that's up to you guys too," I said.

"I'm in. As much as I hate the plan, at least I can slit some more throats, but no judging," Larna spoke, pointing at Arthur when she said the 'no judging', causing people to laugh. "One comment out of you, Pretty Boy and I'll have you."

Arthur then gulped and held his hands up in defeat.

After Larna spoke up, everyone else seemed to agree, nobody backing out, even though they all had a choice.

We had to be smart, we needed to have a back-up plan. My family was the only thing I had, we stuck together, we would do it together, but we needed something as leverage, something that could guarantee some sort of safety.

I looked towards Jessie and Jonas and walked towards them. "Jonas, you said you have everything on that drive, right?" I asked.

"Yeah," he replied quickly, looking confused.

"If nobody comes back, I want you to leak everything."

"Leak it to the world?" he asked.

"Yes, let everyone know the truth about Scarlet, it either ends with me killing Hugo or everyone finds out the truth, either way that man loses," I said.

"That I can do," Jonas smiled. "Payback's a bitch."

Leaking the programme and all its data to the world was the best option we had. The threat of it alone was going to be enough to make him worry, make him cripple under the pressure. I had an advantage, and it wasn't going to be something he would take easy. Truth was I didn't want to leak everything, it would mean all our lives would be on display, they would know everything we had done, all the lives we had taken under his control, putting us on the radar. It wasn't as simple as going to the police or the government, as there was always some worm hiding within who knew everything. Leaking it to the world meant everyone knew and that itself would be enough to put a stop to Scarlet. I just hoped the hurricane of events coming was worth everything.

"You two need to stay here, be our eyes and ears," Jack spoke up, pointing towards Jonas and Jessie. "Hannah…"

"I swear, you have another thing coming and a punch to the face if you tell me to stay here. I'm the only one they definitely won't recognise. They also need to pay for Luke," Hannah interrupted him.

"She has a point, Jack," Malcom mentioned, with a sly smirk on his face from Hannah's comment.

"That's true, she's least likely to be recognised," Amelie agreed, as all eyes landed on me.

"Ok," I sighed, knowing she had a point.

Jack then looked around. "Someone needs to be the getaway driver when we get out."

"I'll do it, I might not be strong enough to fight, but I still want to help," Donald said.

Everything seemed to be falling into place, the plan, the preparation, the knowing. All we needed were the identity cards, some hardware, and a burner phone. Next stage of the game was to call him and surrender.

Chapter Twenty-Seven

T wo days had passed, everyone had been preparing, setting up, making sure everything would run to plan. Everyone had their ammunition ready and loaded, the software download and the identity cards at the ready. There was only one last thing to do and that was to call.

Everyone gathered in the living room ready for the events ahead, just waiting for Hannah and Jonas. After a few minutes, they both entered the room, with Hannah handing me the burner phone and Jonas with his laptop at the ready, taking a seat next to me.

"When you make the call, I can block the signal, they won't be able to find us. Take as long as you need," Jonas explained.

I looked around the room at everyone watching me, making sure everyone was still on board. "You ready?" I asked them all.

They all nodded in agreement.

"Make the call," Amelie said.

I turned to look at the phone, entering the number for

the programme, putting it on speaker, only to place it on the table and listen to it ring.

"Hello and welcome to Scarlet, the place to give your child the best start in the world. My name is Amy, how can I help you today?" a woman asked, causing everyone to roll their eyes.

"I need to speak to Hugo," I answered.

"I'm sorry, but can I ask who's calling?" she asked.

"The bitch he's been after for the last six years," I hissed.

There was a sudden click as I was put on hold and music started playing.

It didn't take long before the music stopped and there was silence on the line. The silence on the line beckoned me to answer, for me to speak first, but I knew it was him, he was waiting, and I wasn't going to be the first.

"Adeline?" Hugo's voice came through the phone.

"Hugo."

"What do I owe the pleasure? Is it smart to ring?" he laughed.

"I wouldn't bother tracking me, if I was you. You know I'm way too smart for that."

"Noted, so why the call?" he asked, clearly surprised to hear from me.

"I'm surrendering."

"You're going to surrender?"

"I'll surrender, but..."

"How did I know there was a catch? Go on... name your price...I'm listening," he interrupted me.

"You stop hunting the others...and let Sebastian go."

"You have demands...you're not in the right place to be making demands..."

"Do you want me or not?" I interrupted him with aggression.

Everyone sat there quietly, hearing him sigh, knowing full well he was going over my demands, not agreeing, but also not disagreeing to them.

"You need to decide now," I said. "Clock's ticking... five... four... three... two..."

"Fine," he interrupted, disappointment and anger laced in his words. "Anything else?" he hissed.

"Nick doesn't come...you send him, and I'll personally slit his throat where he stands."

"Fine. Anything else you want to add to the list?"

"How many you sending to escort me?"

"Why?" he asked.

"How many?" I shouted at him.

"Just to be certain, you're coming willingly?" he asked again, questioning my motives, like he didn't believe what he was hearing.

"I'm coming willingly and unarmed. You know I don't go back on my word."

"Fine, five," he answered. "Where am I sending them?"

"I'm presuming you still have the same email address. I'll send you the details and no, you won't be able to trace it back," I spoke, ending the call.

I looked around the room at everyone, knowing not all of us could go.

"I already said I was going," Jack said.

"Same here," Hannah agreed.

"And me," Amelie raised her hand.

"I'm slitting some throats," Larna smiled, as she clapped her hands to herself. "Like I said," she pointed at Arthur. "I want no judgement, or else." She then slid a finger across her throat and winked at him, causing his cheeks to flush.

"Jack, Amelie, Larna, Hannah and Arthur," I confirmed the names that volunteered.

"Then it's settled," Jack said.

Everyone slowly started to get up and leave the room, only for Jack to shout "Stop! I must do something before you all leave."

Everyone turned to face him and watched how he turned to face Amelie, taking her hands in his.

"Jack what are you doing?" she asked him, her eyebrows furrowing with confusion.

"Something I should have done a long time ago," he stated, glancing at everyone watching and then back to Amelie. "Amelie..." Jack spoke, hesitating, watching her face, looking into her eyes. "I never believed in love at first sight, but the first time I saw you, I fell in love with you, I just didn't know it yet. I'll forever choose to love you every single day. Without you my world doesn't exist. I used to like being on my own, but now without you, I have nothing. You are forever going to be my priority, my first thought of the day and the last thing I think about before I go to sleep. I don't need anything but you in this lifetime and any lifetime that follows. I love you and will love you until I die and if there is life after that, well, I'll love you there too. I want to be with you until the end of the line because every time I see you, every minute I spend with you, I fall in love with you more than I ever thought was possible. My heart is yours for however long you want it. All I want to do is make you smile and with that, I just need to ask you one thing."

Jack slowly got down on one knee and held out a Haribo ring, while Amelie started to cry with a smile on her.

"Amelie, I know this isn't a real ring and once all this is over, I will buy the most expensive ring I can find because you deserve the best. My favourite words to ever leave your lips are 'I love you' and there is nothing else in the world I want more than to hear you say them every single day, so will you please marry me and let us spend eternity annoying the shit out of each other?" he asked.

Amelie dropped to her knees and kissed him. "Yes, Jack! Always!" she cried, only to be engulfed by Jack in a long lingering kiss full of emotion and everyone cheering.

In that moment, my heart burst full of love. I was overrun by emotions myself, seeing two soulmates finding each other and committing to spending eternity together. I had spent years watching them grow together, only for their love to blossom into the prettiest of flowers.

After a few seconds of a longing kiss, Jack and Amelie got to their feet and kissed again. Jack then grabbed hold of her and twirled her around, both overjoyed. Once they stopped, everyone walked over to them, hugging them both in turn and giving their congratulations, including myself.

This was a moment I wanted to treasure and a moment I felt even more guilty over, knowing they could lose everything later today. I realised the secret I was keeping was worth the risk, I had planned something no one would like, but it was my card to play, and I promised myself they wouldn't see it coming, until it had to happen.

Truth was, I had always been prepared, prepared for this moment, but I had never thought it would happen. As much as Hugo manipulated everyone, I seemed to be the only one he manipulated with kindness, by the payment of his love, his loyalty, his devotion. I experienced no torture or bargaining chips; I did what was asked.

***

Everyone slowly started to leave the room, going to get ready because they would be setting off to the location soon. Before Malcom could leave the room, I ran up to him, grabbing his arm, causing him to turn around.

"Wait," I said, and he frowned curiously at me.

I had planned this from the moment I'd sat watching the sunrise, watching the beauty of everything around me.

I always believed love was eternal, a twin flame in the middle of two people as they watched it burn. Love meant everything to me, more than life itself. I loved them all and would do anything for them.

"I'm going to ask you something, but you can't tell anyone else," I told him, only for him to look more confused than he did.

"What is it?" he asked.

"Promise me you won't tell them?"

"I promise," he agreed.

And that single promise sealed my fate.

Chapter Twenty-Eight

Time, location, preparation, everything was set. A ticking time bomb waiting to go off.

I stood there waiting on the barest of streets possible, no people in sight and little to nothing there but brick walls, rusting bins and the occasional rat making an appearance, scurrying to safety, a place I wish I could go.

In the distance, I could see a van making its way towards me, making it clear it was time. It was too late to back out, too late to run and go back into hiding. I had to do this, I had to do this for them, for Sebastian.

The van pulled up and they all exited the van and walked towards me, one woman in particular coming closer than the rest. "Adeline," she greeted.

"Hugo's slave," I said, receiving an eye roll.

She nodded to another woman to step forward after she passed her stuff to one of the men.

"Arm's up, spread your legs," this woman spoke.

"Really?" I sarcastically asked.

"Got orders," she said. I rolled my eyes but complied, holding my arms out and spreading my legs a little further apart.

The women slowly started to feel me down, checking for any hidden weapons, any phones, or any devices on me at all. At least it wasn't Nick. Nick was a fate waiting to happen, a certainty of death if he was to cross me.

"All good," the woman said, making it clear that I didn't have anything on me.

As soon as she did, the others appeared, sneaking up behind them, only to quickly attack and knock them out with a single injection to the neck. It was a concoction of chemicals Malcom had mixed for us, putting them asleep for hours. Once they were out cold, Malcom, Rose and Donald rolled up in another van, putting the unconscious in and quickly undressing them, chucking the clothes they were wearing to the people playing dress up. They quickly slipped on the uniform and attached their own identity cards to their waist, all ready for the adventures ahead.

We all got in the van, while Hannah took the driver's seat, already setting up the satnav for the route we needed to go, knowing it would take a few hours to get there. The possibilities we faced before us felt more real. I wanted everyone to be safe, to be protected. All I ever really wanted was for them to have their own fairy tale.

***

After several hours, we were close enough to see the target, the place where dreams died, and nightmares were born. It was Hell on the land of the living.

As we got closer, everyone slipped on their caps, pulling them down to hide a little bit of their own faces, while the girls put their ponytails through the back, getting ready for what laid ahead.

"You ready?" Jack asked, turning to look at the rest of us seated in the back of the van.

"As ready as I'll ever be," I said, not looking at anyone.

"We're here," Arthur said.

Looking at the compound now, it just looked like an office complex, tall buildings with a lot of windows, encased in fencing with security men posted around, like it was just a normal thing.

Hannah drove up to the grey gates, that were covered in barbed wire, sharp enough to cut skin so deep you would see bone. A man quickly stepped out of the small cubicle, while the van came to a stop in front of the gate. Hannah quickly lowered her window, and the man ever so slightly stuck his head through, taking a look at us all.

"Identity card?" he asked Hannah. She held it up for the man to scan it. "Who you got back there?" he asked her, while he waited for her details to appear on his hand-held device.

"Hugo's bitch, she surrendered," Hannah replied, causing the man to laugh.

"I heard she was making a reappearance," he said.

I knew they all knew I was coming. Hugo would have upped security for me, to make sure I wouldn't 'step out of line'. It would be on a need-to-know basis and gossip always did spread quickly. Chinese whispers were definitely a thing here.

"I know right! Finally!" she laughed with him.

"Agreed! Nice meeting you Emily!" he smiled, just to then turn and walk back to his cubicle and hit a button that opened the gates.

As soon as the gates opened, Hannah started to drive again, only to be directed by another man to drive down the side of the building, leading to a raised shutter.

Once in, the shutter started to close, and someone

opened the back doors. "Oh! Look what the cat dragged in," he smirked, looking me up and down.

"Nick," I hissed, wanting to slit his throat and get pleasure in it, just like Larna always did.

"Princess," he beamed. The arrogant prick.

Watching him turn towards something out of sight for me, he nodded. Not even a second passed before two people appeared and jumped into the back of the van. They instantly grabbed me and dragged me out like a wild animal, being harsh with their movements.

I quickly shot the others a look that said, 'don't move, stay put' because if they stepped out of line, they would know, and this plan would be doomed before it had fully started.

Once out of the van, they pulled my arms behind me, just for Nick to tie them up. "He's waiting for you," he said.

"I know."

"He's missed you."

"Well, the feeling isn't mutual," I hissed.

I felt a shift behind me as Nick walked to my side and leaned in, his lips close to my ear. "I've missed you too princess, maybe when we fry your brain we can kick off where we left off" he whispered.

Seven Years Ago...

Nick. My friend with benefits, my companion, my lust without love. When I needed a break, needed some form of release, I would go to him. After meeting Sebastian it had become a rare thing for me to want or need and I was finally on my way to tell Nick it needed to end. I wasn't telling him because I fancied Sebastian, but because Sebastian had somehow made me see myself better than that and had proved to me I was better off, especially when Nick was sleeping around with multiple women, and I didn't want to catch anything.

Walking into the training room, I could see Nick attacking a punching bag over and over again, sweating heavily. From the corner of his eye, he must have noticed me because he grabbed the punching bag and stopped, turning to face me.

Nick was a good-looking bloke, no wonder he had multiple 'friends with benefits.' His hair was dark blonde and usually slicked back, unlike now where it was everywhere due to his heavy work out session. He had a jawline that was pristine and chiselled, as well as his abs. His eyes were dark blue, mixed with hues of green, a concoction of beauty melting together.

As I got closer, he smiled, so I hesitantly smiled back at him.

"Good morning, Princess," he said.

"Nick, I've told you to stop calling me that," I huffed, just for him to laugh.

"Well, I like calling you it and also, don't friends with benefits bully each other to show their love?" he asked.

I sighed. "About that," I said, his face to dropping. "It needs to end."

"What do you mean?" he asked, letting go of the punching bag and starting to unstrap his gloves.

"We can't do that anymore. I don't want to do it anymore," I said.

Nick abruptly stopped unstrapping his last glove, just to chuck the one glove he had gotten off to the floor and met my eyes. "What do you mean stop? I thought we had a deal?"

"We do. I mean we did. But don't you have other women you're doing that with?" I asked.

"I do, but they are nothing compared to you. I'll put a stop to it," he said, as he went on to unstrap the other glove.

"I want it to end completely. I don't want to do it anymore," I said.

He then threw the other glove to the floor and put both his hands on his hips. "Why? What's changed?"

"I have. I just don't want to do it anymore."

"But what about what I want?" he asked, raising his eyes in triumph like it was some sort of loophole.

"It doesn't matter what you want...it's my choice if I want to do something."

"Come on, Princess," he smiled, reaching out to me.

Swatting his hand away, I shouted. "I told you to stop calling me that!" His smile then disappeared from his face. "I've told you no and no means *fucking* no."

From the way his mouth gaped, I knew he hadn't been expecting me to turn on him. "Listen here," he said, taking a step forward and gripping my arm. "It ends when I say it ends. Got it?"

Soon as the words left his mouth, I smacked him across the face and then pulled my arm free from his tight grip. "Listen here, Nick. I want it to end, it ends. I don't do what you say, I don't listen to you. I thought we were friends?" I hissed.

"Deals change," he stated point blank.

"Well, the deal didn't change for me," I said. "I feel the need for it to end."

"And what about what I feel?" he shouted at me. I took a step back away from him, shaking my head.

"We said no feelings," I said.

"Feelings change," he stated, as he bit his lip, admitting what I thought.

"You feel something for -"

"I'm in love with you, Adeline. I want you and only you," he interrupted me.

"No," I said, taking another step away, just for him to take one towards me.

"It's always been you and always will be."

"I don't love you, Nick," I said, just for him to take a step closer to me again.

"Yes, you do. You just can't see it yet."

"I don't."

"Yes, you do."

"No, I don't!" I shouted.

"I'll prove it," he said. He then chucked himself on me and kissed me with force.

I tried to shove him, but he gripped me tighter as he kissed me. He then stuck his tongue down my throat, so I bit his lip, causing him to pull away and hiss.

"You bitch!" he shouted.

I smacked him across the face again and shoved him back. "You're fucking mental," I screamed at him, before wiping my hand across my lips, getting every trace of his kiss off me. "I told you no. Does that mean anything to you?"

He stood there just, watching me as his lip bled, with the rest of his face turning red with rage. "You will regret that," he finally spoke. I huffed.

Within seconds, he walked towards me and gripped my face. "One of these days, I will have my control, my power and you will be at my mercy, just you wait."

I spat at him, just for him to raise his hand and then retreat it, backing away from his initial reaction. "I dare you. Smack me. Let's see what Hugo thinks then," I grinned.

He then let go of my face with force and proceeded to

walk straight out of the door and back into the hallway, disappearing from view and away from me.

What had I just done?

Present...

From then on, I knew I had fucked up. Any sort of friendship we had died that day. We were tied at the hip since we were kids, growing up together in the programme, before I met the others. We did all our training together, all our missions, until it all changed by Hugo taking me under his wing. There always seemed to be some sort of jealousy that I was chosen, that Hugo had picked me. Over the years that followed, it seemed to be less obvious, and we grew our friendship back, but then we stepped on the cracks that were forming and pushed the limits, just for it to break the moment I ended things, the moment he told me he loved me. Since then, I became the enemy.

No words left my lips, I stayed silent, just staring at him. I could tell from the expression written on his face that he was pleased with himself, pleased to have more control, more power over me, even if it was only for a moment.

"He's waiting for you," Nick said again. He then grabbed hold of my arm with a tight grip and started walking, dragging me along with him and leaving the rest behind.

They knew what they needed to do and now the plan was in full motion.

Checkmate Hugo, your move.

Chapter Twenty-Nine

The office was decorated the same as the last. He always seemed to be a man of similarities, a man of a few specifics. I always remembered it that way, a piece of history stuck in my head on a constant loop. The walls were a dark green, silk, and smooth, a colour I once picked for him many moons ago. The floors laminated, probably due to the amount of blood he would spill; it would be an easy clean up job. He also had a circular green rug, the same rug that I once had in my room when I was here. He wanted something of mine close to him, for a piece of me to become part of his. As much as seeing the rug made a small ache in my chest grow and noticeable, I didn't want to feel any sort of emotion but anger towards the man. All the ache told me was that I still had some part of me that loved him, that would forever love him, but the pang of sadness that followed proved to me he meant more to me than I thought. I didn't just still have part of me that loved him, I still had part of me that cried for bond we had.

Still looking around the room and ignoring the ache in my chest, I saw another stupid but beautiful large chandelier, his very own signature piece dangling from the ceiling. I also noticed the bookcases, a feature he always had, but the difference being what lingered on the shelves. On the shelves were books that I loved, the books that I would read repeatedly, his way of trying to have a piece of me with him again, a way of being ready for my 'comeback'.

As we got closer to the desk, Nick let go of my arm and stood behind me, untying my wrist, just to then force me to take a seat. "Stay seated," Nick demanded, keeping his eyes locked on me while he sat in the seat next to me, luckily not in arm's reach, but close enough.

Suddenly, I heard the door behind me open and several footsteps walked in. I turned to face them, to see Hugo and two men following him, closing the door, and standing in front of it, watching us, watching me. Hugo made eye contact with me, as I narrowed my eyes at him, causing him to sigh. I really did hate the man and he could clearly see it.

Hugo carried on walking closer to me, only to walk around the desk and sit in his chair. He didn't say a word, just sat there looking at me. He then took a glance towards Nick and nodded, a simple gesture of 'thank you'.

He then took a cigar from his pocket, lighting it and placing it in his mouth. "So, you finally decided to grow up and come back home?" he said, blowing out a cloud of smoke.

"If you say so," I scoffed.

"Why do I feel like you have altera motives?" he asked me, as he took another drag of his cigar.

"You tell me?" I asked him, not giving anything away.

"Because you're my daughter," he smiled.

"I'm not your daughter," I said.

"You are."

"Just because you decided to pick me and raise me, doesn't make me your daughter," I scoffed, causing him to laugh.

He leant forward on his desk, looking at me, making me wonder what was really going on. "See...if you didn't try to flee and stayed, you would have learnt the truth," he said.

I frowned. "Truth about what?" I asked.

"That you are actually my daughter, and my DNA does run through your veins," he smiled.

"Bullshit!" I hissed. He laughed. "Prove it!"

He slid open one of the top draws and picked up a file, just to then slide it across the desk. I grabbed it quickly and opened it, reading what was there. In the folder itself were documents, pictures of me and him, a birth certificate, and a test analysis. Looking closer at the test, I could see it clear as day, written down was two forms of DNA, mine and his. Checking it out and looking at it, they matched, I had his DNA, and he was my father.

Fuck.

The Devil was inside of me, I was corrupted. In the twenty-five years of my life, I had been tricked and the truth had been right in front of me all this time. It all made sense, the reason he dragged me out, the reason he took me under his wing, I was special because I was his. I had spent years thinking I had a devil sat on my shoulder, but it wasn't, it was in my veins, in every substance of my being and there was nothing I could do about it.

People always say you have some part of your parents in you, that they become part of you, and you forever carry that imprint. I was half human, half monster and there was nothing I could do about it. All the monsters in my head were so loud, so real because he was a part of me.

I felt the world around me crumble, the ground beneath my feet swallowing me whole. It all made sense. The reasoning behind never stopping to find me, never stopping to get me on his side...he did it because I was his daughter...I am his daughter. It was never a game to him, it wasn't trickery, he did it because he genuinely loved me, and I was his. His devotion, his love, his gifts were all real. But yet...I didn't love him. My heart may have ached for a memory, but I knew for certain there wasn't any love there now.

To me, he wasn't my father.

The blood running through my veins, the organs keeping me alive, the flesh of skin that covered me and the tattoo etched along my ribs, all belonged to him. The only thing that was my own was my mind and my heart, which was something he would never be able to take away from me or gain, even if it meant fighting till my dying breath.

***

I sat there silently, not saying a word, just staring at the paper in front of me.

"I wanted you to grow up like the others," he said, breaking the silence. "The plan was to tell you, but I waited too long. I wanted you to grow up like them and be part of the programme itself, but I loved you too much to be that far away from you, so I came and got you. I was going to tell you when I decided it was time, but you ran before I could," Hugo explained, like it was any better telling me the truth.

His face stayed relaxed, he didn't flinch or give any tell-tale signs of a lie. Everything he was saying was the truth and he meant every word of it.

"Now you're reading me?" he asked me, knowing full well I was.

After all, I was good at it.

"Maybe," I stated, watching him, hoping there was some sort of a lie there, praying this wasn't the truth.

"You're calmer than I thought you would be," he smiled, leaning back in his chair.

"What happened to her?" I asked, avoiding his observations.

"Who?"

"My mother?"

"Not relevant," he said quickly, making me realise he didn't want to talk about it.

What else was he hiding?

"I want the truth," I stated.

"Truth..." he laughed. "Truth is she didn't want you."

The words he spoke hit me hard. I didn't know why. I had spent my life growing up thinking my parents never wanted me. I was nothing to her, like he was to me. He had made me think he was the fool, the fool for loving me like his daughter, but in reality, I was the fool and he had played me.

"How did she die?" I asked.

"What do you mean?" he asked,

I scoffed. "You're forgetting how well I know you. You're telling me you didn't have her killed?"

"Yes, she's dead...car accident a few years after you were born," he explained.

I wasn't even looking at him, I didn't need to read it on his face. I was just happy to take his word for it right now, he gave me the truth about who I really was, so what else was there to lie about?

"So why haven't you killed me?" I questioned him, staring back at him once more.

"You're my DNA and I'd go to any lengths for my own blood," he sighed.

He then took a glance at one of the guards, only for the guard to step forward and grab a bottle of champagne next to Hugo's desk and open it, filling three glasses as he did. He then passed each of us a glass, Hugo, me and then Nick.

I watched how Hugo lifted his glass and how Nick followed. "Let's raise a toast to family," Hugo smiled, signalling me to grab the glass.

I leant forward and grabbed hold of the glass with a smirk, raising a glass up to make another toast. "And let's raise a toast to a worthless shit of a human being, that is as cold as winter and as evil and sinister as the Devil. Ladies and gentlemen...I give you... my biological father, a man who doesn't even deserve the title and will never gain it," I cheered, then downed the champagne. I then chucked it across the room, just for it to hit the wall and smash into a million pieces.

Looking at Hugo's face said it all, he looked disappointed. He then took a small sip from his glass and placed it back on the desk. "Was there any need?" he asked.

"You will never be my father," I stated.

"You will always have my DNA, doesn't change anything," he said. "No matter what you do, I'll have your back, and nobody will hurt you."

"Even if I told you that I could leak everything about Scarlet?" I taunted with a smirk.

As much as I wished I had already released everything to the world, I knew it would start a dangerous war, due to the people Hugo had hidden in his pocket and the control they had over the country, yet the world.

I could tell he was reading me, reading the expression written on my face, only for the colour in his to fade. He saw it, he could see that I was telling the truth, that I had leverage and I was happy to go to any lengths to prove it. His face started to fill with anger, with pain. Pain from the fact his own DNA would betray him, especially when he had just said there was nothing that could ever make him hurt me. He was now clearly wishing he never said that because we both knew in that moment there wasn't anything he wouldn't do to protect his baby, to protect Scarlet. It was his legacy, his lifeline and me, I was nothing in comparison to it.

He sat there not saying anything to me, the silence being the one prominent thing in the room. The fact he sat there not saying anything, that was the most dangerous part, a silent Hugo was a deadly one. The men behind me were nothing in comparison to him; he held the rope, he could either pull it or break it, he was the one in charge, he was king.

After a few minutes of silence and sitting there waiting, he finally took a deep breath. "You would betray me?" he asked, his voice so soft and gentle, like disbelief was taking over him.

"I would."

Words of truth and honesty were laid out on the table and that's when I knew that he knew he had lost me.

"Why?" he asked.

"You have done nothing but kill people, all for the sake of profit. You don't care who gets hurt and don't forget you brainwash them, manipulate them and torture them...Just because they step out of line. Nobody asked for this life. Yes, I know you give everyone who's unwanted a chance, but you never think of what everyone really wants and that's a life, not a mission, not to sacrifice our own life just for you and the programme. This programme will be the death of you, and I'll happily be part of that."

Angry was an understatement, I wanted out and I didn't care if his death was on my hands. It was the only life I would happily accept, the only blood I would happily have covering my hands. He would be my ending.

He chuckled to himself and the love he had in his eyes changed, the man who adored me disappearing. "Well, that just means we have a small problem then," he sighed, turning towards Nick. "A problem we can fix."

He was going to give me to Nick. I was Nick's problem and that only meant one thing...I was in for a reckoning.

"Let me leave with Sebastian and you can have the data, your programme, and the life you want. All we want to be is free," I said, hoping to offer him what he wanted and hoping that a small bit of him would let me.

"Why do you want him back?" he asked me, trying to read me, not knowing the truth.

Feeling sick to my stomach, I wanted to throw up right there and then. I felt every cell within me tingle, anxious about him finding out the truth, knowing he would only use it against me.

"I see! Why didn't I see it before?" he rhetorically asked himself. "You love him. I wondered why he sacrificed himself and made sure you got out. I just thought it was due to all of you being a family and close and that you all just had a close bond, but I didn't see this."

He leant back in his chair and laughed to himself, looking at me. "He did it because he loves you and you came back because you love him...I'm right aren't I?" he asked me, hoping this time he would get a response.

"Yes," I hesitantly spoke, knowing he had already seen the truth and there was no reason to hide it anymore.

"All this time, you both loved each other...I never saw

284

it coming," he sighed. "I knew there was something. I just didn't think it was that. So, you really think that he loves you? That he wants you to rescue him?"

"I do," I confidently spoke.

Hugo let out a laugh and shook his head. "I'll make you a deal," he offered. "If you truly believe that he loves you, that he would do anything for you, and he admits it, I'll let you both leave. If it doesn't work, you come back to me and join me here, side by side, running Scarlet."

"Deal," I confidently spoke, realising I had made a deal with the Devil himself.

Chapter Thirty

'Love conquers all' means love can conquer any hardships, difficulties, and challenges. That anything placed in front of it didn't stand a chance and love would win. I believed it would. I had spent the last few years hiding the truth that I had loved him, only to have the truth of it out in the open for a matter of weeks.

Love is power, it holds a strength over us and makes us do anything for it. We would fight for it, fight to protect the ones we love, fight to be loved. Our love was selfless. It's given without any expectations of receiving anything back.

And I believed in us.

***

Pacing back and forth, creating a sweat, my anxiety accelerated through the roof. This moment was hanging by a single thread. He had to remember me, we had to fight for our love. Nick had gone to fetch Sebastian, while Hugo sat and just watched me pace, while the room remained silent. What was minutes felt like hours, until the door opened, and they both entered, our eyes locking the moment he looked my way.

Before I even knew what I was doing, I was running to him, wrapping my arms around him, but the embrace wasn't returned. Instead of returning my gesture, he grabbed my hands and pried them off him, taking a step back away from me.

"It's me, Adeline," I smiled, tears threatening to spill.

The confusion etched across his face said it all. He didn't understand the emotion I was showing him, but that little glimmer of light behind his eyes I could see was enough to give me hope. Taking one step closer to him made his brows furrow.

I slowly reached out towards him, resting my hand ever so slightly on his arm. "Do you remember me?" I asked, hoping, praying he did.

"I know who you are," he said, small words giving me hope. "But you mean nothing to me."

The words hit me like a cold blade, creating a sharp and deep cut. I felt the warmth around me disappearing and a cool breeze hitting my skin, like the light around me was fading and the darkness was creeping in. Surely, he didn't mean the words he spoke, it was just a lapse of memory, a fragment that was dismantled but easily fixed.

I ran my hand down his arm and held his hand, while my eyes stayed fixated on his. "You love me, we mean everything to each other. I'm your Adi," I explained, with a faint smile on my face.

With a pull of his arm, his hand was out of mine, and he was taking two steps back away from me, shaking his head. "You mean nothing to me!" he stated again, the blade striking and cutting deeper.

"No! You need to remember us! We are in love!" I

cried, not believing him in the slightest, my emotions overruling my brain.

"You're just a spoiled brat!" he shouted towards me, making me realise his memory had been altered to before he truly met me.

Why was he not treating me the same way he did back then? What else had Hugo done?

"No!" I shook my head in denial. "What did you do to him?" I asked, turning to look at Hugo.

"What do you think happened to him?" he asked me, with a wicked grin on his face.

"You brainwashed him and manipulated him!" I shouted, as more tears ran down my face.

"I just made him forget ever meeting you," he smiled, amused by what was happening in front of him. "I may have also told him who you are and fabricated a few lies here and there to make him think of you in a certain way. It's funny how torture can make you believe lies after you beat it into them. Then again, you say you love each other; that your love is strong. Prove it, prove it by making him remember that emotion and the truth about you."

Hearing his words and wanting to prove him wrong, I charged myself forward, grabbing Sebastian by his collar, pulling him forward, just for our lips to lock as I forced a kiss. From the way he didn't move, I could tell I had shocked him, but then his brain clearly kicked in as he shoved me away.

"Get off me!" he shouted, taking two steps away from me again, looking at me in utter disgust.

He wiped his mouth, infuriated. I had honestly thought a kiss would set the flame alight, that it would be that small spark that would set the rest in motion, but I was wrong.

"You're pathetic," he hissed, looking dead set in my eyes. "The only emotion I carry for you is disgust, you're a disgrace!"

All I could feel was my heart breaking, like shattered glass. My heart was falling into thousands of pieces, unable to be glued back together. He must have been lying, I knew this wasn't the Sebastian I was in love with or the one who loved me. I had to remember that this was all a manipulation, this wasn't reality.

"This isn't you!" I cried, "Whatever he has said, don't believe him. He's lying to you! He will do anything he can to manipulate the situation into his favour. You know the truth and you know what you're saying is a lie. The truth is you love me."

I took two steps forward and cupped his face. He grabbed my hands and I saw the small glimmer of light in his eyes watching me, only for him then to chuck my hands down, away from him. "How could someone like me, ever love someone like you! Look at you! You're broken and damaged goods. How can anybody love that?" he shouted right in my face, giving me the final blow of breaking my heart.

I looked into his eyes again, trying to read him, trying to figure out what was really going on and that's when I saw it. The Sebastian I loved, the last glimmer of light in his eyes was gone, it had disappeared into the darkness and now become a distant memory. Hugo had erased everything, every single piece of the Sebastian I fell in love with, every piece that loved me. He wasn't coming back to me; his mind was too far gone.

I watched how the one thing I had in the world dismantled in front of me, how the beauty of the flame went out.

I took another step back away from him, flickering between looking at Hugo and Sebastian. "I know you don't get to keep everyone in life, but I thought I had you…" I broke, looking at Sebastian. "I chose you and will forever choose you, no matter what I'm feeling right now. That's what you do when you love someone."

Broken, damaged, crippling in front of them both. Memories once treasured were being ripped from the roots and burned by a single flame. Heartache, coming down on me like a clap of thunder, striking me instantly, taking everything away from me. I could feel the colour draining from my face, the sickness in my stomach and the tightness in my throat. It was like part of me died with him and without him, she would never come back, that part of me I would forever desperately crave for.

I wanted to reject every word being spoken to me, I didn't believe what he was saying, but I knew it was his truth. I needed to prove him wrong and get him to learn the actual truth himself and the not the truth Hugo had got him to believe.

He had won. A victory well celebrated in his head. Hugo finally had everything he wanted; having me crippling and damaged, broken enough to have enough control and power over me. That was his win, and I was his trophy.

***

I turned to look in the direction of where Hugo was sat, only to be met with an unrestrained smirk plastered across his face, as he sat back in his chair with exaggerated casualness, his hands remaining clasped. The confidence he displayed was shown through his strong posture and the strong glare he gave me, with a small gleam in his eyes. "So, now that I've proven he doesn't love you and it was all a lie... will you come willingly?" Hugo asked.

"If your plan was to break my heart and make me nothing, then congratulations... you succeeded, consider this as your mission completed," I smiled, while the tears still ran down my face.

In a split second, I was across the room and standing in front of his desk, overcome with anger and pain, the rage brewing. Hugo didn't even flinch, he sat there remaining composed and calm, like my rage was nothing to fear.

"To love is to suffer and if all I'm going to do is suffer, then fine...take me. Do what you want to me. Wipe my memories! I don't care anymore!" I shouted, throwing my hands in the air, admitting defeat. I had nothing else to live for anymore. Tears were still running all over my face as I stood in front of him. "Just remember that the one thing you love Hugo, you broke. I thought I had everything I wanted, but you took that away from me! A life without that love, is a life I don't want...I have nothing, you have successfully taken everything away from me, all for your own pride and ego. I have nothing left to lose, nothing else could possibly hurt me like this...so take my life and do what you wish because you have finally taken the last piece of me that will never return, and I'll tell you something now...rewiring my brain isn't going to fix that! I may not remember my story, my life, or my friends, but you will and that in itself will forever be on your conscious. Knowing the truth about me will haunt you, make you question anything and everything I do from the moment you wipe me. You will forever be haunted by the memory that the life you have will be a lie, the love you will have from me will be fiction. So, go ahead, do whatever you want with me, I don't care anymore. All I have is a broken heart, so sure, have the rest of me, there's really nothing left."

As soon as I had finished telling Hugo the truth about how I felt and what was in store for him, I took two steps back, only to be met with a tight grip on my arm and for me to turn my head to see Nick standing there. I didn't fight him on it, he had the power, and I was letting him have it.

With a tug of my arm, I was pulled away, Nick beckoning me to move my legs and follow him. As he started to lead me out of the room, another set of hands grabbed my other arm, another man helping Nick, making sure I didn't put up a fight.

Just before we got close to leaving, I stopped in front of Sebastian and looked up at him, just for him to stare back at me. All I could see was the glimpse of pain being reflected in his eyes, he still had some compassion, it was like he felt guilty giving me his 'truth', in reality, his fiction.

"I know part of you is still in there and I hope you end up seeing the light," I said. "Just know...I'll forever love you, but sometimes too much pain can't be rectified. Once something is broken, it can be fixed, but you can still see the cracks left behind."

He rubbed the back of his neck, like he was thinking about everything he had said to me and what I had told him, like doubt was coursing through his veins.

"Take her away, Nick. We need to know about the device! You have my permission to do anything to get it," Hugo commanded, giving Nick utter control over me.

I didn't even bother to turn around to look at him, or even fight the matter because everything I ever cared about was gone, leaving no fight in me anymore.

Nick then pulled me forward and all three of us left the room with the doors slamming shut behind us.

In reality, love can't conquer all, no matter how hard you try.

Chapter Thirty-One

C hains hanging from the ceiling, wrist bound tight and raised above my head, tiptoes barely touching the floor. I was now the lamb being strung up, being beaten, and bruised. I was the animal I knew I was all along to them, and I was going to suffer the fate everyone knew about.

The room itself had nothing, bare and bloody just like me. The wall had slight cracks that were breaking the walls into fractions, like damage had been done. The floor itself had dark spots, large and small, rotting, and dried blood, torture had been done here before. This room was for the innocent souls, to be battered and bruised and to be silenced.

Reality hitting, it was the room of the fallen, the forgotten souls, the loss of innocence and my time had come.

It was a prison, with a sentence so fitting.

***

From the words I spoke to Hugo not long before, it was the

fate I had sealed for myself. I knew by spouting my mouth I would end up here, in the bottom, underground with flickering lights, to be manipulated and beaten until I spilled the details of my plan, to source information about the device that would leak news of Scarlet to the world.

I hung there thrashing like a fish on a hook, while he stood in front of me with a wide grin on his face and vengeance in his eyes. Nick always loved the thrill of a kill, the slice of bliss in taking someone's last breath, a victory of silence. He was a man of manipulation, written by Hugo himself, the perfect specimen reincarnated in him.

He walked around me like I was his prey, ready to strike and attack. I was now part of the show put on display, like an exhibit for people to watch and get entertainment from. I could feel a hand slowly feeling me up, running from my thigh, past my waist, up my chest and neck, until he grabbed my face in his hand, just for me to pull my head back out of his grip, jerking against the bonds, causing him to smile.

"Finally, I've got you all to myself, Princess," he smiled, looking me up and down, enjoying the view in front of him.

I stayed quiet just watching him, knowing full well I wasn't going to spill anything to him, no matter the beatings that were coming. I was ready.

"So, are you going to tell me what I need? Or would you like me to beat it out of you?" he asked, getting closer to me, until he was right in my face.

All I could do was smile and stare into his heartless eyes, while his lips were only inches away from mine. I let out a laugh, just to then headbutt him and with all my strength I could get by pulling on my restraints, I lifted myself up and raised one of my legs, kneeing him straight between his legs, just to watch him crumble to the floor.

"You fucking bitch!" he hissed, as he cradled his crotch.

"Love you too, Nick," I huffed, proud of my little victory. Even if it meant I got more of a beating, at least I got a hit in.

I hung there watching him as he rolled around on the floor and slowly got himself to his feet, only to strike me across my face and for me to spit blood; the bastard had busted my lip by striking me. "You going to tell me what I want to know?" he asked me again. I spat at him.

In that moment he took his chance and punched me straight in the ribs, winding me. I started to cough, being left breathless, feeling like razors were slicing my lungs, as my body screamed for oxygen.

"I'm going to enjoy this. Especially, if you're not going to say anything," he grinned.

"I've lost everything, so do what you please."

The one person I came to save, didn't love me, didn't recognise me, and basically just broke my heart. What else was there to live for?

He circled me waiting for me to talk, even though he must have known I'd be silent. He pulled a blade out from the side of his pants, spinning it in his hand. The coldness of the blade was then pushed under my chin, forcing my head up to look at him, just to then run the blade slowly down the side of my neck, only to then with his free hand grab my shirt and rip it down the middle, leaving me exposed.

Watching his eyes rake my chest, he bit his lip. "I have definitely missed those," he smirked.

"You're a pig!" I hissed.

He then let out a deep chuckle and looked me in the eyes. "I'm going to ask you again. Where's the device?" he asked, moving the cold blade so it was against my chest.

"Go to hell," I hissed.

He lifted the knife and brought it down, slashing my chest, making me scream. "Where's the device?" he asked again, as his left eye started to twitch with annoyance.

"Go to hell!" I shouted again.

He slashed my chest again, letting my blood run. "Where's the device?" he shouted, like a song on constant loop, only for me to spit at him, causing him to punch me in the face, instantly making me hazy and my vision blurry.

I felt a pair of hands grab my face, barely making out Nick's blurred face. He was holding mine close to his, trying to shake me back to normal.

"Focus!" he shouted, slapping me across the face to get my attention back and for me to regain my focus, only so he could do more to me.

When I seemed focused, he let me go, watching me as my eyes followed him. "What would you do if I hurt Sebastian?" he asked, teasing the idea in front of me.

"Don't you dare touch him!" I seethed, causing him to laugh; he knew how to get under my skin.

"If you don't want me to hurt one pretty little hair on his head, answer my question," he taunted, walking around me again. "Where is the device?"

"I hope you rot. I swear when I get free, I'll slaughter you where you stand," I spat at him again, just for him to slash my chest three more times, with me screaming every single time one landed.

I had to bare it, grit my teeth, and push through it. I couldn't falter because if I did, he would love it. I was happy to oblige in provoking him. I couldn't let him break me. After all, he was nefarious.

I felt the blade against my cheek pressing down once

more, slowly cutting away at my skin, just for the blood to slowly run down my face. He was making a promise to himself to slice me to pieces, and he wanted me to know it was coming, slowly and all so painfully.

He got closer to me and ran his hand down my face, neck, chest, and side. "You always were a pretty little thing. Shame your personality and your mouth didn't match," he smirked. Unease started to creep up inside me. "To think once I found you attractive. Maybe brainwashing you might work in my favour and cure that insatiable mouth of yours."

A scoff left my lips. "I'll never be yours!"

"We had something once, I'll get my way with you again."

"Over my dead body!"

"You're forgetting you won't remember anything," he chuckled.

"You will always be nauseating. Brainwashing me won't do anything," I promised him. He didn't say a word. "Cat got your tongue?" I snickered, knowing I was getting under his skin.

The vein in the middle of his forehead was becoming more prominent as he slowly trailed closer to me, only for one of his hands to reach out and squeeze my cheeks, tight enough for my lips to pucker.

A smirk on his face grew and the light in his eyes screamed at me. "Such a pretty thing with a foul mouth, what a shame," he taunted again. I huffed at his comment. "There are other things I'd rather that mouth did. Then again, I can remember your talents, I dream about them daily."

The words he spoke made my stomach turn and my

body shiver. It was like the feeling of lust had corrupted him, taking over every fibre of his being. He thought with his dick and not his head. After all, this man had more dick in his personality than his pants. If I had to be truly honest, it wasn't even a dick worth trying.

Then again, that was years ago. Never again.

***

His grip loosened off my face. "Just get on with it," I huffed, knowing my fate.

His eyes for a second softened and then turned into a hard gaze. "Everyone's got a breaking point," he said, with the tip of the blade pushing into the bottom of my chin. "I'll find yours."

I let out a laugh. "Good luck with that."

He pulled the knife away, only to walk behind me and for his mouth to appear close to my ear. "I've got all the power, Princess" he whispered, his hot breath sending the hairs on the back of my neck up. "It's a shame because I do like a woman in charge."

I could hear the snicker in his voice as he spoke, trying to turn this game sexual for his own pleasure, something for him to get off to later. Then again, if that thing ever came close to me again, I would either chop it off with the knife he wielded or bite it off with my teeth.

Pain is pleasure right?

He soon pulled away and came back to stand in front of me, still with the sly smirk plastered across his face. The glimmer of light I could see flickering in his eyes gave me hope, maybe that boy I met all those years ago lingered inside somewhere in that dark soul of his.

"What happened to you?" I asked, making him cock his head, like he was studying the random outburst of my question. I knew right there and then that I was opening a can of worms.

The silence that fell made me soon realise he didn't have an answer, that the boy I once knew got lost some time ago. It was like Hugo had taken a sweet innocent soul and ripped that part of him away, a boy so golden now broken, like he was now one of 'Peter Pan's' lost boys. As much as my heart ached for what Hugo had done to him, Nick had made his own choices and he had done things I would never forgive him for.

"Why are you... his favourite?" he asked out of nowhere.

The question alone told me so much, like it had been lingering in his mind for years, a question he so desperately wanted to ask me. By me leaving, he never got the chance. It was like he had so many unanswered questions swamping him, questions that only I could bear witness too.

"Well, that question got answered not long ago, didn't it?" I huffed, knowing full well the answer was because I was his daughter, a fate that I found a curse. "I wish I wasn't."

He turned to face away from me, so I couldn't see his expression as he rubbed a hand over it, like the emotion he had was too much of a weakness for him. "You had everything," he said, with pain radiating in his voice.

The pain in his voice told me he wanted to be me, have my life, that's why he was the way he was. It was all jealousy. He wanted to be the beacon of attention, the one shining star taking all the light, he wanted the spotlight. He had worked his ass off in everything, doing everything possible for Hugo, to please him, for him to be proud of him... all he wanted was Hugo's praise and he never had it.

I felt myself let out a sigh, knowing the truth. "It's not worth it," I openly admitted. He turned to face me. "I spent my life hanging by a thread. It may have looked like a life of luxury and love, but it wasn't. It's all manipulation and a game he played well. You're a puppet to him, a chess piece and nothing more than that. That man can't love anything."

He let out a scoff, then an amused grin filled his face. "Can't love anything?" he laughed. "Yet he loves you!"

What Nick could see as love, was greed, power, and control. Loving people or a person, wasn't in his nature, wasn't in his corrupted DNA. The only thing that man had in his heart was love of power, control and wealth and nothing more. If anyone close to him died, he wouldn't grieve, he wouldn't cry, he wouldn't let it consume him. One day he will cry, that day would be the day he would watch Scarlet fall and that was a promise I was going to make myself.

"He loves power and nothing more," I said, hoping he would see the truth.

"You never really cared about anything!"

"I cared enough to leave!"

"He saved us all!"

"He controlled us! You're just a sheep following the herd!" I screamed at him.

He struck me across the face, leaving a raw imprint of his hand.

I was digging myself a hole, digging my own grave. I was basically drowning in truth and what did I do?

I chucked myself straight into the deep end...

***

I just listened to him laughing to himself and how he found

301

amusement out of me and my honesty, like I had hit some sort of nerve within him.

"You know nothing," he laughed, shaking his head in disbelief, like I was feeding him bullshit.

"Why do you think I left in the first place?" I asked him.

"Because you're weak!" he shouted, as he got right up in my face.

"I'm stronger than you think. If I'm weak, I wouldn't have left in the first place. Get out while you can, Nick and I'm not saying this just because I can, I'm saying this because if you don't get out, this place will be the death of you, and we all have a chance of a normal life…don't let him take that away from you."

All I wanted was him to see the truth, to see that one ray of light at the end of a dark tunnel. There wasn't much more I could say to him, he would believe what he wanted and that was Hugo. He was that far imprinted inside Nick's head; there was no way out. He had broken that small little boy who had a smile that could break any woman's heart and now he was a shell, a ghost of his former self.

Before he could say anything else to me, looking her up and down. "What are you doing here?" he asked her.

"I've come to take over from him" she said, pointing to the only other security member in the room.

His brows furrowed, confusion setting in. "Why the swap?" he asked.

"Hugo said he needed him for other important measures," she quickly replied.

He sighed and looked towards the man. "Go! Give her the keys on your way out," he commanded. The man then nodded and handed Hannah the keys.

The man left the room and disappeared, leaving only

Nick and Hannah in the room with me. Nick was facing away from Hannah, causing me to take a small glance towards her, giving her a small nod, basically saying I was ready when she was.

When he turned to face me again, he was filled with rage, the vein in his head looking like it was going to burst. He took two large steps towards me and spun the knives in his hand, just to smirk once more, a manipulative smirk that I had only ever once seen on Hugo's face. "So, you going to give me an answer yet?" he asked.

This was turning into a mindless game of who was better, where nobody would win. I knew by the end of it that I would end up shedding blood, more blood than what had already been spilt. He was happy to get his hands bloody, a man of cruelty. I had the upper hand though; he just didn't know it.

***

I let out a sigh, a sigh of pretend defeat, like I had given up all hope. The smirk on his face grew more calculating than the last. He seemed to think I had cracked, that I was willing to spill all my secrets.

"If you come really close, I promise to tell you something," I muttered, making it sound like I was finally giving him what he wanted, the one piece of information he craved.

He came even closer to me, his face only inches away from mine, his eyes locked on mine. "Tell me your secrets, Princess," he encouraged. I gave him a sly smirk and his eyes then realised what was happening, but not quick enough to move out of the way.

I pulled my head back and with everything I had, I headbutted him again, only to then pull on my restraints

303

with all the energy I had left to lift my leg, hitting him between his legs once again. He fell to his knees right in front of me, just for me to wrap my legs around his neck, trying my best to strangle him, or at least to apply enough pressure to make him pass out. He grabbed my legs and stood up, trying to pry my legs away from around his neck. He tried a few times and before I knew it, he had picked up the knife and plunged it into my leg, making me scream in agony. I was trying my best to desperately push the pain aside, not letting the agony consume me, making sure I kept my wits about me. As much as my mind was screaming at me to react, to let go, to crumble…I couldn't.

Hannah came towards me and raised her gun, pointing it directly at him. "Move and I'll shoot," she hissed.

The smirk that grew on his face said it all and all he could do was laugh. "Big bad wolf come to save the day?" he taunted her.

"Don't give me a reason to shoot you," she beamed.

He scoffed. "You're just a woman, you're not going to shoot.".

Hannah still stood there with the gun pointing towards him, as I felt the sensation of a knife being pulled out of my leg. It felt like the blade was grinding against the bone, ripping the muscle in my leg, as blood started to spray out when the knife fully departed, causing me to grit my teeth because of the pain. "Last time, Dickhead! Drop the knife or I'll shoot!" Hannah hissed, causing him to drop the knife to the floor, while my legs stayed wrapped around his neck in a tight grip.

"You're not going to shoot me," he smiled.

"Why do people say that?" she asked, as she pressed the trigger.

He dropped to the floor, clutching his leg. "You bitch!" he seethed.

"Don't test me!" Hannah shouted back.

While he was on the floor, Hannah ran up to me and flicked through the keys, just to then unlock the chains around my wrist and for me to finally be on my feet, only for the pain to shoot through me. I looked down at my calf to see the blood oozing. Using the remains of the shredded top I had on, I tied it around my leg, making sure I restricted the blood flow enough to survive the mission.

In the corner of my eye, I saw Nick grabbing the knife, only to grab Hannah's gun and to hit him in the face with it, causing him to drop the knife.

I pointed the gun at him.

"You will regret this," he hissed as the blood trickled from his receding hairline and nose.

"I don't think I will", I smiled, hitting him in the face again with the gun, knocking him out cold. "See you in Hell."

Seeing the handcuffs on the floor, I picked them up and wrapped one around one of his wrist. Hannah then helped me pull him close to the wall, just to then loop them around a bar and hook the other, locking him in place.

"It won't be long till he's out of these when he wakes up, but it will still give us a bit of time," I said. "Where are the others?"

"They are trying to find Sebastian," she said.

I nodded but I knew if he felt the way he did about me, they sure as hell weren't going to get through to him. We would be dragging an unconscious Sebastian home.

"I know where he is," I said. Hannah raised a brow. "He's with Hugo."

I could tell from the look on Hannah's face that she

was studying me and could hear the pain lacing my words.

"What's wrong?" she asked, confirming my suspicion.

"He doesn't remember me…he told me he doesn't love me…Sebastian's gone. We are going to have to drag him kicking and screaming or out cold."

"We will fix it," Hannah tried to reassure me, with a faint smile on her face.

There was still hope, even in the darkness. It was going to be a challenge, a fight, a battle to get him to remember the truth, but he wasn't too far gone to not come back.

**

Within seconds, we had stepped out of the room, only for Hannah to hand me a top for me to put on. I couldn't exactly walk around half dressed. She also handed me a comms piece, just for me to quickly place it in my ear, and to pull the cap fully down to hide my face.

Taking a deep breath, I looked at Hannah to see her watching me. This was the moment, and it was finally time to set this place ablaze, we were ready, and Hugo wasn't going to see it coming.

Game on.

Chapter Thirty-Two

Step by step, we started searching the halls, trying our best to stay out of sight and blend in with the crowd, as we made our way to Hugo's office. It was the last place I had seen Sebastian and the best place to find him and to also end Hugo's life.

It didn't take long before the alarms were raised and war was coming, the lights in the halls flashing red, the sound of an alarm blazing and people scurrying, another CODE RED in action. This only meant one thing, Nick had either been found or he had escaped and raised the alarm, a path I knew was coming, but hoped would take longer.

"They know!" Amelie spoke down the comms.

"I'm halfway in setting up the detonators," Arthur communicated.

Arthur was the one who was going to blow the place up, make the place crumble to the floor and make it just a memory. A memory I was going to watch happily burn, it was just a shame I didn't have any marshmallows to toast over the flames.

In an instant, we both heard footsteps coming from

behind, making us turn to see Sebastian. He had stopped as soon as he had noticed us standing there.

In the corner of my eye, I saw Hannah look at me, but I was too focused on Sebastian and the two knives in his hand.

"This isn't you, Sebastian," I stated, hoping to at least try and get him to see sense.

"You don't know me!" he hissed. "Did I not make that clear to you earlier or are you that deluded?"

"I have known you for the last eight years," I pointed out to him. He scoffed.

"They have brainwashed you in to forgetting us," Hannah pitched in.

"Brainwashing me into seeing the truth," Sebastian said.

"This isn't you; they have taken who you are," I said.

He shook his head. "This is the real me!"

I took one look at Hannah and nodded to her, basically telling her to carry on, go find the others, go, and cripple this place to the ground. I was basically telling her to leave Sebastian to me, he was my problem, and I was going to try and fix him.

Within seconds, Hannah disappeared, leaving just me and him in the corridor. If I had to fight him, so be it. There was no other option up for grabs, Hugo wasn't getting him back and I sure as hell wasn't going to let him die.

The smirk on his face that crept upon him said it all; he was willing to fight me on this and was up for the challenge. "Looks like I just need to take one of you out then."

Before I could even respond, he lunged for me, knives at the ready. I blocked his incoming hand and knocked one of the knives out of it. As we were slightly bent over, I felt his knee come up and get me in the ribs, winding me. I dropped to the floor on my knees.

Taking my chances, I stretched one of my legs around, swinging it under his, only to take them both out and for him to crash. I got back up and watched how he was only down for a few seconds, before he flipped himself over and pulled himself back on his feet, a trick I had seen many times before when we trained in the gym. He went to strike me, but missed and the next thing I knew we had started fighting each other again, both landing and blocking blows.

In a second of misjudgement, Sebastian had his hand around my throat, and I was pinned to the wall. I instantly felt my heart race, as the one person in the world I thought wouldn't hurt me, was trying to kill me. The air became thin as my hands went to grasp his, but then I just left them resting on his, letting him do as he pleased.

"I'm...not going...to fight you," I barely got out, as the air got thinner and thinner.

He pulled me forward and chucked me back into the wall, clearly hoping it would cause me to fight him, but it didn't.

"I'm...not going...to fight you," I said again and once more he threw me.

"Fight me!" he shouted, causing me to smile.

"No."

"Fight me!"

"No!"

"Fight me!" he shouted, slamming me against the wall one more time, hoping he could get something out of me.

"I'm not going...to fight you," I slowly said, as his grip had ever so slightly eased.

He still held me tightly, but I could breathe. He just stood there trying to read me, with his head slightly tilted, like he was curious to why I wouldn't. I watched how his eyebrows raised and how he repeatedly blinked, like he was imagining my response, and this wasn't real.

His lips then slightly parted and his face came closer to mine, still not letting go of the hold he had on me. "Why not?" he asked.

"Because I know you and I love you," I stated.

He just stared into my eyes, my soul, beckoning me to touch him without even asking. I slowly ran my hand up his arm, until it rested against the side of his face. After a few seconds, his eyes closed and his face tilted into my touch, like he felt something he remembered, something he liked. His eyes then opened and carried on watching me, giving me a yearning look and that's when I saw it. In a passing second, I saw the glimmer of love being reflected at me, like the feeling was coming back to him or he was relearning what love felt like.

"Come back to me," I soothed, watching as the flicker in his eyes kept changing, like something was stopping his mind from fully switching back.

The hold he had on me soon loosened, and his hands dropped away from my neck. He then rested them against the wall beside my head, as his eyes remained locked and focused on me. I felt him slowly inch closer, our lips almost touching like we were going to kiss, only to see the glimmer fade and for him to slap my hand away from him.

Taking a few steps back away from me, he shook his head, his eyes ping ponging in all sorts of directions, as he ran his hand through his hair. I could tell he was conflicted, he was weighing out both sides of his brain, trying to figure out what was happening to him, like his head was telling him one thing, but his heart was saying the opposite.

Taking a step towards him, I reached out, holding my

hand out to him. "Come back to me, Sebastian. I will help you, we can fix this," I stated calmly.

"No!" he shouted.

"It's only me, It's Adi," I tried again.

"I don't want to hurt you," he mumbled, knowing something was going on in his head, something making realise I was of some importance to him, but he didn't know what.

"You won't hurt me," I weakly smiled, as I took another step forward.

In a flash, my back was against the wall again. Sebastian had charged forward and pushed me. Barley a second passed before he took a few steps back and looked at his hands, like they had acted without him knowing, like he had lost control of himself. Without warning, he ran, disappearing down the hallway, leaving me standing there, confused.

All it did was confirm what I knew, part of my Sebastian was in there and he was trying to break free, trying to get out of the confined space Hugo had locked him in, in his own mind. With enough effort, I knew he could be broken, the cracks were already forming and all I had to do was give them a final blow and Sebastian would break free.

All I wanted to do was chase after him, but I had to do one other thing first. I crouched down and picked up the knives and my gun, hooking the knives into my waistband. Once I had done what was needed, then I could go and find Sebastian again.

But first, I had to go and kill the snake.

Chapter Thirty-Three

Hugo wouldn't be in his office anymore due to the alarms now blazing and I didn't know the layout of the building that well, only the blueprints Jonas had showed us all. When chaos came, Hugo fled, that was his thing. He wouldn't fight, he wouldn't stay, he would run and hide and stay in the safe zone. He was going to run.

Testing my luck, I started running down the halls, knowing there was a helicopter pad somewhere close by on the roof, but I had to go in search of the staircase. As I ran the best I could with a leg injury, I could see shards of shattered glass from broken windows and specs of blood on the floor. Chaos had hit the whole compound and people had been fighting, but there weren't any bodies, it was like everyone was fleeing instead of fighting. As much as I wanted to believe we had caused all this, we hadn't. The damage that had been done so far, was too much for just six of us, there must have been others taking a stand, breaking free, joining the war. We had luck on our side.

Suddenly, I felt my surroundings shaking, only to see

out of the broken window, that the top floors of building one, the one we escaped from, exploding. Flames started to break out and smoke descended into the air; this place was falling, and it was coming down fast. I had to hurry.

"Shit! Sorry! Forgot to make sure nobody was in there," Arthur spoke through the comms.

"Luckily I'm in three," Amelie responded, with her words uttered in disgust at the fact he was late to think she could have been killed.

"Same here," I stated.

The compound had three buildings, all interlinked by a bridged corridor, three floors up. I was at the opposite side of the compound to what Arthur had just tried to destroy, but still in the middle of the 'U' shaped compound, was a pond of water, that looked more like a gigantic pool, with flowers and benches around it. As much as this was hell, Hugo had tried to make it beautiful and homely, but that would have only been for the naked eye to see, the truth lay down in the depths below.

"We're behind you," a female voice spoke. I then turned to see Amelie and Larna, both sweaty from the events that had occurred.

"Let's go and find the bastard," Larna wickedly grinned. She wanted him dead, and she was going to love watching every moment of it happening.

If it was up to them, torture would be the ultimate start. The goal being to do what he did to them and many others. Punishment for his sins. If it was up to them, they would rip that man, limb from limb, bone by bone and piece by piece, dissecting him into tiny little pieces and feeding them to the wildest of animals, a death well suited and truly deserved. Me, however, I just wanted to look him

Scarlet

dead set in the eyes with a gun pointed towards his
forehead and for him to watch me pull the trigger.

***

Carrying on down the halls, we made our way to the
second floor, still searching, only to look down the corridor
and see a set of men and within them, Hugo. All eyes locked
on us, and Hugo could see me clear as day looking at him,
he knew I had come for him.

"Now!" he shouted towards one of the men.

The man reached forward, scanning his ID, just for an
electronic door to start coming down slowly. I knew
instantly if that door was to lock, there would be no way of
getting to him and I couldn't miss the opportunity. It was
now or never.

"Run!" Amelie shouted, causing us all to pick up our
feet and with it, all the strength we had to run towards the
closing door.

As we got closer, it was only a few feet left from
closing. Amelie and Larna quickly ducked under it, but I
was slacking, the pain in my leg slowing me down. I had to
take my chance, or I was going to be locked out. Picking up
as much strength as I could, I put my foot down and
sprinted, only to dive onto the floor just managing to slide
under the gap, barely getting through and making it to the
other side with it closing behind me.

Opening my eyes, I looked up to see Larna and Amelie,
leaning over me, both smiling. "Smart move," Larna lightly
laughed, offering her hand to help me get to my feet.

Turning to look further down the hall, we saw Hugo
and his men turning into the lift. He was heading to the
helicopter pad. We instantly sprinted again, reaching the
lift doors as they closed.

"Fuck!" Amelie shouted, slamming her fist against the door.

"Stairs! Now!" Larna pointed, only for us to see the stairs sign and a helicopter pad icon on the notice.

We all instantly ran more, out of breath, but accepting the challenge up flights of stairs, only to hear a door slam below us. We looked over the banister and saw a march of men running through, charging up the stairs, coming for us.

"Fuck!" I shouted.

"Tell you now...I'm not fit enough for these stairs but come on... let's go," Amelie tried to get out between breaths.

"Just kill me now," Larna breathed out, causing us all to have a small laugh.

"Not just yet," Amelie winked, causing Larna to flip her off.

We took it step by step, dying from how much energy we had already used and from the pain that constantly shot through me.

We reached the top, pushing open the door, pointing our guns at the ready. We started firing our weapons, only to hit the helicopter, causing the bullets to bounce of it. We fired as much as we could, trying our best to shoot through the glass, as we saw Hugo looking at us. The helicopter started to move faster, getting higher as our ammunition started to run out.

I wanted to scream, every part of me raging with anger, wrath, rage, however you wanted to describe it. Today, was supposed to be the day his life ended, but today was just another day he survived.

It hovered above as Hugo signed to me, basically saying 'better luck next time and I will find you'. When I was younger, he taught me to sign, taught me to be able to communicate with everyone, so we had some sort of communication with others, a friendly gesture that made me think kindly of him.

I signed back. 'The next time we meet, I'll be putting a bullet through your head...count on it'. Knowing what I had signed, he laughed at me, before speaking to someone. The helicopter then set off and disappeared into the distance. He had escaped...for now.

Chapter Thirty-Four

Looking around, we knew we couldn't turn around and go back down the stairs, due to the men that where running up them, coming to capture us. As we faced the exit, smoke started to fill the air, fire coming through every crack, surrounding us. The place around us was burning and we needed a way out.

Amelie kept looking around, hoping to figure something out, but there wasn't one.

"What do we do?" I asked, looking at my gun. "I'm out of ammunition."

"Same," Larna agreed. "We haven't got long; they're right on our tail."

I had lost all hope and didn't know what else we could do. We only had our knives, our fist, and feet. The men behind the door were loaded and ready to fight. I was willing to give everything I could, but it was a battle I knew we couldn't win.

Watching Larna, her eyes lit up. "I know that look. What's the plan?" I asked, only for Larna to wickedly smile.

It was a smile of a calculated plan, a solution and

knowing Larna, it wasn't going to be that straight forward, especially seeing the way she was with blood.

"Do you trust me?" she asked.

"Not really, but I feel like I'm going to have to," I stated, looking around me, knowing this was going to be our only option.

"Ouch, I'll pretend you didn't say that. But, when I say jump, you jump," she smiled, looking to the other end of the building.

I knew there was a pond down there of water, but I had no idea how deep it was, and we were six floors up.

"You have another thing coming if you think I'm jumping," Amelie sarcastically laughed.

"Just trust me, ok?" Larna stated.

I closed my eyes and rubbed my forehead. What could possibly go wrong?

"Fuck!" I stated. "Ok!"

"Jesus," Amelie said. "If I die, I am coming back to haunt you, mark my words."

Larna laughed. "Noted."

Within seconds, we were halfway across the roof, facing the edge of the building, waiting for our moment.

I stood there shaking my arms and legs out, hyping myself up. "You better know what you're doing," I huffed.

"When I say go, just go," Larna said, as the door behind us burst open with multiple men running through, charging towards us.

"Go!" Larna shouted. We instantly started running, sprinting towards the edge.

In the corner of my eye as we ran, I saw Larna quickly pull out a small object and chuck it behind us.

"Jump!" she screamed, as we got to the edge.

As we jumped, I heard an explosion coming from

behind, only to see more fire, smoke and pieces of the brick flying around us. That's when I realised, Larna had chucked a grenade and she had pulled the switch.

Falling six floors was an adrenaline rush. I could feel my heart beating out my chest, the fast-paced air hitting me in the face and my limbs going stiff, as we fast approached the water.

As we landed into the water, I felt myself sink to the bottom, being submerged by the water breaking my fall. Opening my eyes, I was met with the blurry image of two people, Amelie, and Larna, they too had landed safety in the water. The water around me started to change, I could see the red, the blood coming from my wound surrounding me. I then saw a hand wave under the water, turning to see Amelie, who was pointing up, telling me to swim to the survive. Feeling myself needing to take a breath of fresh air, I kicked my legs to feel the pain shoot through me. As my head came up above the water, I finally took in my first breath of fresh air after being submerged, just to come face to face with Amelie and Larna.

No one said anything and we just kept looking between each other, just for us all to start laughing.

"Did that just really happen?" Amelie asked.

"Yes," I laughed.

"Good thing you guys trusted me," Larna said.

"Can we do that again?" Amelie asked, with a massive smile across her face.

She had clearly loved every minute of the adrenaline rush and so had I, but I was definitely not volunteering to do that again.

"Come on let's get out of here and find the others," Amelie said, just to then swim to the side and pull herself out, with me and Larna following.

Scarlet

Standing at the side of the large pond, dripping wet, we all stood there getting our breath back, while the buildings around us burned and crumbled to the ground slowly.

"Where are we going?" Amelie asked me.

"Last I knew they were heading to building two, the engineering building," Larna mentioned, causing us to look behind us and see the engineering building burning.

Just from looking at it, I could tell we didn't have much time and we would have to get in and out quickly.

Before we could even take a step forward, we heard a loud bang and turned towards building one to see Hannah running towards us. As soon as she got close, she chucked a duffle bag on the floor in front of us and let out a deep breath.

"More ammunition, guessing you might need it," she smiled, getting her breath back from running. "We haven't got long. Arthur has nearly finished rigging the place with explosives."

"Arthur?" I asked, remembering the ear comms.

"I hear you!" he replied.

"How long?"

"Ten minutes and I'll be ready. Just let me know when and I will."

"Be careful, we're going to find Sebastian."

"And Hugo?" he asked.

I sighed. "He got away on the helicopter," I said, feeling defeated, knowing that was the goal, to rid the world of him.

Inside I was raging, I wanted nothing more than to put a stop to him, but I couldn't do it, I couldn't complete my mission.

"Let's go get Sebastian," I said, turning towards the building with smoke still circling and fire burning around us.

***

As we walked through the corridors, we walked over bodies of our deceased enemies, people who had fought for Hugo and failed. There was blood everywhere, mixed in with glass, brick, smoke and fire, a fight had broken out and we sure as hell were about to enter another.

As soon as we entered the main warehouse of the building, we could hear voices, causing us to look up at the metal structure of floors and see Sebastian and Jack stood before the metal bridge that led across to the other side and out to building three.

We went to step forward and head towards the stairs, but before we could, I saw two figures move in the corner of my eye. We stopped and turned towards them to see two men charging towards us, weapons in hand.

Turning towards Amelie and Hannah, I nudged my head in the direction of the stairs. "Go! We can handle this!" I shouted, causing Amelie and Hannah to run off and help Jack get Sebastian.

Turning back towards the men, I noticed one of them was Nick himself, the skin on his face and arms burnt by the flames, forever scarred for life. Within seconds, they started to shoot, causing me and Larna to duck behind some of the engineering equipment, opposite sides to each other. I took a glance around it, only for shots to be fired at me, just missing. I quickly stood up, turning to fire my gun, only to miss Nick and for him to fire back. I ran to another place to hide, shooting at Nick as I ran, while Larna tried to take down the other man.

"Give up now!" Nick shouted.

"Over my dead body!" I shouted back.

"That can be arranged!"

"I thought he wanted me alive?"

"Accidents happen!"

Taking another glance around the box I was hiding behind, I took another shot, catching his hand. "Fuck!" He shouted, just for me to hear the clatter of his gun dropping to the floor.

I went to fire again, but it didn't work. I was out of ammunition. Taking a glance around again, I noticed Nick's gun had travelled closer to me, meaning we were both unarmed. Getting to my feet, I stepped out of hiding and came face to face with Nick, who had hold of his bloody hand.

"How about I give you a head start?" he laughed, while he ripped part of his shirt and wrapped it tightly around his hand.

"Don't need it!" I smirked, knowing full well this was going to be a hell of a fight.

"You don't have to do this," I said giving him the out I wish someone would have given me.

"I'll forever follow him," he said.

"You're only a chess piece to him."

"So be it, play your piece. Let's see who reaches checkmate first...shall we?" he asked, signalling a come-hither motion, with a smile on his face. "Bring it, Princess!"

Without a second thought, I charged towards him to try and strike him. He avoided me but I didn't hesitate. With my second strike, I hit him in the ribs, winding him. As I had the advantage, I swung my leg to the back of his and wiped his feet from under him, causing him to hit the ground. Having quick reflexes, he sprung back to his feet, only to take my feet out from underneath me, causing me to crash to the floor. He quickly went to punch me as I laid there, but I moved my head, causing him to punch the

322

concrete floor with his already injured hand.

"Fuck!" he hissed.

Taking this as my chance, I sprung back to my feet, just to make out the gun he had dropped not too long ago, a few feet away. I turned back to Nick to see he had also noticed it. Both of us then looked at it and then back at each other, waiting to see who was going to make the first move, only for us both to charge towards it. He suddenly grabbed the back of my shirt and pulled, pushing his foot out in front of me, making me fall, but I then grabbed his leg, making him too drop to the floor. As he fell, I pushed myself back to my feet and ran past him, only to feel myself being grabbed and chucked into the wall, a hand wrapped tightly around my throat and a tip of a blade pressed against my stomach. I tried my best to fight his tight grip around my throat as he strangled me and pushed the blade in, feeling myself being sliced open. In the corner of my eye, I saw something shiny, to notice a loose nail sticking out of the wall. Feeling Nick standing closer to me, as his breath hit my neck as he slowly carried on pushing the blade in, making me suffer, I tried to reach for it. My fingertips barely touched it, but I knew I had to do something, and I had to get it quickly. I tried once more and finally grabbed it, instantly shoving it into the top of his shoulder, causing him to let me go and for me to drop to the floor coughing, trying to get the air back into my lungs.

As he ripped the nail out his shoulder, I quickly pulled the blade out of my stomach and chucked it to the floor. As he remained briefly distracted by the nail, I quickly got to my feet and dived back to the floor. Grabbing the gun, I quickly flipped myself over onto my back to see Nick standing above me.

"Checkmate," I stated, firing the gun with no hesitation, no remorse, no second chance.

The bullet hit him dead set between the eyes, and I watched how his body dropped next to me with his eyes still open, staring directly into mine as the blood started to pool around him.

Truth was, staring into those soulless eyes, my heart sank. It sank for a death of a friend, a boy I held close to me years ago, but I wasn't mourning the man he was now. My grief was for the boy who had a heart of gold and may that boy rest easy, but I hoped the man he became suffered in Hell.

Hearing steps to my left, I turned quickly, pointing the gun, to see Larna with her hands up. "Watch it, girl! It's only me!" she said.

Lowering the gun, I sighed, "Sorry."

Larna instantly held her hand out towards me. I accepted it, just for her to help me stand and stare at Nick's body.

"He had it coming," Larna stated.

"I know," I said, wishing this wasn't the end for anyone, but a starting point of freedom, a freedom he had the chance of but didn't want.

"I need a hand here!" Arthur shouted through the comms.

"You go and help them. I'll go help, Pretty Boy," Larna winked at me.

"I heard that!" Arthur spoke again, causing us both to laugh.

"Be careful," I said to Larna. She nodded and ran back the way we came in whilst I ran up the metal stairs to whoever was waiting for me.

Chapter Thirty-Five

A landing of chaos, fire, and clouds of smoke, that's what I entered. A place burning to the ground, crumbling, and turning to ash. Destruction was brewing and the nightmare was quickly coming to an end.

I stood there looking at what was in front of me. Jack was talking to Sebastian, but I couldn't hear a word he was saying over he noise of the building around us falling apart. The compound was falling to ash, the roof above us already gone, as I looked up at the rain that started to descend above us, but not enough to put the flames out. It was like the rain had come to mourn the fallen, innocent souls that had fought against Hugo.

Before I could even take a step forward, Sebastian lunged for Jack, only for Jack to try and defend himself. Within seconds, Sebastian had Jack against the wall, only to punch him straight into the face, knocking him out cold. I suddenly saw Amelie appear from nowhere, just to charge herself towards Sebastian. Sebastian struck her without hesitation, sending her to the floor before she even had the chance to touch him. I stood there frozen, unable to move to go and help as I watched Sebastian stand above her and raise his leg, bringing it down with all his force to stamp on her right arm. A snapping sound filled the air, a sound that sent shivers down my back, just to be followed by a scream that rippled out of Amelie. It was a scream so bloodcurdling, it made me sick to my stomach.

The grin that was plastered across Sebastian's face said it all, it wasn't the Sebastian I knew. It was Sebastian's alter ego, the pure and innocent man I knew gone and replaced by something much more sinister.

Satisfied with the injuries he had caused, he turned away and headed straight towards the metal bridge. Not noticing me standing there in front of him, I quickly ran to Amelie.

She waved towards Jack with her good arm. "I'll be fine, go and help Jack!" she said.

I did as she said and diverted my attention to Jack, quickly approaching him and crouching down. Putting my hands on his shoulders, I shook him. "Jack! Jack!" I shouted, just for his eyes to flutter open and land on me. He slowly lifted himself up and placed his back against the railing and clutched his chest.

"Think I've broken a few ribs," he spoke, "but I'll live."

I turned my head to see Amelie still sat on the floor, watching as she tried her best to strap her arm into a sling, as fire and smoke started to lap around us. I knew this was all my fault and Hugo wouldn't have done any of this if it wasn't for me, after all I was his flesh and blood, his daughter.

It was honestly getting too much to bear, the feeling of smashed glass being twisted at the bottom of my heart, a vice wrapped around my chest, crushing me from the inside out. I knew they all needed a new life, a life without pain, destruction, and death. It was a life they couldn't have if Hugo was after me. The number of times they had sacrificed everything for me was becoming too much and I knew it had to come to an end.

Broken faces of broken souls being crushed and mangled into the chaos. I knew I was the front runner all along. I was the one who had dragged them into this mess a few weeks ago, starting this plan, I now had to be the one to end it.

I took another glance towards Jack and watched as his eyes watched mine, as I looked towards the knife next to him.

Without second guessing myself, I grabbed the knife. "I have one more trick up my sleeve," I explained, as Jack's eyebrows furrowed.

I knew he wouldn't understand what I had to do to stop this, to get Sebastian back, but it was one thing I knew would work and it was the only way.

Bringing the knife towards me, holding it close, Jack's eyes widened. "No!" he shouted, knowing the plan I had set in motion.

I reached my other hand forward and rested it above one of his, as the rain started to pour heavier over us. "I have spent a long time wondering why you all sacrificed your freedom to help me. You did it because I'm part of your family and I'll forever be grateful for that. Now it's my turn to save you all and set you all free," I softly spoke, with tears slowly running down my face. "Promise me you will get them all out?"

Jack eyes started to weep, and his lip started to quiver as he sat there silently, clearly saddened and in shock with what was happening.

"Promise me, Jack!" I shouted.

He grabbed my hand and gave it a squeeze. "I promise," he cried, tears running down his face more, knowing the ending of the story. "There must be another way."

I squeezed his hand back, knowing there wasn't another and I knew deep down I had to do it.

"I wish there was," I cried, knowing full well I had to play my last card. "I have to do this, it's the only way it's going to end."

Jack sat there knowing he had to let me do what I intended, and he knew he didn't have a choice, the plan I had set out to do was already in motion and he knew I had accepted my fate and it was a fate worth taking.

Jack pulled me to him, hugging me tight, a hug I returned and with that, it was the reassurance I needed that everyone would be okay, and it was my time to go.

I quickly got back to my feet, causing me to wince at the pain I was feeling. I had to be quick with my actions because time was running out. I looked down at Jack once more and met his gaze, while I held my hand on my upper abdomen, where the pain was coming from.

I turned away in seconds, running towards the metal bridge, noticing that Sebastian had just got to the other end, while the flames around us grew stronger, bringing the building around us to the ground. I caught up to him quickly, without him noticing and stopped a few feet away.

"Sebastian!" I shouted, causing him to stop and turn towards me.

His face said it all; his eyes lit up with joy for the fact I was standing in front of him. He was happy to see I was there presenting myself to him, stopping him from searching for me, so he could take me to Hugo.

He let out a sly smile and stepped forward. "I was about to come and find you."

"I know," I told him, only for him to take another step forward. "Wait!" I shouted. He stopped and his brows to furrowed, a look I had seen only seconds ago from Jack.

"Stop wasting time, he wants me to bring you to him."

"Just give me five minutes and then you can take me to him," I said.

He shook his head at me. "No!" he shouted, taking another step towards me.

"Five minutes and I'll willingly go, that's all I ask."

"Five minutes and it's all over?" he asked, confused.

I gave him a weak smile and nodded. "Five minutes and it will all end."

"Nothing you say will change my mind," he scoffed.

I knew deep down there was a possibility it wouldn't, but it was the only time I had left, and it was going to be the last thing I could try. I was willingly putting all my eggs into the basket, playing all my cards, letting it all seal my fate.

"Maybe not, but it's worth a shot," I said.

"Fine," he huffed.

Truth was, the shuffle of pain that radiated up me, shocked me a little, but I knew why. I had to tell him and start now; time was running thin.

After all, if only he knew, time itself was my enemy.

***

The questions I must ask, I already knew the answers for. Truth was, I just needed the reassurance of what I knew, so I could play my final card and make it work. Even if it did work, it wouldn't be me who benefited from it, it would be them.

"Do you remember anything? I asked.

"No," he replied.

"I know there is nothing I can say that will make you remember and there's no point of me travelling down memory lane."

"So, why bother?" he interrupted me.

"Because I just want to thank you," I smiled, as the rain started to get heavier, but still not enough to put the flames out.

"Thank me for what?" he asked.

"Thank you for loving me," I cried. "If there is ever a day you remember everything, I want you to know that. I want you to know that I love you and everything you have done from the moment they did this to you, isn't your fault. You're forgiven."

"That it?" he asked.

"No... give me a second," I stated, taking in a breath, knowing I finally had to say what I had to say. "Just know, that anything I do, isn't your fault either, I did it because I chose to do it."

Feeling the wave of pain taking over me, I let out a small hiss, my own body feeling weaker, knowing I was going to crack.

"This is my last trick in the book," I sobbed, letting out a small smile, knowing I had smothered myself in tears and there was no hiding how heartbroken I felt for doing what I was doing.

Without even a second thought, I chucked the knife I held close towards his feet, causing him to look at it and then me.

"What's a bloody knife got to do with anything?" he scoffed, making me realise I had to reveal the truth now.

"The knife signals the end," I weakly smiled, only to look down at where my hand was placed and move it, with Sebastian's gaze following mine.

All this time, I had hidden the truth away from him. By me moving my hand, I had exposed the truth. I looked down at my hand and looked at how it was covered in blood. Looking back at Sebastian, I could see that he had clocked I was bleeding, that something was happening.

"There was one thing you told me..." I paused, holding my bloody soaked hand out in front of me, remembering the moment we shared only days ago.

A Few days ago...

"What if they catch us and make us forget?" he asked.

I knew that deep down this was his recurring nightmare, one of us being taken and being made to forget the other, or even worse one of us being killed.

"I could never forget you; I love you," I stated, words as true as they could ever be.

"What if we do forget?" he asked again.

"I'd find my way back to you," I said.

"I'd find my way back to you... the fear of losing you, would make me remember," he softly spoke, the pain reflecting in his voice.

Present...

"The fear of losing you, would make me remember," I said out loud, repeating the words once spoken to me by the man in front of me, only for his eyes to widen.

He finally knew what I had done.

Only moments ago, when I was with Jack, I had picked up the knife and plunged it into my own side, making Jack cry out. I had to be the sacrifice they needed for it to all end, my life to save them all.

I felt my legs turn to jelly, only to drop to the floor, but before I could even hit the floor, I felt someone catch me. Opening my eyes, after they fluttered briefly closed while I dropped, I came face to face with Sebastian. He had caught me.

He was on his knees, holding me in his arms, with tears in his eyes. Looking into them properly, I noticed the light, the glow, the sparkle, I had flipped the switch. Tears were running down his face, as the rain mixed in with them, both of us drenched.

"No!" he cried, watching me as I weakly smiled at him, knowing I had got my Sebastian back, even if I only had a small moment of time left to witness it. "Stay with me!"

I wanted to stay with him more than anything, but it had to be done. The love I had for him was pure, it was a love from the fairy tales, where there once was a happy ending, but that fate was for another life.

I slowly lifted my hand up towards him, placing it on the side of his face, with him relaxing into my touch. "Please don't blame yourself," I said, knowing full well he would. "This is my choice."

"Please stay with me," he begged, holding onto me with dear life, just for him to try and lift me.

I shook my head, causing him to stop. "I won't make it," I said.

I could see the pain in his eyes as he held me. "I can't lose you; I need you," he cried, tears freely pouring down, falling onto me.

"It's time for me to let you all go. You guys no longer need me," I cried, knowing it was only a matter of time.

"Stay awake. We will save you!" he tried to reassure me.

"It's ok," I weakly smiled, "I'm ready."

"But I'm not ready." He held me tightly, as I felt a wave coming over me, causing me to wince. My body was shutting down. "I'm not ready to say goodbye."

"Thank you for saving my life and loving me. There has always been one thing I've always been sure of...and that's you," I soothed him, knowing time was growing thin. "You will love again," I said, just for him to kiss me.

The kiss was soft and gentle. It was a kiss goodbye, a goodbye full of love, pain, and heartache. A kiss I treasured and one that made my heart beat stronger, even for a tiny bit of time. He soon pulled away and looked at me again, but this time only inches apart. I could feel his tears dripping on my cheeks, as my hand remained gently placed on the side of his face.

"This isn't goodbye...I'll see you again," I promised him, my words getting weaker.

"You can't leave! You can't leave me," he cried, "I've not finished falling in love with you."

I really did wish I could have had a life with him, I badly wanted it, but I knew with all my heart we would get it in the next.

"And I-I..." I muttered. "Love you."

I felt myself fading fast, my eyes closing, the darkness creeping in, taking over, shutting me down, dragging me away from my lifeline. I let out one more smile as he kissed me on the forehead. The love he had for me was something I had treasured the most in my life, besides the love of my friends, my family. If my life rested on love, then I would forever be eternal. There was one thing I knew I didn't have the strength to say to him, one thing he had said to me, that I couldn't say back. I hadn't finished falling in love with him either.

In the final seconds of light, I could see it, see them. I could see the souls of our future selves dancing in the flames surrounding us.

My family had become the light in the darkest of places, a light I knew I was for him that I was dismantling, a star that led the way just for him. I could no longer feel the pain, the torment, the nightmares, or the danger that surrounded us. Everything I had built with them was their starting point, but their new start was my end, my last call, my last ring of the bell at the end of the night. My light was fading, and I was at peace with it, like the serenity I would feel from looking at the stars above. It wasn't the ending or the story I wanted, but an ending I never knew was coming until now. The flames around me meant a beautiful start and an ending to the nightmares, with them burning away history that once was the Devil and turning it to ash. It was ash that could one day be rebuilt into a better story, a better chapter, a better ending for all the ones around me that I loved and with that I welcomed my ending. Knowing the ones I love would be safe, be free because I was dead and Hugo had nothing to come for anymore, I welcomed the darkness, letting my eyes close and letting my last thought be...I loved him.

Chapter Thirty-Six

Four days Later...

Sebastian

Gloomy grey skies, clouds blocking the sunlight, rain pouring and making puddles everywhere and soggy grass, with my shoes sinking in every time I took a step. The grass itself glistened in the rain, leaving only a few raindrops in perfect form on a few strands of grass itself.

The day represented how I felt. I was heartbroken, every time I saw the stars I cried, I cried till I couldn't breathe, or I threw up, I cried till I couldn't cry anymore, and my tears just ran dry. My sleep was scarce and scattered, my dreams had become nightmares again, a recurrence of her leaving me, the vacant look in her eyes, her soul departing. I would toss and turn and lose all sense of time. I was barely functioning, but I had to play my part.

We all stood there in our line, dressed in black, with umbrellas above us, protecting us from the rain, but not the tears that fell. We stood there in perfect form, watching the shiny black casket that was covered in blue roses, her favourite flower, get lowered into the ground. It was our final farewell to the one person we all loved the most; a friend, a sister, my soulmate, making her final journey.

Nobody wanted this day to come, nobody could have done anything to save her. Adeline had decided to do this and all we could do was honour it, honour her sacrifice, and honour her life, even if I was losing the one thing I wanted the most.

I stood there dead centre in the line, as I dismantled in front of everyone, tears I didn't know I still had running down my face. I honestly despised myself knowing she did this all for me, to get my memories back and not only that, to set us all 'free'. She believed if she was out of the picture, he would stop hunting us, as he had no reason to chase us anymore because she was gone. Truth was, she was forever bewitched and imprinted on my heart, in all our hearts.

As the casket disappeared into the ground, everyone dispersed besides Amelie and me.

I heard the squelch of soggy feet, sinking in the grass as Amelie walked closer to me, only to feel her place her hand on my shoulder.

"He's here," she said. I looked into the tress in the distance and saw a figure stood in black, with a cane helping him stand and an umbrella in the other, protecting him from the rain.

"I should go over there and kill him," I hissed, watching as he watched us, paying his respect to his 'daughter'.

"As much as I am in agreement, you know that isn't what she would want you to do right now," Amelie reminded me, as she too watched him with me. "We must respect her wishes; due to everything she has done for us.

This was her final wish, she told us to do everything like this because she knew he would be here."

"I know, I just wish everything was different," I cried, causing her to pull me into a hug.

"So do I, but all we can do is have faith. She would want that," Amelie lightly smiled at me, as tears ran down her face. "Come on, let's go."

"I'll be there in a minute," I said. She nodded and walked away, leaving me standing there alone.

In this moment it was silent, only the sound of the wind rustling in the trees was present. Truth was, as much as it was as quiet as a mouse...I wanted it to be as quiet as a dinosaur because she was never quiet. I wanted her.

People say those we truly love never leave us, and now I know it's true; she will forever be with me. I'll forever remember staring into those beautiful hazel eyes of hers and getting lost in them every single time. I could picture every single moment I shared with her as friends and eventually lovers. How her laugh was contagious, how she would let loose by sticking her head out of the car window, letting the wind blow in her face as we drove places. Every moment we shared played in my mind on a continuous loop, every...single...moment.

I took another look towards Hugo to see he had gone. He wouldn't be coming back; his last string of hope had vanished and that's all she wanted. With a heavy sigh, I turned back around and made my way through the countless of headstones that were dedicated to endless amounts of people loved, back to the black car that waited for me and the open arms of my family, waiting to bring me home, but even though they were my family, my home was with her.

Scarlet

***

Few hours later, I was in a bleak grey room, like the world I now lived in. I sat there in a chair with a piece of paper in my hand, a piece of paper I had kept with me for the last four days, since the moment Malcom had given it to me.

Adeline had given Malcom three letters. One letter to explain how she wanted everything to go for her funeral and where, so Hugo would come and how we shouldn't do anything about it. The second letter was a group letter for everyone, how she loved everyone and why she did what she did and then there was the third. It was the letter dedicated to me and only me, with words that I had read repeatedly, to the point I had lost count of how many times I had read it. She had written it already knowing the outcome. It was a final goodbye.

Sitting there reading the letter once more, the tears ran down my face, and I couldn't get through it without hearing her speaking the words to me, like she was next to me reading it word for word. I wished there was another ending to the story of how it all came to be, but I knew she did what she needed to do. I wasn't going to fault her for that, for her sacrifice because I knew the reasons behind her actions. I just felt broken inside, wishing there was a loophole that would let me restart, so I could have the love of my life in my arms again. Just so I could hold her, kiss her, and take in her warmth, a constant loop of happiness I wished I could be smothered in.

My Dear Sebastian,

In a world of nightmares, I never believed I would get my own dream. We grew up in such a world that dreams for us were literally pixie dust. We always pictured how our life may have

338

turne• out an• how we wante• it to go, but the truth was, I never thought I ha• mine or woul• get it. But I •i•.

The one thing in life I always •reamt about was having a family, being love• an• being in love with someone, having those moments I woul• forever treasure. I always •i• people watch, imagining the stories an• lives they live•, won•ering when I woul• finally get my happy ever after.

I foun• it in you.

My Sebastian, you were my everything an• more. You ma•e a worl• so •ark come to life. Just being your frien• was enough but being love• by you an• being in love with you was the greatest gift I coul• ever ask for. My own •ream became a reality. With you by my si•e I starte• to •ream bigger an• brighter because I •reame• of waking up to you every morning, watching you sleep so peacefully un•er the glow of the sunrays creeping in. I coul• see us cooking together, cherishing every moment while we create• a new worl• for us. I coul• see us fighting like cats an• •ogs, only to make it up to each other in a thousan• •ifferent ways, with one of them being the best way possible. I truly •i• want to grow ol• with you, watch you turn grey an• wrinkly, but still look like you were create• by the Go•s. I wante• to grow our own family together, while we ha• our moments of kissing in the rain. You will always be my rainbow come rain or shine.

What I'm •oing, what I'm going to •o is the har•est •ecision I have ever ma•e. It hasn't come easy, an• I wish I coul• say there was another way an• maybe there woul• have been, but none of you woul• have been safe until I was gone. In or•er for you all to get a future, a life, a happy en•ing, mine has to en•.

To you, I'm going to be a moment, a small fragment of your time an• story, while you are my written piece, front to back, wor• by wor•, my whole story.

Our love is going to be one of the great ones, like all love *stories, ours will die with us. Romeo and Juliet, Bonnie and Clyde, Jack and Rose and Hazel and Augustus, great love stories that end with tragedy, but love stories, nevertheless. With some love stories, love demands sacrifice and with that, I happily pay the price.*

I'll be watching you from the stars, making all the stars fall to grant your wishes.

I'll find you in the next life, but until we meet again, until I can feel your touch, breathe the air you breathe and to love eternally and forever, I will be your guiding light. I love you more than words can express.

I wish one more star would fall and grant my wish, reuniting us now.

I love you always,
your Adi xx

Folding up the letter once more, I could feel the pain she had writing it all down and see the tears that ran down her face. I could imagine it clear as day, even when I wasn't there to see it.

"I love you Adi," I spoke out loud, looking at the folded paper in my hand.

Taking another glance up, I looked at the one thing I wanted most in this world. "Grant me my wish and make that star fall by opening your eyes."

TO BE CONTINUED IN 'Something Blue'

Acknowledgments

Thank you, to you the readers. For spending your money and time getting lost in Scarlet with me! You are the amazing people helping make Scarlet happen and the adventure isn't over yet! There is more to come with 'Something Blue', that I am currently trying to get finished so you guys can carry on the journey...as you all will hate the cliff hanger.

My book was born out of a world of darkness that consumed me and made me feel small. I couldn't be prouder of the journey I have taken and how it has helped me write the world we are now living in. Mental Health is important and shouldn't be frowned upon, one of the many reason I am making a series based around it. By writing my own struggles and thoughts and creating a world around it, I hope I make you feel less alone. With Scarlet, I want to make a community, a group where we can all thrive and live in this world together, making the world a brighter place for everyone!

So, once again...Thank you! The love you share means everything and more. Love has the power to bring light to anyone's darkness.

I also want to thank a few people who have help me make this happen!

My parents: Tony and Jane…Thank you so much for everything you have done by supporting me and pushing me further! You have helped me through my darkness and helped me see the light. I am honestly extremely lucky to have you both and blessed to call you Mum and Dad. Without you both, I can't even imagine where I would be today and you're the most important people in my life… I love you both to the moon and back.

My sister: Hannah, thank you for being your annoying self. Tough love and all that works, and you have helped me more than you think you have! I'm lucky to have a sister like you and couldn't be more blessed to be going through life with you by my side…even though you drive me up the wall sometimes.

Jade and Alex: Thank you for being my idiots. You are my people, the ones I love, the ones who are mentally crazy like me and my little rockets! Thank you for standing by my side through thick and thin and being there for me through everything, including the darkness and filling it with utter nonsense. You're both dicks, but I love you.

Ryan: Thank you for your endless support and everything you do. I'm lucky to have you.

Ed and Kirsty: Thank you for being the duo that helped kick my ass into gear and for reading my book and helping me improve. You have both helped me massively and have done wonders for me. Thank you from the bottom of my heart. I love you both!

My other friends/work friends: Though you haven't been named, I still thank you for being there, no matter how small of a role you played. You still are a small part of the big picture.

My Editor: Morgana Stewart, thank you for taking your time with my baby and helping me improve everything throughout. I honestly have the loveliest of editors I can't wait to carry on with this journey with you as my editor and see the world we create!

Lena Yang: Thank you for your beautiful artwork that has put a picture to Scarlet! I can't wait for the rest to fall into place as we continue the Scarlet journey!

Lorna Reid: Thank you for formatting my book and helping me get it ready for self-publishing. Without you, it wouldn't have made it to print!

My Beta Readers: Thank you for your kind words, for volunteering to read my work and all the love you all gave me during my rough drafts! I honestly don't know what I would have done without your help.

My Arc Readers: The ones who got the book first in paperback! Thank you for helping me get my book out there and for being the first people to read the final draft! Let me know if you want to be my Arcs for book 2! You all get first dibs.

And to you, the man that will never be named... I thank you for all the pain and torment you showed me because pain has the power to create beauty and without that, I wouldn't have created Scarlet.

<3

About The Author

My name is Kayleigh Hilton, and I am a self-published author from Preston, United Kingdom. When I am not busy creating the world of Scarlet or future books that are brewing. You can find me working for the NHS and spending time with my family and friends and my parents three West-highland Terriers Amelia, Lia, and Milo.

I am a strong supporter when it comes to Mental Health and Domestic Abuse, not matter if its mental or physical, as I am a survivor myself. I will forever strive to try and make my voice heard when it comes to these topics by bringing them up within my own creations, so people know they are not alone. Please feel free to join me on my journey by following my socials and lets create a community where we can help each other.

Facebook: Kayleigh Hilton-Author

Instagram/Tiktok: Kaylzbookadventures

Printed in Great Britain
by Amazon

23183065R00198